wicked

Celestra Series

Book 4

ADDISON MOORE

WICKED © 2011 ADDISON MOORE

Edited by: Sarah Freese
Cover Design by: Gaffey Media
Interior design and formatting by: Gaffey Media

Copyright © 2011 by Addison Moore
http://addisonmoorewrites.blogspot.com/

This novel is a work of fiction. Any resemblance to peoples either living or deceased is purely coincidental. Names, places, and characters are figments of the author's imagination. The author holds all rights to this work. It is illegal to reproduce this novel without written expressed consent from the author herself.

All Rights Reserved.

Books by Addison Moore:

New Adult Romance

Celestra Forever After (Celestra Forever After 1)
The Dragon and the Rose (Celestra Forever After 2)
Perfect Love (A Celestra Novella)

Someone to Love (Someone to Love 1)
Someone Like You (Someone to Love 2)
Someone For Me (Someone to Love 3)

3:AM Kisses (3:AM Kisses 1)
Winter Kisses (3:AM Kisses 2)
Sugar Kisses (3:AM Kisses 3)
Whiskey Kisses (3:AM Kisses 4)
Rock Candy Kisses (3:AM Kisses 5)

Beautiful Oblivion (Beautiful Oblivion 1)
Beautiful Illusions (Beautiful Oblivion 2)
The Solitude of Passion
Burning Through Gravity

Young Adult Romance

Ethereal (Celestra Series Book 1)
Tremble (Celestra Series Book 2)

Burn (Celestra Series Book 3)
Wicked (Celestra Series Book 4)
Vex (Celestra Series Book 5)
Expel (Celestra Series Book 6)
Toxic Part One (Celestra Series Book 7)
Toxic Part Two (Celestra Series Book 7.5)
Elysian (Celestra Series Book 8)
Ethereal Knights (Celestra Knights)

Ephemeral (The Countenance Trilogy 1)
Evanescent (The Countenance Trilogy 2)
Entropy (The Countenance Trilogy 3)

Preface

Perfect knowledge is hallowed ground. It caresses you, cradles you with the barbed wire of truth. It grazes and tears at your flesh as though it ever really mattered—as if there were anything you could have done to stop it from penetrating you so completely.

Revenge in the hands of your enemies is a loaded gun. You can beg them for mercy, wave the white flag of surrender, but the only true elixir for the vitriol they bestow is a measure of hatred dispensed of your own. Never lie down for the enemy. Never hand them the knife with which to slaughter you.

The truth is a labyrinth. Secrets are truths as sharp as razors ready to spread like a virus—ready to saw your existence in half.

My truths came to light. They took shape in the form of my enemies until all of the color bled out from my world. It lacked the beauty and majesty of a black and white portrait. The landscape had glazed over in rusted tones of sepia—rancid—tarnished—with urine colored sky.

My world glittered from the fragmented glass it had become.

This is what I know.

These are my truths.

1

The Gift

"Happy birthday, Skyla."

Chloe.

Her eyes gleam a peculiar shade of black, her pupils unnaturally dilated—her flesh, a rosy shade of pink just under the cheeks, so healthy, so alive. The white sheath she wears is perfectly tailored to her hourglass figure. It glows against her deep warm tan. You would think she had been away on a tropical vacation. She looks straight out of a fashion magazine rather than a casket.

The room falls silent. A hypnotic hush filters through the facility save for an errant bowling ball rolling towards its destiny far in the distance.

The sound of glass shattering splinters the silence. An ear-piercing scream that sounds vaguely like Brielle comes from over my shoulder. I hear the sound of retching then a splash of vomit splattering between Chloe and me. Brielle doubles over, exposing the slightly digested contents of her stomach.

"So glad you could make it," I say to Chloe. I don't believe the words as they fly out of my mouth, sarcastic as they might be.

Chloe moves forward. Brushes past me without another glance, and walks right up to Logan. She hikes up on the balls of her feet and whispers directly into his ear. It looks sensual as though she were sweeping her mouth over him with all of the passion and zest you would have after a lengthy absence.

Logan cuts me a quick glance. Lets me know by his inability to be discrete that I'm the subject matter of Chloe's tender words. I wonder if her hot breath is enough to ignite any feelings he might have once felt for her.

Chloe steps back and examines the crowd.

Helpless, lost faces—paper white—filled with awe, fear, and relief, as she henpecks for one in particular.

"What is going on?" My mother hisses as she sops up the mess on the floor with a roll of paper towels. She whisks Brielle out for fresh air before I have a chance to answer, not that I was going to—not that I have plans of ever speaking to that woman again. Let the Counts fend for themselves.

"Gage." Chloe sings his name like a desperate song that's been over rehearsed. You can practically taste the obsession in the air—the sour bite of rejection clings to your palate.

She lunges at him with a tight embrace, sways on her heels as she rocks her body into his.

The crowd exhales, and a spontaneous round of applause breaks out in a disorganized fashion. It's as if a long drawn out movie had ended and the princess has reunited with her prince. A low rumble of murmurs circles the room, and the vibrancy of life begins to fill the bowling alley once again.

Michelle peels Chloe off Gage and shrieks into her as she gives a long vibrating hug. The bitch squad moves in, and I can't watch anymore.

"I'm so sorry," Logan fills the small of my back with his hand. "I had no idea my uncle planned this."

I pull away reflexively as though his arm had somehow morphed into a snake.

Logan with his perfect features, his bright amber eyes lit like two eternal flames. I reach up and touch his face, run my fingers loose over his eyelids, cheeks, and lips.

"I don't know you," I whisper. In one swift move I pluck off the ring he gave me moments before and thrust it back at him. While his palm is still open, I fish out the key to his father's car and press that in as well. I don't want birthday gifts from him, now, or ever again.

I race over to Gage, and we collide into one another.

"I'm sorry, Skyla," he shudders ever so slightly, "I never thought there was a reason to tell my dad to abandon the project once you stopped giving blood." His eyes close briefly, appalled at his own misgiving.

I look back at Logan who lingers on the periphery of the crowd that has amassed around Chloe.

Voices shout at random. "Where were you? Are you OK?" Questions fly like arrows from faulty bows.

She pats her hands, and half the crowd sits as though she were about to deliver a modern version of the Sermon on the Mount—the parables of the dead and the restless.

"I..." She looks over at me as both my arms circle around Gage.

I want him to get me out of here, teleport me anyplace else on the planet.

Her dark glossy hair is pulled back into a ponytail, broad even features, and perfect full lips can take the breath away from any living creature. I don't remember Chloe ever looking so beautiful. For sure I don't want Gage to see her like this, see her at all.

She clears her throat before returning her attention to those faithfully bowed before her. "I ran away," she lowers her head in a dramatic fashion, "I don't know whose body they found. It must have been a mistake," she gives a contrived sigh, "I guess after the funeral my mom had it cremated, so we'll never know."

All lies.

"Why the hell would you run away?" Emily hiccups through a steady stream of tears.

"I had a nasty fight with my parents," she shrugs apologetically, "I'm embarrassed to say it, but after I found out that Carly and Brody had a baby, I..." A sharp collective gasp fills the room. Half of the faces turn to a stunned Carly Foster gripping at her throat.

Shit.

I hadn't even noticed Carly was here, but there she is, hunched over like she's just been socked in the gut.

"Oh, I'm sorry. I thought everyone knew." Chloe zips the pendant from Logan's grandmother across her neck in one quick motion.

Carly darts across the room and hits the exit so fast she's nothing but a blur.

"I didn't know it was a secret," Chloe calls out after her. She turns to face Gage and me. "It's such a burden to know great things. It can drive you insane." She takes a bold step forward. "Make you forgo love." She caresses his cheek with the back of her hand. Chloe sweeps into me with a cold, sterile gaze. "It could make you stab a friend right in the back."

2

Chaos

In a matter of moments the bowling alley explodes in tears and drama—cries of joy and relief as throngs of students from West and a few from East descend upon Chloe.

"Skyla," Logan's forehead is creased with worry. "I know this is turning out to be a strange night—but what's going on?" He holds up the ring and key still nestled in his palm.

Marshall pushes between Gage and me, completely ignoring the fact Logan is speaking and glides into an easy grin. "Nice show. The two of you really know how to throw a party. Any other little ghouls ready to pop out of the woodwork?"

Logan steps into me a little too close, and the tip of his nose touches mine.

"What's going on? Can we talk?" His hot breath sears across my face in agitation.

I step aside, so I can see Marshall again.

"Mr. Dudley, if it's alright with you I'd like to spend the night at your house." It's almost a joke to ask.

Marshall straightens, biting down on his lower lip at the prospect.

"What?" Logan and Gage hiss in unison.

"I'll have the guest room ready Ms. Messenger." *You, however, will not be using it.* He gives a suggestive smile. *I would have resurrected the Northern Hemisphere had I known it would drive you into my arms—bedroom—same difference.*

He's practically purring.

"Listen," Gage takes me by the hand and walks me a safe distance away from Marshall, "I know you're freaked about Chloe, but I can't let you spend the night at that whack-jobs house." His cobalt eyes bolt around my face perplexed and wild.

"You can't *let* me?" My ears thump in rhythm with my adrenaline. "Just like you wouldn't let me in on who was in that book of Counts?" My entire family—my mother, my sister—*Logan*. "Maybe it's because you were too busy trying to protect someone close to you." I free my hand from his. "Too bad it wasn't me."

"Crap," he moans tipping his head back to look at Logan.

"Yes. Marshall showed me everything." I turn to leave and run right smack into Chloe.

"Sorry if I've ruined your party." She holds me by the shoulders pretending to straighten me. "I really do hope we can get to know each other." The bitch squad flanks her on either side—and surprise, surprise, Brielle holds up the rear.

"Well, I really don't want to know *you*." I spit the words out with venom.

"Skyla!" My mother runs up gripping her chest in horror. "This is the girl everyone thought was *dead*." She leans into Chloe apologetically. "I'm so sorry. My daughter obviously has you confused with someone else. Please forgive her. It's her birthday. She probably thinks you're a party crasher. Skyla has never been good at sharing the limelight."

"Oh, I'm certain I don't want to know you," I dig my finger into Chloe's chest. "Or ..." Before I can point the finger at my mother and say *you,* Gage wraps his arm around my shoulder and calls out an *excuse me* as he whisks us towards the kitchen.

He slows as we approach Logan. "Put that fire out." He cocks his head towards my mother and Chloe still gaping in my direction.

wicked

"How can you talk to him?" I try and wrangle out of Gage's death grip as we spill into the newly remodeled kitchen. Gage takes up both my hands. His eyes soften, and I have to hold back the urge to run my fingers through his jet-black hair, lose myself in the splendor of his dark symmetry, and forget about the nightmare that's unfolding all around us.

"I'm mad about you." The words project out of me broken, on the verge of tears. "I mean *at*," I correct.

He gives a slow long blink. "Swear to God, I was going to tell you everything, tomorrow. Your mom called and wanted to throw this party."

"You let me sleep under the same roof as those people!"

"And nothing happened," he pleads for me to understand.

"Maybe you would have fought to protect me a little more if I was family." Funny, because with Gage I sort of thought I was.

"You are family." He pulls me in. "You're already a part of me." He breathes the words before pressing in a kiss.

Gage has a way of softening the blows the world has to offer by way of his lips.

"Here you two are." My mother calls from the entry. "Skyla don't let any of this commotion get you down. It's like a huge celebration out here now. Camera crews are on their way and everything! Gage, tell her to get over herself and join the fun." She motions for us to come back out before disappearing.

"She's right," I say. "Why should we let Chloe ruin our party?" I cut a beastly look into the crowd before heading back into the bowling alley.

The chaos is steadily rising with the decibel level threatening to test the eardrums of both the living and the dead.

Mom and Tad are happily bowling with Mia and Melissa as though our lives were normal, as though I didn't know their secret. Dr. Oliver and Emma fast approach, and I manage to ditch Gage just before they hit us. I don't have it in me to even hint to Dr. Oliver—Barron, that I can't find it in me to appreciate his gift.

I hightail it to Ellis over by the banquet table and join him glowering at Chloe.

"Look at her," I scowl. She's buried nine deep in a circumference of overeager bodies just waiting to touch her as though she's got some sort of healing properties. "She ruined my party." I was going to say, she killed my dad, but that's not what came out.

"You should kick her ass," Ellis suggests.

"OK." Really I didn't need the nudging. I hardly think Ellis meant for me to do it or even entertain the idea as if it were something that could actually morph into reality. But it is my party—I could kick some ass if I want to.

I push through the first layer of Chloe worshipers, the tangled middle—the final membrane of bodies part for me wide like the Red Sea.

Chloe gives a serene smile, but it's the cutthroat look in her eyes that tells me she knows it's coming, that she's been expecting it all along.

"Thank you for coming to my party, Chloe." The words struggle through my vocal cords. "If you weren't here, I couldn't do this." I take a clean step forward and latch onto the silver chain around her neck with both hands and crisscross until a silver line cinches deep into her flesh—until her nails claw into my arms in an effort to stop me from strangling her.

"Shit!" Michelle blows into me with a series of hard pushes. She tries with tireless perseverance to shove me away,

wicked

but I've screwed my feet into the floor and become an impenetrable wall.

Chloe's face lights up a delightful shade of purple, so close to blue, so close to death for real this time.

I increase the velocity in which I hope to asphyxiate her—tug harder at the chain—tighten its noose effect around her throat until her eyes bulge, until blood vessels burst in the whites of her eyes just like fireworks on the Fourth of July. Her arms and legs begin to flail.

It's the laborsome distress—the abnormal hyperactivity of watching someone in death throes that makes people uncomfortable when observing the art of dying.

It is all out confusion, screaming at unimaginable octaves, and yet, it's like I'm off on some desolate planet with Chloe—all alone in our own psychotic world. I'm murdering her in front of dozens of witnesses, and I really don't mind. If I'm going down for this, I'll gladly do it with an audience. Hell, some of them might even thank me.

People tug at my clothes, try to peel my sweater right off my body, my hair is pulled out in handfuls leaving hot patches of pain all over my scalp—my skin carved into with fingernails, but it's my Celestra strength that buoys me. Ironic how there is only one other Celestra in the vicinity, and I've made it my mission to publically decapitate her.

"Skyla!" Gage shouts, penetrating the crowd in an effort to reach me.

A body falls over me, then dozens.

The world gives a soft spin. Everything becomes unnaturally quiet as I land hard on the floor with a thump.

My eyes flutter open.

Gage and I are no longer at the bowling alley.

3

The Promise

It's dark. Molasses-colored dew falls over the world as I try to make out my whereabouts.

Gage rolls off me, and I hear his footsteps shuffling away until he flips on the lights. It's then I realize he's teleported us to his bedroom.

"Nice move," I say trying to right myself.

"You were going to kill her—again," he smarts as he helps me up off the floor.

We head over and sit on the edge of his mattress. There's a towel on the floor, and the bed isn't made, but other than that his room is immaculate and holds the scent of his woodsy cologne.

"Do you forgive me?" He wraps an arm around my shoulder and leans in.

"Should I?" Of course, I forgive Gage. I've lost everything tonight including my sanity. The last thing in the world I want to lose is Gage.

"Yes." He gives a wry smile. "Neither Logan nor I knew anything about Chloe coming back." He looks down remorsefully. For a brief moment I wonder if the remorse is because he said Logan's name, as though reminding me of Logan were enough to make me fall in love with him all over. "Anyway, I'm gonna let him fill you in on the details about his bloodline."

"Whatever." I have a feeling I'm going to have a hard time believing anything Logan tells me. "So where am I gonna live?"

"Home?" He pulls me back onto the bed, and we land side by side.

"Can this be my new home?" I'm only half kidding.

"I wish. How about," he presses a series of soft kisses into me, "after you go to bed, I'll come over and keep you safe."

"Do you really want me to go back there?" I'm petrified at the thought. My so-called mother has probably been poisoning my food all these years. Forget the theory that eating her cooking was a slow suicide—it's probably been a slow homicide.

"I don't get the feeling they're going to hurt you. When I found out, I was in shock, but we had the away game and—"

I cut him off.

"How could you have found out just before the away game? Logan had that list for weeks."

"It took us that long to comb through it. Their names were buried in the back. And Logan wasn't mentioned until the final few pages under a list of hybrids."

"Hybrid," I say it just above a whisper. Logan's face impresses itself upon me. He's always had that extraterrestrial godlike quality about him. Something deep and knowing that lies just beneath the surface of his sublime features—that pitch perfect body that I'll never know to touch because now I can't stand to.

"I know you're upset." He pulls me in close until my chest is pressed up against his, and I can feel his heart pummeling out of control. "I beg of you, don't be upset with my dad, he honestly had no clue we didn't want Chloe around. He mentioned he had a gift for the both of us, but I had no idea about her showing up tonight, or breathing for that matter." He shakes his head in disbelief.

Chloe was quite the unbirthday present.

"I could never be mad at your dad. I already think of him as my own." I dig my fingers into the back of his hair, and like some unwanted alarm, Logan pops into my mind again. Logan tugs at my heart, interrupts the moment. He is the constant quivering nag on the outskirts of my love for Gage, fighting to be let in, only now, knowing who he is, it's impossible to even entertain the idea. How could I have ever been so stupid to wrap myself around him so completely? And now letting go of him feels like peeling off a layer of skin.

"Things are going to be different with Chloe around," he laments.

Something cinches inside me when he says her name. She's the demon I've called into being through the labor of my marrow. We're blood from the same bowl, literally.

"Promise me something?" I whisper.

"Anything." His eyes sparkle in the light like the ocean on fire.

"Promise we'll never change. That you'll never leave me, or lie to me, or hold anything back from me ever again."

"Skyla." His hand runs down my hair, swift as a waterfall. "There is nothing on this planet, in heaven or hell, that can keep me from you. I more than promise."

His cobalt optic spheres dart through me, and I know his words are true.

We fall into a bliss-filled kiss that spans decades, time, and space. Loving Gage is more powerful than Chloe and her venom, stronger than Logan and all his lies. Gage washes me in his truth, the deep rich colors of his love. It feels eternal—right.

A light knock erupts at the door.

We both know who it is.

4

Don't You Forget About Me

Logan steps in and gives way to a sigh. His blonde hair catches the light and gives off an aura of otherworldly superiority, makes me like him less.

I don't bother getting up, but Gage is already bolting for the door so Logan and I can 'talk'.

"I'll be right downstairs," Gage drops his gaze before exiting.

I can't believe he's leaving me with Chloe's minion.

Logan comes over like he owns the place, like he owns me. I leap off the bed and take three long strides in the opposite direction.

"Whoa." He holds up his hands in defense. "Skyla," he latches onto me with those eyes of orange fire—magnetizes me with an intense pull, but I won't give in, "did Gage tell you we found out before the game? Your mom—"

"He told me." I interrupt his flow of excuses.

He takes a step forward and sends me sailing the other way.

"So, I have Marshall to thank for this."

"You have *you* to thank for this," I shoot back. "You should have told me." An unnatural chill fills the air. "But then, you never tell me anything. I bet it pleasures you to keep me in the dark. Some kind of me-Tarzan-you-Jane, cerebral high you get off knowing things."

"No—never. Skyla, I love you. I want to share everything with you. You knew I wasn't a pure Celestra. I—"

"Why should I trust you?"

"How can you not?" He looks genuinely perplexed and hurt at the same time.

"When Chloe and I were light driving to see my father, she mentioned that she wished the Logan from the future would visit her." I stare off into the black of the window. "At the time, I thought it was strange."

"Wait, you think I'm in on something with Chloe?" His eyes spring wide as though he's just digested where this might be headed.

"Why wasn't your name on the list of people she hated in her diary? Gage and I were both on it. So why were you omitted? Didn't you supposedly piss her off by breaking up with her? Didn't *she* decide the end?" I ask, mockingly.

"I don't know why I wasn't on it. I don't know why Chloe does anything. Maybe she wrote the list while we were still together?"

"Sure," I whisper acrimoniously.

Logan swallows hard as he eyes me with the distinct look of fear. I can't dissect it enough to know if it's because he's genuinely afraid or afraid of getting caught.

His hair looks so pale in the wash of moonlight streaming in, soft as feathers, and I want to touch it and put this entire nightmare behind me.

"What did she whisper to you?" I ask.

His eyes round out in alarm.

"At the party," I demand. "The first thing she did was go over to you. You remember. Also, can you try to remember that you said you'd never lie to me?"

He lets out a heavy sigh.

"What did she say?" I repeat.

wicked

Logan compresses his lips until his entire face looks as though it's made of plaster.

"I thought so." I scan over the desk in an effort to hide the hurt in my eyes.

I miss Gage. Just looking at his things makes me long for him, his open math book, his backpack where he once carried a poem to school for me. My heart perforates at the thought of Logan being incapable of loving me the way Gage does so freely. I wish I never gave my heart to Logan. I wish Logan were who I thought he was.

A dark amber bottle sits collecting dust on the top shelf. It catches my eye as the light filters through the bronze glass. I snatch it down—let it warm in my hands as I examine it. Root Beer. I wonder what prompted Gage to save it. I wonder what makes guys do anything. According to Marshall they run porn reels twenty-four seven—I suppose that hardly affords the time or energy to find the recycling bin.

Logan surveys me with caution like a predator ready to pounce.

"Tell me," I say, rubbing my hands over the circumference of the bottle. Let it roll around between my palms before grasping it by the neck with my left hand. A slow building rage pumps through me. I can taste the anger inside me, dull and bitter like sucking old coins.

"She said, 'well done.'" His head dips when he says it, resigned to the fact the words were loaded, that they testified against him in the worst way possible.

An impervious silence lodges between us.

"So you were the well-placed boyfriend," I say it as fact. No wonder Chloe laughed when I suggested Ellis. It was Logan all along.

"It wasn't me. I would never do that to you, Skyla."

"You looked right at me when she spoke to you!" The words rattle out of my lungs in a heated scream.

"Because I knew she was setting us up for something."

"There is no *us*!" I crash the bottle down against the edge of the desk and send a series of brown glittering shards all over.

"There is." Logan's voice is low and pressured. It's as though he wants me to believe there was something real there between us as though he weren't hiding anything else in the world.

"I can't believe you." Tears spike up unexpected, and I blink them away. "I'm so freaking angry!" I push hard into his chest over and over. "You tried to make me believe you were putting me first, but you were always with someone else! And this whole time Chloe had you on a string like some kind of puppet," I shout in his face.

"I love you."

"I hope you really *do* love me!" I roar. "I hope it hurts like hell when you see me with Gage. In fact, I'm going to give you something a little more permanent to remember me by."

My hand flies up over his face with the broken bottle. I give one clean swipe down the right side of his cheek until a line of crimson emerges on his flesh and awakens me to what I've just done.

My hand opens in horror, and the glass drops with an unimpressive thud onto the hardwood floor.

"I'm sorry," I whisper, covering my mouth reflexively.

But I'm not sure I really am.

5

Far Away From Here

I lean against the kitchen counter with Gage as Dr. Oliver stitches up the side of Logan's face. A stack of clean dishes lie on the granite with a dishtowel over them, and the fragile scent of coffee lingers from the reserve left in the pot.

Lucky for Logan, Dr. Oliver took the time to invest in quality invisible thread since the last time he stitched up the living.

I finger the roll of flesh that runs the length of my neck courtesy of Chloe. It feels as though Chloe is responsible for every single scar in my life, both visible and invisible. I'd take a million physical scars from her if I could go back and stop her from killing my father, or at least giving the orders to do so.

"I'm really sorry," I bleat out once again. Even if Logan is one of Chloe's drones I still feel bad for running a piece of broken glass down the side of his face.

"It's not your fault," he says, trying to stay still as the needle digs in and out of his flesh, lifting and pulling his skin as though he were made of elastic.

"I gotta get out of here," I whisper to Gage.

"Let's go upstairs, or I can take you for a drive."

"Will you take me to Marshall's?"

"No." His eyes swell with disbelief. "I had Brielle tell your mom you were spending the night with her. And, I really don't think my parents will mind if you stay as long as you sleep downstairs." He leans into me with a pleading expression. "Stay. I want you to."

I look over at Logan with his face contorting in pain as Dr. Oliver continues to prod at him mercilessly, and yet I still can't feel sorry for him. Instead, I resist the urge to go over and start stabbing at him with a scalpel, because my heart feels like it's just been puréed.

"All done." Dr. Oliver snips the edge of the remaining thread. "Please refrain from playing with broken glass in the future, even if it was accidental."

"It was intentional," I say, under my breath.

Logan wasn't one hundred percent truthful regarding our little mishap, which is par for the course with Logan.

"I hope you enjoyed the surprise." Dr. Oliver beams in our direction.

"Yeah." Gage gives an apprehensive glance before looking over at me.

"Great," Dr. Oliver nods, "Skyla, the Bishops are dying to meet you. I hope you don't mind joining us tomorrow evening at their home for dinner. They're so thankful to you for giving life to their daughter." He looks over at Gage. "I realize it's your birthday, but they simply couldn't reschedule. The Bishops thought it best before the media descends. Perhaps we'll go out for dessert after?"

Dinner? Didn't he see me trying to kill her? But then, probably not. She was mobbed with bodies the entire time, and for all I know people could have been trying to strangle her all night. She's indestructible with that necklace on, she's worse than a cockroach.

"We'll be there." Gage wraps an arm around my waist and nudges into me, as though he'd like for me to agree, but I just give a little smile. I can't promise anything.

"I hope you'll excuse me," Dr. Oliver heads out of the kitchen, "it's been a long day."

We each shout goodnight out of turn then just sit there staring at one another as though the planet were about to explode.

"I'm going to need some space," I say looking up at Gage. If I stay, my anger might percolate, and God forbid I go after Gage with a broken shard of glass, or worse, slaughter the two of them in their sleep and really give Dr. Oliver a project.

"Don't go," Gage whispers, bumping his nose into mine.

"It's not you. I just don't trust myself. I'm insane right now. I need to clear my head."

He expels an exasperated sigh. "OK, I'll take you."

Logan migrates over with his arms stuffed in his pockets. His face is swollen and bright red, with a glossy row of X's dripping down his cheek.

I can't even look at him, so I turn away.

"I'll find someplace else to sleep tonight," Logan offers.

My neck whips back in haste. "Don't flatter yourself."

"Alright," Gage starts us towards the door, "let's get out of here."

Logan speeds over and snatches his keys off the counter.

"I'll drive."

🦋 🦋 🦋

As soon as Logan's truck pulls alongside Marshall's entry, I hop out and bolt to the door. I made Gage sit in the middle. There was no way I was going to rub my thigh up against Logan all the way over and let the heat of his body try to lure out any feelings I might have left for him like rattling a coffin full of bones.

I give a series of harsh knocks and ring the doorbell in triplicate before Marshall lets me in.

"I've been waiting." Marshall looks resplendent, still in the same black shirt and jeans from earlier. I swear it smells like he took a bath in cologne. Any minute now I suspect my allergies will kick into overdrive and choke the living hell out of me.

"Sorry," he holds back the two of them, "neither of you are welcome." Marshall espouses a level of calm that he seems to reserve for trouble, or Logan and Gage.

I turn in time to see Logan speed through the door with his shoulders back and a pissed off look galvanized on his face. In all honesty it melts me a little to see him this way. Pissed off is probably the hottest look for Logan, and judging by the linear direction our relationship is taking, I'd say he's pretty lucky that it's a good look for him.

Logan picks Marshall up and spins him 180 degrees before pitching him hard against the wall a good twelve feet away.

"Holy crap!" I jump back.

Gage walks over to me with a horrified look on his face.

Logan starts in on a series of well-concentrated punches right to the ocular area. He's rearranging the face of a man who, as far as Logan is concerned, is just his *math* teacher. In a stupid fit of anger, Logan is going to clue Marshall in on the fact I ratted him out as a Sector. I'll be bound and gagged and shipped off to the Counts by midnight. Ironically that might be just as harsh a punishment as going home.

"Holy freaking shit!" I scream at Logan. "Get the hell out!" An entire volcano of adrenaline purges through me. I'm not going to stand here and listen to Marshall moan before he obviously gets up and assaults Logan—until the entire place is trashed, and there's nothing but broken glass and blood covering every square inch like the time Chloe slit my throat.

wicked

Before Marshall has the chance to retaliate, I snatch Logan up by the back of the shirt and send him flying across the width of the room like a Frisbee.

It feels so good, I pant from the sheer bliss of watching him smack into the wall.

"Nice work." Marshall rises and dusts himself off. "But do stay out of this. I rather enjoy hand combat. It's a rare occasion anyone chooses to go against me."

Marshall strides over and picks Logan up by the back of the neck and stands him up awkwardly as though he were made of rags. He wastes no time in pummeling Logan's face—powerful punches that split open his newly sewn incision. His eyes and lips swell almost instantly.

"Enough." Gage struggles to pluck Marshall off Logan before putting an end to the brawl.

"God!" My hands clamp over my lips. "You could have killed him!"

Well then, you could have replicated your voodoo magic and resurrected him from the dead, Marshall sneers in my direction.

"Very funny," I say out loud.

Just when it looks as if Logan and Gage are making their way out the door, Marshall's feet are knocked out from under him, and he lands hard on the floor.

"Shit," Marshall seethes.

I've never heard an expletive fly out of Marshall's mouth before, like *ever*, so I know this isn't going to be good. I almost feel sorry for Logan—almost.

Marshall bounces to his feet in one quick move. He picks Logan up and holds him by the stomach high up over his head.

"Shall I give him a ride?" Marshall looks to me for approval before spinning Logan like a basketball—like a propeller on a freaking beanie. "Do you like amusement parks Mr. Oliver?"

"He's gonna puke!" I warn. Logan is limp as a corpse. "That's enough Marshall!" I scream in disbelief.

Marshall flexes on his knees before tossing Logan up in one powerhouse move launching him with his back flat against the vaulted ceiling. "Oh dear, it looks as if you've adhered yourself." Marshall feigns concern as Logan hangs like a fixture, writhing in pain. "The grommets on the back of your jeans must have latched onto the magnetic studs I had the builders use. Magnets are excellent for your overall wellbeing. The therapeutic benefits are innumerable. An hour or two up there, and you'll be thanking me for the next solid year." *Are you amused Skyla? And in the event you're wondering, the only magnetic stud in the room is me.* He gives a sly smile.

"Get him down," Gage demands.

"I'm afraid I can't do that." Marshall walks over to where Logan dangles from the ceiling. "I won't hold your erratic behavior against you. I'm aware puppy love has its fair share of undesirable side effects. However, do refrain from attempting to injure me in the future. You may not come off so lucky. I can remove three of your limbs before you realized what's happened." *I've done that twice before. It's a skill I don't want to get too rusty at. Somehow I believe I'll have opportunity to practice again in the very near future.*

"How do I get down?" Logan shouts. His face turns a violent shade of red as the blood rushes unnaturally, pooling in the veins around his temple.

"You'll have to crawl." *Like a roach.* "Do be careful. I'd hate for my insurance premium to rise."

Well, Ms. Messenger, now that I've had my testosterone riled up, I'll be glad to let you reap the benefits.

wicked

Perfect.
I'll need a suit of armor to keep him off me tonight.

6

Stranger Danger

Surprisingly there wasn't a whole lot of blood trailing from the ceiling. Logan jumped down the last ten feet, and then they left.

"I'm going upstairs to shower, you care to join me?" Marshall is intent as though this were a real possibility.

"No thanks." I plop down on the couch and stare at the splatter of blood dotting the bone colored floor. Count blood. Count and Celestra—a hybrid.

Marshall ditches upstairs at supersonic speeds, creating a suction with his overeager sprint. God only knows what he expects to happen tonight. He's had some seriously disturbing Sector-Celestra fantasies ever since we've met. Now that Chloe is here, I wonder if she'll be interested in him like I hoped. She's so emotionally tethered to Gage—*my* Gage—she can't see straight. I mean the way she leeched onto him right after giving Logan the attaboy, you would have thought she spent the last year pinning after him in her grave. Speaking of which, I'll have to ask Marshall where exactly was it that Chloe spent the last twelve months. Was she in some holding tank in hell like Gage was, Halloween night? In Sectorville—pissing off every angel in the celestial sphere? I bet they were glad to give her the boot back down to earth.

A knock erupts on the glass slider that leads towards the backyard, inspiring me to pull my feet up on the couch and curl into a ball of fear.

"Marshall?" I call out.

More intense knocking.

Shit!

Why am I always alone when crap like this happens? I can tell a million miles away this is going to be bad, bad, bad, so I bury my head in my knees and sit there like a turtle hoping it all goes away.

The knocking picks up to a frenetic pace, so I cock my head sideways and take a quick peek.

It's a girl about my age with jet-black hair and a cadaverously pale face. She's smiling and waving like crazy as if she knows me or something. She does look kind of friendly. I unfurl myself a little bit.

She motions me over, rubbing at her bare arms to keep warm.

It *is* freezing out there. I should at least let her in. She's probably Marshall's eleven-thirty. For all I know he has them arriving at regular intervals all night long. I'll have to put a do not disturb sign all around the property if I plan on getting any sleep.

I head to the door and slide it open. A harsh wind whips in a few stray leaves as she jumps into the house, and I shut the door behind her.

"You mind if I give you a hug?" She says it sweet enough, but there's something strange about her that sparks in me the urge to run.

"Yeah sure," I'm so stupid. This is probably the part where she sticks a spirit sword in my back. I'm going to die getting a hug of all things. But she doesn't stab me or do anything weird like feel me up. She gives a quick non-lethal embrace and pulls away. She smells sweet and clean, like strong aloe vera.

"So, you're here for Marshall, right?" I head back over to the couch and take a seat.

"Nope." She lands next to me and scoots up on her thigh, taking me in like she's never seen another person before. "Was I any good?" Her eyes sparkle a familiar shade of deep sea blue.

"At what?" She's super pretty and very strange—a totally dangerous combination.

"You know, the hug. I've never done that with a human before."

"Shit!" I leap off the couch backwards and head for the stairs. "Marshall!"

"Oh no!" She yells over to me and pats her hands in a panic. "Please stop. You don't know me, but you know my brother."

Holy crap, it's Emerson.

I open the front door and shout into the night for Nev.

It takes less than three seconds for Nevermore to fly through the door in all of his midnight splendor. He makes three revolutions around the room before attacking something in the far corner.

She starts in on a giggle. I'll give her one thing—she's a happy little spook.

"What do you want?" I head back over feeling a bit more protected now that Nevermore is here. A lot of help Marshall is. I can still hear the water running upstairs. He's probably busy scrubbing down every orifice of his body in the event I wish to further myself into this newfound insanity.

She points just shy of the piano. "That's Holden Kragger," she whispers almost secretively, so Holden won't hear. "Oh look, the bird's got him by the hair." She laughs.

"Sorry I killed your brother. He was sort of a jerk though." I slide onto the couch just opposite her.

"I'm not too concerned over who you kill, Skyla." A dimple depresses itself on her right side without the effort of a smile. "I'm here because your mother sent me."

"My mother? As in my mother the Countess or another mother?" I seem to be collecting them these days.

"The mother who birthed you."

I scoot in quick as a cheetah and snatch up her wrist. "Who's my mother?"

"It's not my place to tell." She takes back her arm. "Ask your father."

"My father?" Yes! I totally will. "What does my mother want? Does she have a message for me?"

"You're quick," she says, massaging her wrist.

There's more than a familiar quality about her. I swear I've seen her before, those eyes, those lips.

"She wants to let you know there is a very real threat of losing something that is rightfully yours. Danger has fallen upon you like a shadow. It's close. It's time for you to be the person you were born to be. Run fast and hard, the race is yours to win. You'll need much endurance, but if you educate yourself you can outwit your enemies."

There's a lengthy gap of silence.

"That's it? That's your basic pep talk like before a history test or a sample sale in the fashion district. There's got to be something more."

She pulls a face at my oversimplified analysis.

"That's it," she adds, rather bored. "One more thing, and this is just from me."

I nod in anticipation.

"You and my brother," she sighs. "I really like you. Be extra nice to him. Trying times have come, but he really does love you."

"He loves me?" I examine her fully—smooth pale skin, translucent as rice paper. I can see her veins ever so slightly along her jaw, around the hollow of her eyes, an entire track of green and blue threads race across her eyelids. "What's your name?"

"Giselle." Something in her flares when she says it.

"Giselle? Did they used to call you Emerson? Is it Pierce that loves me?" I've clearly dislodged myself from any kind of reality I was loosely holding onto.

"My name is very much Giselle. I was hit by a car when I was three." She spreads her hands out and sticks her tongue out the side of her mouth as an added effect causing me to shrink back a little.

She gets up and heads to the door. "That's not my brother." She flicks a finger over to where Nevermore sits mid air. She steps outside, leaning in to look at me one last time. "My brother is Gage."

7

Love Me Tender

Marshall speeds down the stairs, still patting cologne on his neck. He's wearing a t-shirt and sweats and looks about ten years younger, this never ceases to freak me out.

"You—" He snaps his fingers in Nevermore's direction. "Be gone."

"No," I shout. "Let him stay."

"I'm not talking to the bird." Marshall slides the backdoor open and motions towards Nev. "Come now, you too."

Nev glides over with his wingspan as wide as a baseball bat and flies out the door.

"So, you see ghosts like I see people? What do they look like?"

"They retain the impression of their former selves. Rotten *ghosts*," he says in a mocking tone, "like that one, are tagged with a foul spiritual odor—sort of a universal calling card, like excrement or urine."

"Lovely."

Giselle's face looked pretty darn human. What if it was just some stupid prank from Chloe?

"I think I saw a ghost myself while you were upstairs. This girl came to the door and—"

"You let her in?" He narrows in on me.

"She was cold."

"Ghosts neither need to be let in, or have their body temperature adjusted. Who did she claim to be?"

"A dead Oliver—Gage's sister. She said she died when she was three."

"Giselle," he says it as fact. "And what did she want?"

"It's true?" The hairs on my arms prickle to life.

"That's true. However it doesn't quantify what you saw as being true."

"She said my birth mother sent her. So I guess that's pretty quantifying, right? Anyway, she wants me to run a race and win what's rightfully mine. Then she told me to be nice to her brother and took off."

"Excellent." Marshall lands hard on the couch next to me and wraps an arm around my shoulder. "Can we drop the subject now? I think I've had about enough of the living and the dead for one night."

"I happen to fall into one of those categories." I lean into him and let Marshall hold me. I love the steady intense rhythm that surges from him. He has a way of scrubbing away the grit of reality and replacing it with something simpler, far more relevant to the joy of my soul. "I can fall asleep like this." I close my eyes and nestle my head into his shoulder.

"Then let's." He produces a white-cabled blanket from beside him and covers the two of us.

Really I thought Marshall would put up a sexual struggle. I thought for sure he'd slip the glibbery member that lurks in his mouth down my throat and give me a glimpse into another unwanted future event. But this? This is a nice change of pace.

❦ ❦ ❦

Logan waits for me in my dreams.

It's dark save for his countenance. His body is entombed in an otherworldly glow, provided by something much brighter than the sun, something that would make a fire jealous with its captivating reflection.

I should have figured he would be here. I should have asked Marshall to penetrate my mind with a shield of some kind to prevent this very thing from happening, although now that I'm here, under a sad frosted moon and full night sky of pink glittering stars, I don't seem to mind so much.

We sit on a grassy knoll with an overgrown willow tree nearby. I listen as her branches whistle in the breeze like a wind-chime made of microscopic seashells.

Pretty. Logan smiles over at me bashfully.

Yes, it is, I answer.

I meant you. He carefully picks up my hand and scoots in closer.

So I guess everything changes for us now. My voice swirls in the night, encapsulates us with its sad broken whisper.

Nothing changes. I still love you, and I can feel your love for me, even though...

Even though I've painted it black with anger? I ask.

Yes, that. Logan pushes into a smile, and the right side of his face depresses into a long comma-like dimple. Even in my dreams, he wears his scar for me.

I run my fingers over the dent I left by way of a broken bottle. Still not sure how sorry I am, although I suppose it's not his fault he was born a Count.

I'm going to visit my dad soon. I shrug. I say it more as a peace offering than anything relevant to the situation.

I'm planning on paying my parents a visit, too. I'll go with you, if you come with me. I'd love for you to meet them. He pushes his chin into his chest uncertain of my reaction.

I don't know. I'm sure Gage would come with me. You could probably talk him into going with you, too. Or Chloe, or

Lexy, or Michelle, whoever the flavor of the month happens to be. I thought it was impossible, but there it is. I've managed to drag all of our relational garbage right into a perfectly good dream.

There's no one else, Skyla, just you.

We lie back on the grass and stare at one another, puzzled. There might as well be prison bars between us. Not even in our dreams should we be together. How could I have been so deeply drawn to the wrong person? How could I still have an unrelenting ache deep inside that won't let him go?

I love Gage. I'm going to marry him eventually. We both know it's true. There's not one ounce of sadness in me when I say it.

I know. His eyes dip down swallowed up in sorrow. *But I know something else that's true.*

You do?

He nods.

Tell me. Even in my dreams I need to pull information from him, like extracting milk from a stone.

That our love is eternal. That it can never be broken.

I don't ask if Gage told him that. I don't want to know. I'm not sure whether or not I like the illusion of the kind of truth it projects, or the fact it could be a blatant lie.

He runs his fingers soft across my face, leaning in until our noses touch, and I close my eyes.

Logan dives in with a deep ocean of kisses. Kisses like a life raft, like a pool of shimmering water in the dry thirsty desert. I can feel the stars wrap their attention around us—peering down from their heavenly perch, riled up with intense jealousy at the purity of our love.

Wake up! Logan shouts.

I moan and push deeper into him. This dream—this is the only arena, the only microcosm of time that this eternal love will ever exist in.

Skyla! Wake up! It's not me. Open your eyes—please!

I rouse to a warm body nestled to my side. Deep throaty kisses that linger and... oh crap!

I start to slide off the couch in a panic only to be pulled into another round of Marshall's bad intentions.

Then a vision appears—me in the forest, running in the rain, arrows stream by, missing me by inches.

I get up on my elbows exhausted, far worse off than before I closed my eyes. I can see the sun coming up over the barn from out the back window.

"And I suppose that was my immediate future?" I pant into it.

"You suppose right." Marshall pushes out a sigh.

"And do I get speared by these vagrant arrows?"

"You might. I believe the question you want to ask is, who was shooting them at you."

"Who?" Pierce, Chloe, Mom, Tad, the list could go on forever.

"Me." He gives a shameless wicked grin.

8

There's No Place Like Home

Gage picks me up from Marshall's early in the morning and drives me to Casa Count where I once laid my head secure, not realizing it held the promise of a guillotine.

"Happy birthday," I say once again, carefully watching the Landon house as though it were a black widow lingering behind him.

"Thank you." He gives a warm kiss that momentarily makes me forget about my harsh new reality.

"Come on." He nudges me towards the house.

"I'm going to confront them," I tense up as I say it.

"I wouldn't do that, at least not yet. You're holding all the cards, Skyla. Once you let it out that you know—things could change fast. And," he pauses to run his fingers through my hair, "there's always the chance they don't know they're Counts."

I find this doubtful.

I don't dare go in the house alone, instead, I secure myself to Gage and hold my breath as though I were heading into a minefield.

"Here she is!" Tad shouts craning his neck up towards the stairs.

My mother glides down in her pink bathrobe, the flap opening with every other step.

"Where were you?" She slits the words out.

"I was," I look uneasily towards Gage, "with Brielle." Is that right?

wicked

"Ha!" Tad barks pointing a finger at me. "See this, Lizbeth? We fork over hundreds of dollars for a birthday party, and she thanks us by blatantly spending the night with her boyfriend!"

Brielle and Drake come racing down the stairs, then abruptly turn around when they see me in the doorway.

Great.

"Mia ran next door to tell you something early this morning." Imposter Mom hitches her hair behind her ear. "Darla said you weren't there. What's going on? Did you spend the night at the Oliver's? Just the truth please."

I look to Gage for answers. The truth is I don't ever want to speak to these people again. In fact, I want nothing more than to rush upstairs and pack all of my crap and never lay eyes on any of them, not even Mia who I totally suspect turned me in on purpose because she's a maniacal little Count.

"OK, let's try this another way." Mom's voice spikes a little. "Gage—did Skyla spend the night at your house?"

"No." He doesn't even hesitate.

I firm my grip on his hand and move in a little closer. A sharp bite of perspiration explodes all over me at once, and for the first time ever I'm nervous just standing here, in the entry with the people I thought I knew so well.

"That's too simplistic," Tad scolds. "Were you in a hotel? His car? On the beach?"

"We weren't together at all. I spent the night at Mr. Dudley's." I head upstairs to my room and pull Gage behind me.

"We're going to finish this later!" The sound of my mother's voice fills the void between the walls and sends a tremble of fear through me—as though it means something—as though a part of me still considers her an authority figure in my life.

I lock the door behind us, then push the dresser completely over the entry and give a mock smile. Now that I know they're Counts I realize they can bust through, easy as toilet paper.

"You're in deep." Gage wraps his arms around me. A soft rumble of laughter ripples through his chest.

"They're not my parents. Do you think there's some kind of youth hostel on the island I can hole up in?"

"No, I don't, nor would I send you there."

"Can I live in the doghouse with Charlie? I won't even eat food."

"Charlie doesn't have a doghouse. He's an indoor dog, and you have to eat food. You were designed to be filled with delicious hot meals." His dimples ignite on either side, and my stomach bottoms out.

"Thank you," I whisper.

"For?"

"For making me feel safe." I pull him over to the bed, and we sit down. Everything about my room feels foreign now as though it belonged to another girl—a girl who believed anything anybody told her. I feel lost, like the whole planet is swaying, and Gage is the only anchor to keep me from flying out into the atmosphere.

"I'll always be here for you." He tucks his head into my shoulder and gives my neck a string of soft kisses.

"Oh, hey." I pull back a notch. "Did you have a sister?"

"Did I have a sister?" He gives a quick blink. "Yes," he says, looking confused. "She died when I was five."

"And she was three." A surge of tears brim to the surface. "I'm sorry."

"What about her?"

"I was at Marshall's and this girl, she looked at lot like you, she came to the door and said she was your sister." I tell him about the bizarre encounter. "And I think it really was her."

His eyes glitter as fresh crimson tracks explode.

"I wish I could have been there," he whispers.

"Yeah well, I have this distinct feeling she'll be back. Don't leave my side, and you won't miss her." I pull him up towards the headboard with me. "You know when I said I thought it was good idea to slaughter all the Counts?"

"No, but go ahead."

"OK, so I may have been thinking it. Anyway, I had no idea it was going to include just about everyone, but you."

"Do you really think Tad and your mom are aware of this? That they're after you?"

"I don't know what to think. For sure I don't want to find out the hard way. Chloe arranged for us to end up on Paragon. Maybe Tad's in on it—*that* I'll believe every day of the week. And to be honest, it might explain some of Mom's strange behavior. Anyway, I don't want to call her Mom. She's not my mother. I'm going to take a nice little light drive one day soon and visit my dad. He'll explain things to me."

Gage looks away briefly and scratches at his cheek.

"What?"

"Nothing."

"Yes, it's something."

"It's just that I got stuck the last time we were there." He gives a wry smile. "I'm not letting go of you."

"Deal."

A rumble erupts in the hall. Voices escalate—Tad and Mom's.

"How dare you say that," My mother's voice muffles through the wall, "when *your* son also happens to be locked up in his bedroom with his girlfriend!"

"For your information, they're watching TV," Tad booms back.

"Yeah, well you know what we do when we're *watching TV*." Her voice is hard.

"I trust my son." I can hear his footsteps stomping down the hall towards their bedroom.

"And I trust my daughter!" She storms after him.

"See?" Gage nudges me. "She thinks of you as her daughter. She's sticking up for you. That's perfectly acceptable behavior."

"It's probably just an act." I shrink into his arms. "And by the way, some creatures find it perfectly acceptable behavior to eat their young."

9

Dinner with the Devil

I barely escape the grasp of my faux parents as Gage and I head over to the Bishop's for dinner. Apparently Mom called Marshall who, in turn, fed her a load of crap about my whereabouts last night and now all is seemingly right with the world.

"Hey," I whisper to Gage as we head up the walkway to the Bishop's house. "Maybe I can have Marshall convince my parents that I should live with him?"

"No." He gives a stern look. "Logan told me about that dream. Marshall is a predator."

Gage looks magical under the three quarter moon. I push up on the balls of my feet and press a kiss into him.

The door opens, and Chloe appears like a stain in the night.

Her lips curve up unnaturally, and her brows peak skyward. It's a demented feat that only a person with evil flowing through their veins can achieve.

Oh wait, that's my blood running through her veins. She's evil nonetheless.

The Oliver's car is already in the driveway, so is Logan's truck. He and Chloe have probably been strategizing how to best ruin my life and take over the world.

"I've been waiting." Her voice sounds almost hypnotic. "Happy birthday!" Chloe takes Gage by the hand and bounces us inside.

The Bishop home is normal, normal in size and contents in comparison to my own home with the exception that it smells divine.

"Everyone, you remember Gage." Chloe fans her hands over him like she's presenting him to the Queen of England.

"Yes, and you must be Skyla!" A tall brunette with a slight pug nose embraces me. She gives a rocking hug for so long that I'm half convinced we're slow dancing to the instrumental music playing in the background. "Thank you. Thank you for bringing back my precious baby girl. Anything you ever need, just name it and I'll do it for you." She pulls back and examines my face. Her lips quiver with gratitude. And for a frightening moment I almost ask if I could live with her.

"I'm Hal, and this is Glendora." A tall man with broad shoulders and a handlebar mustache comes around the table and gives a quick embrace. "Anything we can do for you, we're eternally grateful."

Wow, Chloe has nice parents. Like really nice. The apple must have rolled way far away from the apple tree, to an entirely different hemisphere for this to be possible.

It's dark in the formal dining room, and it's not until I strain my vision that I see Dr. Oliver and Emma waving to me, lost in murky shadows.

"Let's get started, shall we?" Glendora ushers both Gage and I over to the other side of the table. I try to sit next to him, but Chloe guides me over two seats.

"Follow the name plates," she says it cool as though the nameplates themselves were responsible for the geography of the seating arrangements and not her manipulative self.

The name *Skyler* is scrawled out on a folded piece of parchment in between Logan and her mother.

I pull a face and sit down next to him.

wicked

"Hello," he whispers.

He's got two dark circles under his eyes thanks to Marshall, but for the most part he looks like his brutally handsome self.

Gage is seated far to my left, so I can't even see him without leaning in past Logan.

A group of waitresses stream out from the kitchen each carrying a covered dome and erase all illusions I had of Chloe's family being normal. They stand in a neat row like a drone army of servants.

First, I've never seen real women wear French maid's costumes like the one Gage picked out for me at Halloween at any restaurant, let alone at someone's house. And second, I half expect a hand to pop up when the lid comes off the dome that was just set in front of me.

But there is no hand, there's cubed steak, undercooked—correction raw, sitting in its own juices, and oddly there's nothing else to go with it. Clearly these people are insane. I mean couldn't we start off with a nice salad? That is, until I notice that everyone else *is* starting off with a nice salad.

"Skyla," her mother purrs into me, "I thought you might need something to bring back your iron levels. I'm a nutritionist by trade, and I designed this meal just for you. It's steak tartare."

Gah!

I stare down at my food expecting it to moo or scream or slither away leaving a bloody trail.

"It's wine," Logan whispers.

"What?" I ask confused. There's not enough wine in the world to make me eat this bowl of rancid meat.

Emma and Glendora seem completely accepting of my meal as they engage in a titillating conversation regarding the nutritional value of blood.

"It's marinated in wine." Logan gives a brief smile. "You might like it." The right side of his face depresses unnaturally. Oddly it makes him more attractive in a rogue— bad boy sort of way.

"If you like it so much you eat it," I whisper.

Without warning my hand dips into the bloody mixture and sloshes it around.

"Oh God," I whisper. Before I know it, I'm inadvertently chucking pieces at Dr. Oliver and Glendora and Hal. I snatch up my fork and stab violently into the largest portion, catapulting it at Chloe.

"Skyla!" Dr. Oliver stands and brushes off his white dress shirt with a napkin.

"I'm so sorry! I can explain." My hand jerks forward and forces me to pick up the wine bottle off the center of the table, causing my arm to gyrate from the heft of it. "No, Holden please!" My body rises. I'm pushed over to Chloe who's cowering in the corner and I douse her with it.

A series of screams and groans emits from behind as Gage and Logan restrain me like I'm some sort of a lunatic.

"It was a total accident." I call over my shoulder, but by the time I turn around everyone has disbanded into the kitchen complaining of permanent stains, and I swear I hear Emma say something about trouble following me around like a rabid dog.

"If you didn't want to eat it you could have said so." Chloe spits the words in my face.

"It's Holden Kragger's ghost," I hiss. "I killed him just like I killed you."

wicked

"You killed Holden?" There's a promise of a smile on her lips. "I almost respect you."

Dr. Oliver and Emma step out from the kitchen.

"We're going to reschedule." Emma smiles sweetly in my direction, as if she didn't secretly hate me. Although, in her defense, I make it nearly impossible not to.

Glendora comes out and looks terrified at the sight of me. Her hand clutches at her neck as though I might snatch a steak knife off the table and slit her throat with it—little does she know that's her daughter's department.

"I guess I'll run up and change. We should go someplace." Chloe says it directly to Gage.

"Double date," Gage says, heavy with sarcasm while eyeing Logan.

Chloe turns to face me fully. Her dark hair frames her sharp features. There's something lurking beneath the surface of that condescending smile, something heartless—hazardous.

"We'll go to Devil's Peak." She trails her fingers on the side of my face, pressing her lips to my ear. "I hope you're wearing good shoes, Skyla. I hear it's slippery up there—a fall like that could be fatal."

10

If I Fall

The night glows a gentle shade of blue as the island drapes itself in the crystalline breath of God.

It's cold out in the Bishop's driveway. Thankfully I haven't spilled too much blood or wine on myself, not that I was afforded to run upstairs and change into a sequins jumpsuit that reeks of my-mother-bought-it. Still, it looks pretty good on her. Chloe seems to be able to pull off just about anything—sequined jumpsuits, other people's limbs and eyeballs—*death*.

"I'm driving with Gage," Chloe announces it loud enough for her parents and the Olivers to hear. She knows full well they're the only barricade keeping me from pulling her out of his car by the hair.

"It's a two-seater," I say. "You'd better go with Logan. I can't drive in his truck. I'm allergic to the upholstery or something. Plus it smells like crap." I add that last part under my breath. It doesn't really—it's just that every time Logan opens his mouth bullshit seems to fly out.

"Oh, Skyla, you're so insecure." She buckles herself into the passenger side of the car that Gage is still borrowing from his mom no thanks to me—well, Holden. "It's just one way." She rolls her eyes. "I'll hitch a ride back with Logan." And with that she slams the door.

Logan and I follow Gage on the long desolate stretch of highway that leads back to the western portion of the island. The Bishop's live way out in the middle of nowhere. It's like her

wicked

parents wanted to shelter themselves after that whole I killed their daughter thing went down.

"Isn't it ironic that when we were together we were so afraid of being seen, and now that we're not, here we are in your truck like it's no big deal?" I say.

Logan glances over at me before rounding out his hand over the wheel.

"You're with Gage. And when the faction war is over..." He expels a soft sigh.

"I'll still choose Gage."

He nods into the dark as though on some level he knows he should accept this, but the expression on his face is determined to do otherwise.

"I'm going to fight for you," it comes out with angry overtones as he stares down the double yellow line in the road. "I'll bring down the Counts, and Chloe, and every Sector in the universe that gets in my way without thinking twice." He cuts a look in my direction. "I'm not interested in what the future has planned. I want to share everything with you, Skyla. I'm in love with you."

My stomach does a soft roll. Logan knows how to say just what I want to hear just when I least need to hear it. He seems to have a real problem with delivery, and timing, and bloodlines.

"Has Gage ever told you anything about you and me?" Gage seems to use his gift of knowing as sparingly as Logan does the truth.

"Just once." He winces into the road as we pick up speed.

"Anything you want to share?"

"No," he says it low, doesn't say another word the rest of the way to Devil's Peak.

Once we hit the parking lot, I fly out of the truck and rush over to Gage who's standing there having some intense discussion with Chloe. A ton of kids from West are here just hanging out, smoking and drinking. It's a lot like a party at Ellis' house, minus the shelter.

"Hey you!" Brielle dive-bombs on top of me. "I'm spending the night." She lets out a ripple of laughter.

"Are you drinking?" Suddenly I feel like the Count wellness protection program. I'm pretty sure Counts in the incubation stage shouldn't consume alcohol and probably not those out of the incubation stage either.

"Nope. I'm the designated driver." She leans in and whispers, "For the next six and a half months."

Six and a half months to go?

I drop my gaze to her stomach, still flat as a textbook.

That means Marshall couldn't be the father. That means my step-Count, a.k.a. the golden child of Landon manner, has officially knocked up his girlfriend. Suddenly I feel lighter than air, and a spontaneous smile breaks out on my face. For the first time, I'm actually looking forward to all of the drama that's about to unfold, no thanks to Count Chocula senior's lame ass supervision. I, for one, can't wait to bear witness to Tad's head exploding when he hears the news.

Of course, Gage will be practically living in my bedroom, which makes things almost better than OK at home.

Hey? Maybe faux-mom was right? I should send out that sexual invite to Gage real soon. OK, so maybe those weren't her exact words, but it did go something like that.

"Yeah, well, Gage is spending the night, too." I wrap my arm around his waist and draw him in like a hook.

Chloe's face contorts into all kinds of stupid directions while Logan openly glowers over at Gage.

This is great. Who knew that even *hints* of me sleeping with Gage could set off an entire forest fire of hatred in both Chloe and Logan? So I decide to run with it.

"And," I bite down on my lower lip suggestively while looking at Gage. "I've been working on a private cheer just for you." I force a smile as though that weren't the lamest thing possible that could have floated out my mouth.

"A cheer?" Gage lowers his eyelids in a seductive manner. Clearly, he's more than a little amused.

"Uh-huh. It's not so much about the words as it is about the moves and what I'll be wearing. Or not." Just the thought of me cheering in the nude sends me biting down on my lower lip once again, this time in an effort to stave off a look of disgust.

"Wow." Gage gives a little laugh as his face sifts through ten shades of crimson. "Sounds like it's going to be a great night." He looks over to Logan with the slightest hint of a guilty expression.

Chloe steps forward and takes Gage by the hand. She doesn't acknowledge the fact I'm holding him, or that I'm his girlfriend, none of it matters.

"How about that walk you promised?" She tugs him in her direction.

"*No*," I say, irritated. "No walk." *Throwing*—pushing maybe—but no freaking walk.

Gage gently dislodges my death grip from around his waist. He's saying something to me with his eyes, but all I pick up from his mind is white noise.

"I'll make it quick." He shakes his head just barely before taking off towards the dirt path leading to the woods. Chloe is still holding his hand as though it belonged to her—as though all of him did.

"What's that about?" I run my fingers through the back of my hair and watch until they're out of site.

"I don't know," Logan stuffs his hands in his pockets. "But for your sake, I hope it's not a sign of things to come."

11

A Walk in the Night

The fog presses in, gives the impression that the whole world is nothing but an illusion. I can hardly make out the bodies less than ten feet away.

I try not to acknowledge Logan, who insists on leaning up against the railing with me as I wait for Gage to finish taking his new pet Chloe for a walk. We'll probably laugh about this later. Gage and I will make up all kinds of jokes about how Chloe's been acting like a real bitch ever since she came back, in more ways than one. Of course, they'll be private jokes. I like the idea of Gage and I building up our intimacy around Chloe and her canine ways, I would say, *how much we hate her,* but I'm starting to think maybe Gage doesn't hate her as much as I do. Not by a long shot.

I'm sure he's only doing this because he feels bad she's been dead and all, I mean, it's not like he's going to drive down to her house every night and take her out on a leash. He's not right? I glance up at the voile-covered sky for an answer.

Right about now I can't help feeling a little betrayed by Gage and his unrelenting kindness.

"It's been a really long time," I say. I'm secretly hoping to induce a panic in Logan, so he'll rush in and pluck them out. "Maybe he's hurt. You know, broken leg."

"He would have called." A plume of fog escapes his lips like smoke from a pipe.

"Oh, right." Great. I've got Mr. Logical on my hands. "I guess I'll have to go in and get them myself."

"They'll come out eventually, or you can call him, tell him to come back," his voice drops a notch. "I'd come back for you. But then, I never would have left."

"I'm not calling him," I shoot a sharp look. Its getting old listening to Logan profess his love for me now that I don't want it, now that I can never have it. "I'm not insecure. Besides, if I go in and accidentally run into them, it'll come off as totally natural." I take off down the same dirt path they started on well over an hour ago. Maybe they're lost? Worse, maybe *I'll* get lost. Maybe Chloe accidentally took a lethal U-turn, and she's dead for good this time right here at the base of Devil's Peak. How would that be for irony?

Logan appears by my side, slightly out of breath, and walks shoulder to shoulder with me as we enter the dark canopy of stalwart pines.

The absolute blackness of the dense forest drowns out the paper moon. It tones down the puff of visceral fog that blankets our world, and heightens our senses to a perfumed eucalyptus nearby.

"You mind if I come along?"

"Sort of," I say.

"OK then." He turns to go.

I snatch his hand before I can even process the fact I'm still mad at him—that I really shouldn't care if he leaves.

"Stay." I let his fingers drip off slow like honey.

He gives an impish grin. The smooth unblemished side of his face that I didn't graffiti with a shard of glass seems a stark contrast to the scarred rougher version. He's like two people in one. It seems almost representative of who he's become to me. Old Logan and new Logan—the before and after of our demise. He reaches over and takes a hold of my hand.

"You mind? I'm afraid of the dark." His words whistle past me in a swirl of lies.

"Just this once."

The forest floor hums with the thunder of bass from car doors swung open so the speakers can unleash their fury into the virginal night.

The clamor starts to dissipate as we delve deeper into the thicket, until all that's left to fill our ears is the sound of our own hushed breathing.

Logan?

Yes? His eyes glint into mine a haunting shade of glowing embers.

You think Gage has feelings for Chloe? I guess in the middle of an inky dark forest with its arms raised high like an impenetrable membrane, it feels safe to fess up to the fact that maybe this was a possibility.

Nope. Not one, I promise. He gives my hand a gentle squeeze as if to annunciate the fact.

I'm not sure if Logan's promises are worth much anymore. I still don't know if he's ever been true to me, or if he's been working with Chloe the entire time.

Hey. He stops and tugs at me gently. *Skyla, I love you more than I've ever loved anybody. I've never been anything but genuine, I swear to you. And if it weren't for the fact I put you in danger, I would never have let you go. I meant what I said about waiting for the faction war to end. There has to be hope for us because it will drive me insane to think there's not.*

I try not to consume his words—*reciprocate* them. Instead I try to let my mind filter through any other topic, my lit paper due next Thursday, Marshall and his prehensile tongue, but I can't fight it, Logan drifts to the surface like a cork each time. So I address it head on.

I don't know why it feels like there should be hope. I'm madly in love with Gage, and I'm destined to marry him. But, I feel it, too. Shame consumes me upon my admission.

The soft crush of leaves disrupts the silence.

A crackle emits, the distinct sound of something stirring to life ignites a steady stream of pops and whines until it becomes apparent we're not alone.

"Gage?" God—what if Chloe sent an invitation, and he accepted? What if Logan and I are walking in on some private moment between the two of them? I'd rather be eaten by Fems or captured by Ezrina or—

The ground shifts beneath us. Something brushes up against my back, and instinctively I jump towards Logan.

"What was that?" I hiss.

"I think you're getting your wish."

A slither of something thin and frail wraps itself around my ankle.

"Snake!" I try and shake it loose, but my other foot is being wrapped as well. In a moment that defies logic and reason, the evergreens bow down and secure their fur-lined arms around us.

"Fems," Logan says, trying to struggle free. The branches retract and pull us into the air, slowly, as though we were being strung onto a stealth hunter's bow.

"No! *No*—I'm afraid of heights." The words squeal out of me as I'm catapulted up hundreds of feet in the air, up higher than the puff of fog lying over the island like a dream, up high enough to count the stars in detail, to touch the moon, or to scream into God's own ear if I wanted.

I catch a glimpse of Logan stretched back with his arms pulled tight, his legs and torso no longer visible due to the unnatural coiling of branches cinched around his body.

"Skyla!" My name vibrates through the pitch and the gloom—it merges with the crashing ocean waves in the distance.

It's the last thing I hear as I plummet straight back to earth at a velocity that promises only one thing.

Death.

12

Terminal

The ground fast approaches, and I shut my eyes.

I can only assume it approaches because it has to eventually. It's the law of physics, when you fall, you will undoubtedly land somewhere, and that somewhere in my case is going to be the cold hard earth of Paragon.

Then I feel it. That strange tuning fork feeling rattles through me, and my lids fly open hoping to find Marshall wrapped around me, flying me off to L.A., back in time two years ago when everything was simple, so seemingly normal. If he did, which he's not, I could outsmart Chloe and save my father. But I'll never do those things. I might never do anything again because I've passed through sky and earth, and now I'm falling through a blank colorless world that I hardly recognize.

A white glossy floor crops up out of nowhere, and my face slaps against it so hard I'm convinced I've crushed my jaw to dust.

A dull thud lands besides me. I can see the tip of Logan's sneaker through the slit of my left eye, and I feel safe and thankful that I let him tag along in the forest with me.

"Skyla?" He groans crawling over to me. "Can you breathe?"

"Yes." It comes out like the hiss of an expiring balloon. "Where are we?" I think I already know—Ezrina's funhouse. I sit up trying to ignore the intense wave of nausea rolling through me.

"I don't know." Logan rises to his feet and helps me do the same.

"You think Chloe and Gage are down here?" That would make so much sense. Of course, the only way Gage would spend gobs of time with Chloe is if they were taken captive together. She'll have to hold him prisoner if she ever wants him to spend time with her.

"I have no idea," he says. "But let's you and me get the hell out of here."

It's a stark white room, which solidifies the fact we're in Ezrina's lair. A row of steel tables sits up against one wall and then nothing. No door, or window, or attic, just a full-blown well sealed box.

I try my phone, but there's no reception—big surprise there. We pat along the walls for a hint of some way to escape, and just as we're about to meet in the middle a door opens.

"Well, there you go," Logan looks disgusted with himself.

Two men walk in, both with sickly grey skin as though they've never seen the sun, as if they wouldn't believe you if you told them about it. Pale as though they just crawled out from underneath a rock. The shorter one with dark hair treks over and checks my pulse. It's as though he's reading it to see how viable I am.

"What's going on?" Logan asks point blank.

"Celestra." The taller one shouts over after examining the inside of Logan's wrist.

"This one too. Looks like cupboard steak tonight." They break out into goofy grins.

"He's a Count," I say, annoyed that I've landed myself here yet again.

"Countenance?" The tall one pads his fingers across Logan's wrist again. "Where's your allegiance?"

I scoot over and take up Logan's hand, low near my thigh.

Tell them you're a Count.

"I'm a Count," Logan spits the words out with great difficulty.

They look at one another steadily as though conducting a telepathic conversation of their own.

"Where does your allegiance lie?" The tall one reiterates.

"My allegiance lies with Countenance," Logan doesn't hesitate.

I marvel at how easy it came for him.

"Follow me." The tall one starts to pull Logan away.

I'm not leaving you. He gives a panicked look in my direction and resists walking out the door.

It might be the only way you can save us, I say.

Logan is yanked out violently. The shorter one follows suit, and the door seals into the wall once again.

I'm alone.

I start pounding the walls in a panic. "Marshall?" I scream his name like a chorus as I make my way around the room. Whatever happened to the just say my name and I'll be there bullshit? Or did he ever even say that?

"Nev?" I continue slapping the walls until my entire body vibrates and ripples, until it feels as though my bones are going to splinter right through my skin from the effort.

A wobble sets in. The walls start to lose shape. My feet fall in and out of the floor as though it were made of marshmallows. I don't know if it's a good thing, or if I'm going to land myself in a treble that has me walking with Logan in the forest again, or even one that goes as far back as me plunging the knife into Chloe's back, but I keep pounding and shouting, and the room keeps melting until I fall right through the floor and land hard on a carpeted surface.

wicked

I open one eye with caution. The room is dark and unfamiliar, and yet somehow the lack of white shiny walls brings a strange comfort to me. I bounce up onto my feet and dust off the back of my jeans.

Around the corner a blue glow emits, calling me with its soft expressive tone. I steady myself against the wall as I walk towards the shimmering pale light and poke my head over.

It's an entire room full of giant tube shaped tanks that run floor to ceiling filled with blue water or goo of some kind.

It's so still in here—so unearthly quiet, it fills my ears with a pressing silence. I make my way over to the tanks and hold my hand to the glass—warm to the touch. Each one is brightly lit from above. The whole room feels toasty as a bath. I turn around and bump into another row of tubular tanks before a scream gets locked in my throat.

Shit!

Bodies—*bodies*, floating! They're freaking human aquariums! Only the bodies aren't swimming, or evidently breathing, they're bottled up corpses.

A series of unintelligible noises garble in my throat as I stagger backwards away from the bizarre site.

In the first tank is a boy around my age. He looks familiar, reminds me a little of Drake with the sharp widow's peak. He's wearing a bright blue skin suit sort of like the one Gage had me wear the time we went snorkeling. His hair floats up in animated suspension and a light row of bubbles peppers his eyebrows. I wave my hand in front of his face to see if he'll move, but nothing.

In the next tank is something less than human, something with hair and teeth and flesh—

Crap!

I jump back a good three feet. Whatever it is, it's decomposing. The remains are twisting in a slow macabre spin, exposing the very fact that one eyeball is missing from the badly misshapen head. I take another step back before taking a quick peek at the last body on the end.

It's a girl. Long black hair dangles soft like seaweed. I take a step forward as morbid curiosity grips me. She's wearing the same blue body suit, but it's her well-manicured fingernails that catch my attention. Bright pink. The color alone disarms me, and I go over without hesitation to observe her. She spins slow and lethargic from the generated whirlpool like a suspended ballerina. Her long hair swirls in a circle as though it were alive, the only part of her to so much as quiver. A silver band near the bottom of the tank catches my attention. I stoop low to read it.

In tiny font etched into the metal reads, Emerson Kragger.

"Emerson," I whisper.

I look up at the girl in the tank. It's the girl Chloe killed.

I take in her sharp beauty, full lips, almond shaped eyes. Chloe is so narcissistic she could have killed Emerson for her looks alone. That brings a whole new meaning to *looks that kill*. I stand and gaze at her sideways. I wonder if Gage found her attractive—if he could have loved her? Why else would Chloe kill her?

Just as I'm about to pluck my phone out of my pocket to take a picture, a hand flops over my shoulder and gives a gentle squeeze.

13

The Air up There

I don't hesitate unleashing a wild drawn out scream. A scream that last for miles, that feels like it's pulling my intestines out right through my vocal cords.

I can feel myself being lifted. That familiar tuning fork feeling emits all over, and I gasp for breath as I open my eyes.

"Marshall!"

He lifts his finger to his lips and places my feet down safe in a bedroom bathed in moonlight that happens to be my own. I run over and push the dresser over my door and flick the lights on. The alarm next to my bed reads two-thirty.

"Logan and Gage are still down there."

His eyes track over me with a look of serious disdain. "Are they all you ever think about? Does it ever cross your mind that maybe Marshall's down there? Gee, I wonder if Marshall's safe today?" He postures himself as though he were me.

"Very funny." I fish my cell out of my pocket and speed dial. I meant to hit Gage, but my thanks to my incompetent muscle memory, I automatically hit Logan's name instead.

"Hello?" He sounds groggy as though he's been asleep for hours.

"Where are you?"

"I'm in the woods looking for you," he whispers. "Are you OK?"

"Yes," I say, looking hesitantly over at Marshall. "I found a backdoor and crawled out a latch. Um, I saw Mr. Dudley, and I hitched a ride home with him." I'm sure Logan can read between the lines. "How'd you get out?"

"I sold my soul to the company store."

"What does that mean?" I'm almost afraid to ask.

"I'll explain another time."

"What about Gage?"

"He's out here with me. He says he'll be over as soon as he drives his car home."

Marshall cocks his head to the side. *Tell him it's not necessary. I'll stay the night. It's the least I could do after you spent the night at my place.*

I avert my eyes at his offer. "Tell Gage to get here as fast as he can," I whisper into the phone.

Marshall looks indignant. *I'm not taking no for an answer. I won't relish having to alter your boyfriend's limbs in a horrific accident. These things are known to happen.*

"On second thought, tell Gage I've got Brielle, and I don't think he should come." I don't think those lines were quite as easy to read between.

"OK. Hey, Skyla?" Logan sounds winded.

"Yeah?" I watch as Marshall flops onto my bed backwards and fans his arms out.

"I would have done anything to save you," he whispers almost secretively, "I'm glad you're alright."

"Thanks." For once I believe him.

I hang up and toss my phone on the nightstand.

"Get up." I make sure my irritation comes in clear.

Marshall vaults up to the top of the canopy and watches as I get under the covers and turn off the lamp. His body illuminates a gentle shade of butter, and he dims it just right until I can look up without hurting my eyes.

"Where the hell was I?" I'm hoping Marshall will demystify the events of the last few hours.

"None of your business," he says it curt, lets me know he means it.

"What were you doing there?"

"Second verse same as the first."

"Emerson was in one of those holding tanks."

"You wield aggressive observational powers. That, and I believe the tank was labeled."

"Is she alive?"

"Did she wave hello?"

"No," I pause. "Did you come because I called you?" A cold shiver runs through me as I anticipate his answer.

"I was conducting business."

That's exactly what I was afraid of. I draw the covers up around my chin and try not to move as Marshall lands soft besides me.

It's going to be a long, long night.

✺ ✺ ✺

In the morning, I wake to a silent room with no Marshall, and no Gage, and very little light emanating from the outside world. A steady stream of rain pats softly against the window as I pull myself up to get a good look at the bleak pines on the other side of the glass. Their branches dance and sway to the rhythm of the wind. They look more than eerily alive, capable of anything, even launching me into wherever the hell it is I went.

I pick up my cell and call Gage.

"Hey." He sounds beyond tired like I just woke him up.

"Were you in Ezrina's lair?"

"No. Chloe had us climb down to the waterline. She wanted to see where they found her."

"Oh." That's morbid—hardly romantic if you ask me. I tell him all about the walk through the haunted forest and falling flat on my ass in Ezrina's little shop of horrors, Logan's sudden conversion to Counthood, and Emerson's involuntary suspension in liquid blue mouthwash. Then reluctantly I let him in on how Marshall swooped in and saved the day. Deep down inside I know Gage hates Marshall.

"Can you come over? We can get breakfast if you want," I say hopeful.

"I want—but I can't."

"Why not?"

"I have to get an early start," he gives a heavy sigh into the phone. "I need to run down and pick up Chloe."

"What?" I hiss a little too loud while jumping back on the bed. "Is this because of Marshall? I swear I didn't want him here."

"No, no. It's something else. Look, I can't really talk about it," he depresses into another heartfelt sigh. "You need to find a ride."

"Are you kidding?"

"I wish."

"Tell me right now why you're doing this. Is it because you can't help playing Mr. Nice Guy, or does she have you by the balls?"

There's a lengthy pause.

"Look, I gotta go. And Skyla?" There's a tempered silence. "I love you." He expels the words with rendered sadness, just before the line goes dead.

He hung up on me.

I sit there in disbelief just vegging out at the wall until my mother thumps against the door and sings something far too chipper to care about.

Leave it to Chloe to so effectively and quickly turn everything to shit.

I pull on my tightest jeans and a cropped white sweater before examining myself in the mirror. I pull off the sweater and try on three more, before settling back on the white one. I can't let Chloe get the upper hand with Gage. No matter what she has in mind there is no way in hell I'm letting her steal my boyfriend from underneath me.

I race downstairs to let Drake in on the fact I'm hitching a ride.

"Well *here's* the birthday princess." Tad screws the lid back on a jar of orange marmalade. "You enjoy yet another jaunt around the island? What time did you finally drift in? Five? Six in the morning?"

"Two-thirty," I say, heading over to Drake seated at the bar. "Can I catch a ride to school with you?"

"Maybe. Take a shower, show the world you care."

"I did."

A tiny quiver of flesh lands on my foot.

"Sprinkles!" Mia drifts in and picks up the tiny furless beast.

"Sprinkles." I test his name out before giving him a quick pat.

"You don't hump Skyla," she scolds, leaning in close, "that's her boyfriend's job." She gives an obnoxious grin before disappearing back down the hall.

"Skyla, what's going on with you?" My mother stands at the stove frying up eggs for Tad who salivates by her side.

"It's just this whole Chloe thing." That, and the fact you're all Counts. "It's sort of freaky."

"Mr. Dudley said he found you asleep in the barn Saturday night. You kids sneaking in there and partying or something?" She scrutinizes my features for clues.

"Sure." Tad plucks a dish out of the cupboard. "It's called a party for two, otherwise known as a roll in the hay." His lip curls up on the side as though he were certain.

Maybe I should blow them away and tell them I'm sleeping with Dudley, that Brielle is too, hell—that everybody is.

"I've invited Mr. Dudley over for Thanksgiving," Mom says shoving a piece of toast in her mouth. "The Olivers, too. I really like that Emma." She stares off dreamily as she moves the eggs around in the pan. I admire the way she didn't acknowledge any of the insults Tad hurled my way. It's as though the words from his lips were as irrelevant as he is.

"That's great." I'd rather have them here anyway.

I turn to head back up.

"And Skyla?" Tad shuffles over with his arms still folded tight. "When you get home from school, your mother and I have a gift for you." He narrows his tiny eyes in on me, and for the first time I feel the undeniable presence of evil.

"No, it's OK, whatever it is, you can take it back. The party was more than enough." The less I have to do with them the better.

"We can't take this back." He tips his head and peers at me through slotted lids. "But you might wish we could."

14

My Boyfriend's Back

First thing I do when I spot Gage at school is leap on him with my legs wrapped around his midsection and indulge in a deep throaty kiss that lets him know exactly how much I've missed him.

He pulls back and gives a naughty grin that assures me Chloe is the last thing on his mind. His dimples explode as he lands me safe on the ground.

"So why the ride? And can you please stop being so damn nice?" I push in another quick kiss. "Except to me."

Gage straightens. He scans the area as though he were looking for little miss bitch herself.

"What's going on?" He's scaring me.

Gage doesn't say anything. So I pick up his hands.

"Tell me."

I can't.

🦋 🦋 🦋

The hallowed halls of West Paragon High are alive with the demonic whispers of Chloe's name. It echoes off the walls like a Gregorian chant, moves through the courtyards like a voodoo rattle.

A film crew has set up shop in the quad and interviews Chloe before the start of first period. She sits on an elevated canvas chair across from a woman I recognize from local TV.

Chloe is poised and well versed in her lies. She reminds me a lot of Logan in that respect.

I can't watch, so I tuck my arm around Gage, and we head off towards the English building.

Every person I see gives me a mistrustful eye. The death rays come from every direction. I've quickly become the girl who tried to asphyxiate Chloe Bishop.

Gage, too, continues to give me the mysterious cold shoulder. We head into second and find Chloe standing at the desk nodding into Marshall as though it were perfectly normal for her to be living and breathing and in my Algebra Two class. I hope she's been rendered speechless by his beauty. Marshall could ignite a forest fire with his cutting good looks—just touching him is explosive.

As if on cue he reaches over and lays his hand over hers. He's saying something to her—sympathizing. I watch Chloe's face light up like a glowing coal. She's feeling it. Maybe she *is* the one who'll procreate with Marshall. Maybe he'll get his dream race after all.

Gage and I take our seats behind Ellis.

"You think she'll sit next to me?" Ellis appraises her with his glazed eyes.

I'm surprised Ellis would want her anywhere nearby after the way she treated him, or mistreated to be exact. But then knowing Ellis, he's probably up for some midnight visits and impromptu light drives despite Chloe's erratic behavior.

"Don't know, don't care, " I say, digging into my backpack.

Chloe heads on over.

Great.

"So where we sitting?" She doesn't bother acknowledging either Ellis, or me.

Gage glosses over the room before hitching his thumb at the empty seat behind his back.

"Skyla," Chloe twirls her fingers through her long, dark ponytail. "Would you mind sitting in front of Ellis?"

"Yes, yes I would." I open my notebook and settle in.

"Have it your way." She ticks her head, and Gage gets up and follows her clear across the room.

"Holy. Freaking. Shit." I'm so stunned I can't breathe.

"Looks like the wicked witch cast her spell." Ellis blows a breath through his cheeks.

"Yeah, only I don't think it's a spell."

The bell rings as the last few stragglers file in.

Well Skyla, Marshall gives a gloating smile in my direction. *Looks like your competition has eliminated you with minimal resistance.*

I cut my eyes in the opposite direction. There is no way I'm going to watch Marshall thrive over this.

Aren't you the least bit relieved to know that the final Oliver standing has a fondness for corpses? It's best to be apprised of such wicked fetishes at this stage of the game before he promises to marry you then leaves you at the altar for a casket. He's probably got the entire cemetery mapped out of long departed beauties.

I catch Gage sitting there staring off at the wall with a clear look of irritation. No, he's definitely not into this.

Chloe's got him by the balls.

But with what?

🦋 🦋 🦋

Gage pretends he doesn't even know me for the better half of the day. He spends lunch in the cafeteria with Chloe as the other students continue to glom onto her every word as though she's just been dropped back onto the planet after an alien abduction.

Before sixth, I do a lightening change into my cheer uniform and wait outside the boy's gym for him to emerge.

Gage and Logan come out at the same time.

"Hi stranger," I say, pulling Gage back by the elbow. "Are you mad at me?"

"No." His eyes soften into twin pools of cobalt sky. His dimples tremble before digging in, but he doesn't say a word.

"So can I have a ride home?" A heavy feeling coats me from the inside—already I know the answer.

Gage squints across the field. I can see Chloe flagging him down with a big toothy grin.

"I'll come over tonight," he rubs the side of my cheek with his fingers. *I love you.*

He takes off running in her direction.

"You have a funny way of showing it!" I shout after him. Clearly my role as clueless girlfriend has just begun.

"You're on the schedule for tomorrow." A single beam of sunlight casts its light across Logan. He shrugs as if to ask if I still want the hours. Of course I do, just not with him.

"Will you be there?" A part of me is hoping he'll say yes—explain everything to me.

"I will."

"So, do you know what's going on here?" I glance over at Gage who's busy speaking with Chloe.

Logan shakes his head. "He won't say a word."

I'm slightly relieved to know it's not just me he's keeping this from.

"I'll be there," I say as we walk out onto the field together.

wicked

I land on a patch of wet grass next to Brielle.

Ms. Richards blows her whistle and claps her hands together to get our attention.

"I want to welcome back one of the most competitive and best disciplined team captains the West Paragon Dawgs have ever seen." She breaks out into spontaneous applause as Chloe steps up.

I look over at Michelle, our newly dethroned leader, and I swear it looks as though she's scowling at Chloe. She slides the rose of deadly dreams across the chain on her neck, over and over as though it were an act of sorcery—and the birth of an idea starts to percolate in me.

"So," Chloe begins, "I just want to thank all you guys for all the support since I've been back. I want to apologize for taking off and letting you guys worry about me—*bury* me. I feel terrible. Anyway, one of my best friends, Emily Morgan," she flexes her fingers in her direction, "was nice enough to organize a get together at her house this Saturday night, and it would really mean the world to me if all of you guys would come." She leers over at me when she says it.

"No way Messenger is going," Emily barks. "Not after she jumped you and tried to twist your neck off."

"Skyla!" Ms. Richards' red hair dances up above her head like a fire. I'm still dying to find out more about her great, great grandmother a.k.a. Ezrina.

"I thought she was someone else," I say, half convincingly.

"Oh no—I want Skyler there." Chloe gives a quick wink. "We haven't had the chance to sit down properly and get to know one other. I think that's just what we need."

"It's Sky*la*," I smear the correction heavy with attitude.

"Well, Sky*la*," she hides her true intentions behind a thin veil of benevolence. "I have a feeling we're going to be fast friends. In fact, I think you'll fit in real well with my inner circle."

The bitch squad gapes openly as though Chloe were unaware of the social demotion she were impinging on them.

I fall back on my hands and take it all in.

Chloe wants Gage as her boyfriend and me as her bestie. I don't believe that last part for a minute.

I can't stomp her out of existence because she's got a protective hedge around her neck that rivals the missile shield, and she single-handedly ruined my family and my birthday party.

I may not be able to kill Chloe, but for sure I'll have fun trying.

15

The Surprise

"Ok!" After school, momma Count leads me by hand as I pretend to keep my lids shut.

She and Tad have lured me out into the backyard—probably to a giant stone altar where they plan on tying me to a pile of brush and setting me on fire.

We head off into the desolate tip of the property far away from the house. I can feel the air cool around me significantly. The scent of crushed fern and pine needles is so robust—the fragrance sets off a bitter aftertaste in my mouth.

It feels blank out here, too quiet. It's doubtful any human foot has trekked into this distal portion before, perhaps a cartographer studying the lay of the land, then after him just the three of us. I open my lids a little more, only I don't see a stone altar, I see something shiny and *purple*?

"Open!" My mother shouts with glee.

It's a bike. A brand new shiny bike that looks vaguely familiar, and now I'm staring to appreciate the gift Logan tried to give me just a little bit more.

"Wow," I don't bother hiding my sarcasm as I circle around it. "A basket and everything. Golly gee, can I take it to school tomorrow? Thundershowers are in the forecast for the rest of the week, but I can make a game of it. You know, dodge the lightning bolt."

"Very funny." Tad pulls his lips into a line. "Told you she wouldn't appreciate it."

"She doesn't know what it is," Mom steps up and takes me by the hand. "Hon, this bike belonged to your dad. I thought it'd be a nice touch to have it renovated for you."

"Dad?" His name comes out in a pale puff of air, evaporates just like he did.

I touch the now all too familiar frame—the pedals, run a finger over the top of the back tire. I remember him peddling me to the store on the handlebars and how my mother would scream that we were going to crash. "It's his bicycle." I loved this thing, so did he. "Thank you." I hop on and bounce into it.

"Told you she'd love it," Mom chides.

"Yeah well, if she knew how much we paid to have that thing stripped and painted she'd probably want the cash for that '66 Mustang."

"No, this is perfect," I say. "I think when the weather clears I really will take it to school."

"Won't Gage mind?" My mother twitches her nose at me.

I shake my head as I envision Chloe dragging him around by the hair.

"I don't think so."

I don't think he has a say.

※ ※ ※

Gage shows up a little after eleven that night. I've showered and shaved and pushed the dresser in front of the door. I'm totally ready to do whatever it takes to get him to tell me what Chloe's holding over him.

I pull him towards the bed and push him backwards onto his elbows. Hopping up beside him, I give the sexiest, albeit awkward, sideways kiss.

"Hello to you, too." He lets out a lazy grin and kicks off his shoes. They hit the wood floor with two very distinct thuds. The noise causes me to simultaneously freeze and stop breathing just before I lean over and turn off the light. Not that my mother could ever successfully evict Gage from my bedroom.

"That was smooth." He pecks a kiss on my forehead. "Sorry."

"So what's going on?" Now that the lights are off, I doubt he'll notice the pink lace boy-shorts and matching bra that I spent hours debating over. Or the fact I redefined forever by applying false eyelashes until my fingers cramped up from almost adhering my lids together, twice.

"Nothing's going on with me, but you've definitely got it going on." He pulls me into a series of mind numbing kisses, taps into my soul with aching throws of desperate passion that only Gage is able to emanate so well.

We build a blaze on the bed, an inferno that transcends any stupid invitation I was told to send out. It feels right like this with Gage. I trace my hands down his chest and into the edge of his jeans. I don't bother with the button or the zipper, just glide my fingers into the waistband of his underwear and push in a little deeper.

Gage snaps me up by the wrist and brings up my hand as though he's just made the interception of the year.

"Where you going?" He gives a husky laugh.

"I was checking—you know, boxers or briefs." I pull a face and scoot in towards the wall to give him more space.

He brushes my hair back with his fingers in long continuous strokes. A perfect seam of moonlight falls over his face—highlighting him like a black and white picture, save for the eyes, which remain true to the deepest part of the ocean even in this dim light.

"You know that I want to," he leans in with a sarcastic inflection, "help you demystify my clothing preferences, but not like this, not on your bed in your room with a dresser barricading us from your parents."

"They're not my parents, if that helps."

He shakes his head.

It makes me think of Logan, how he had Chloe right in this very room, twice to be exact. He wasn't quite as altruistic as Gage, but then again, he wasn't really in love with Chloe to begin with. And I can't judge Logan. I would've jumped at the chance if Gage let me.

"So you prefer the downstairs sofa?" I shrug.

"No—nowhere in the Landon residence to be exact. I'd hate for Tad to be right about me."

"Who cares about Tad? This is about us." I reach my hand inside the bottom of his t-shirt and trace a heart onto his smooth bare chest. "It's going to happen eventually." I bite down on my lower lip and magnetize him byway of a bewitching stare. "But then you probably already know about it, which totally isn't fair." I push him in slowly by the back of the neck until I can feel his warm minty breath on my face. "So tell me about it."

He shakes his head in reluctance. "It's a very naughty bedtime story."

"You do know." I give a quick scratch at his chest. "I bet its prom because I secretly love clichés."

"No." The curve of a wicked grin waits to explode on his face.

"OK, Christmas," I whisper. "I like Christmas better anyway because it's practically almost here."

"Nope." There's a gleam in his eye because he's so obviously enjoying this.

"Two days—Thanksgiving. Right up on the table in front Tad and my fake mom, Marshall will be there did I forget to mention that?" I giggle at the thought.

"Yeah, well, Marshall might try to knock me off the table and take over, so that's definitely a no go."

I swallow hard and just stare at Gage, perfect in every way—every way, of course, except for the fact he continues to willingly allow Chloe to insert herself as the thorn in the side of our relationship.

"I want to know what the hell Chloe is up to." I needle him with a suspicious gaze.

He doesn't say anything—*think* anything, other than graze over me with his eyes, as he focuses in on the color of my skin, my clean scent.

He's so keyed into the moment, almost forcefully so, as if he were acutely aware of the fact I was prying into his thoughts, waiting to pick up the slightest clue to Chloe's latest and greatest way to unravel my life. Obviously Gage isn't going to tell.

"Why does she hate me so much?" I breathe the words out in a sigh. "I mean, other than the fact I killed her, but that was totally called for." I blink into my own stupidity.

"It's not that she hates you, it's that she loves herself and her own ambitions. She doesn't let anything stand in the way of getting what she wants."

"And right now she wants nothing more than you." I let my hand fall out from under his shirt.

"Yes, but she doesn't get me." His dimples sink in deep. "You do." Gage pulls me on top of him and traces a line up the side of my neck by way of his tongue. "It's worth the wait. I've seen it."

16

Off To Work I Go

Tuesday and Wednesday go in the same direction with me trying to lure an explanation out of Gage and Gage artfully avoiding the conversation by way of his lips.

After school on Wednesday, the weather is its regular crappy self as a morose cloud stretches over the island like a layer of dusty gossamer. Instead of begging Drake or Brielle for a lift to work, I decide to ride my bike down to the bowling alley.

"What happened to you?" Logan strides over examining me curiously as I walk through the door.

"Nothing." I catch a glimpse of myself in the mirrored paneling.

My hair is plastered, completely drenched, and my mascara has bled two inches down my face. I don't even look this bad when I get out of the shower.

"I rode my bike," I blow out the words as I try to wipe down the makeup atrocity with the sleeve of my jacket.

"Your bike?"

"My parent's gave it to me for my birthday. You know, the ones who will probably fork me over to the Counts in exchange for cash and prizes? How could you not tell me I was living in enemy territory?" I watch as his face smoothes over. "Never mind, you're one of them." Logan is the enemy. How's that for irony.

His eyes close momentarily as though he were truly sorry about something, and I'm betting it's the fact he got caught.

wicked

"Look, I have rules about hygiene and," he motions towards my chest, "a dress code to maintain, so I can't let you work like this."

I look down to see my lace bra peeking through my t-shirt that apparently decided to dissolve in the rain.

"Crap," I whisper.

"I also moderate employee language." His cheek rises on the side, forcing his newfound dimple to wink at me.

Really it doesn't seem fair, in the one moment I want to hurt and deform Logan, I only managed to make him more unbearably handsome.

"Are you firing me?" A part of me hopes so. It's too difficult to be around him, close enough to touch him, close enough to feel his constant yearning. Just breathing the scent of his musky cologne is like letting Logan swirl around inside of me.

He stands there with his arms folded low, looking at me with those citrine lenses, over a thicket of long black lashes that any girl would kill for.

"No, I would never fire you. You could do just about anything and on your worst day, you couldn't get fired," he says it mournfully. You could feel the longing exuding from him. Even though he's resigned to the fact I'm with Gage, he can't seem to control his aching expression of sadness. "I have Brielle here—Gage is coming in at six."

I take in a quick breath at the thought of working with Gage. I miss him insanely. He said four words to me today. Pass me the paper. And that was in lit, first period. It's like he's afraid he's going to accidentally divulge whatever the hell Chloe is lording over him. I begged him for hours last night to give me one hint, and nothing.

"I'll go home and change. My mom can give me a ride back." I almost said, that lunatic who claims to be my mother, but somehow I really believe she has maternal feelings for me even if she does plan on eating me or setting me on fire one day.

Logan twists in his shoes looking back into the kitchen.

"You know, I think it's better if you and I just hang out."

"Did Gage say he didn't want to work with me?" It hurts just to think it.

Logan swallows hard and ushers me towards the entrance. He pulls his keys out of his pocket and shouts over to Brielle in the kitchen that he'll be stepping out for a while.

"Logan," I pull him back by the arm. "Are you keeping me away from Gage, or does he not want us working together?" Logan has managed to keep Gage and I off the same schedule for weeks. It makes me wonder if my makeup and fashion disaster are all a lucky coincidence for him.

He gives a slow blink. "This time it's not me."

꙳ ꙳ ꙳

Logan tosses over the keys to his dad's '66 Mustang and asks me to follow him. The night glows a gas lamp yellow as street lights dot the main highway like a series of miniature moons as far as the eye can see.

It's scary being in a car alone. Well, as alone as I can get with Holden's ghost, only I try and blank the thought of him out of my mind because the last time I drove, Holden gave me a formal introduction to his brother by way of a major car accident.

Logan makes a turn into the Black Forest. I hate this place. Maybe it's Logan who's going to set me on fire, chop off my limbs, or whatever it is the Counts do to Celestra for kicks.

A swarm of trees lean in with their long fingerlike branches as I drive along the dirt road. Every now and again, one gets too close, and a horrible screaming sound arouses the silence as its fingernail scrapes against the metal. The car hobbles in and out of the muddy potholes in steep unnatural gyrations. It feels as though I'm riding on an over-laden mule, only this one holds the promise of blowing out all four hooves.

Logan parks up on the side, and I pull in behind him and get out of the car.

"So, what's going on?" A puff of pristine fog encircles us as I make my way over.

"I thought we'd hang out. You know, we could talk."

"Here?" We could have talked in the office, or over the phone while I relax in my room. It's so murky his face is lost in the evening shadows.

Logan pulls a blanket from the driver's side and spreads it out in the bed of the truck.

"Here." He lends me a hand as we hop inside, and suddenly I'm feeling rather kidnapped even if I did voluntarily drive myself here. Come to think of it, that's probably exactly how my capture will take place. The Counts will invite me someplace, and I'll mindlessly go right along.

I sit opposite him as far away as possible and press my back into the hard frame of the truck as a way of showing my loyalty to Gage.

"Skyla." He crawls over on his stomach and lands just shy of me. "I had no idea I had a drop of Countenance in me. I swear, and neither did my uncle."

"That's nice." Never believe a Count, ever. It's my own rule, and I think it's a damn good one.

I watch as the black fur of the evergreens waves limp against the dark purple sky.

"Nev!" I shout, just in case I need him. Truth is I'd rather be here with Logan the Count than with Gage who won't tell me why he's suddenly Chloe's chauffeur and personal book caddy. "You know he walks her to every class? I spent lunch today with Ellis. He's my favorite Count by the way," I sneer half playful.

"Oh really?" I can see his tongue rounding out the inside of his cheek.

A thread of light gets caught in the line of his scar.

"I can't believe I hurt you." My fingers stop shy of touching his face.

"It adds character," he says dropping his gaze to the blanket. His face darkens to soot when he takes the light of his eyes away like that. Sort of the way my life has darkened without him.

"I really love Gage." It comes out like a proclamation. "So what do you think is going on with him, anyway? And what happened to you when we got separated in Ezrina's lair?"

He sits up besides me as the night dulls out in a fairytale wash of amethyst.

"It's not called Ezrina's lair," he corrects, bumping into my shoulder. "It's called the Transfer."

"The Transfer." I think I like Ezrina's lair better. "So, now that you're a Count you know all of their big bad secrets?"

"No, but I'm going to." The whites of his eyes illuminate in jags like a mirror reflecting the sun.

"And how are you going to do that?"

"I'm going to renounce myself as a Celestra."

17

The Deal

I put on my fuzzy leopard print robe and nothing else as I wait for Gage to drop in through the butterfly room, but he doesn't come. Eleven turns to twelve, so I decide to text him.
    Why are you being a turkey? ~S
    It's officially Thanksgiving, and I hope he reads between the lines because being a turkey on Thanksgiving pretty much sucks.
    I was held up. Can Marshall sub for a while?
    Is he freaking kidding?
    Are you kidding? ~S
    A lengthy pause ensues.
    I'll be right there.
    Gage appears in the doorway and comes over to the bed.
    "Thank you." It comes out laced with sarcasm. I want to say something fun and light, but it feels like a jackhammer has impressed itself in my gut, and any minute now I'm going to cry out from the pain.
    "Hey." He rolls in next to me and pulls me into a hug. "I swear I love you." A warm kiss lands on the top of my head as I sniff back tears.
    "I think I'm going to kill her." It comes out flat, more like a fact than anything euphemistic. I did it once for my father, and it didn't take. I think I'm entitled a do-over.
    "No," a soft rumble of laughter ripples through his chest.

"Then you need to tell me." I pull back and glare over at him. "Right now, tell me what she's doing to keep you away from me."

"No." He doesn't even hesitate. "I can't. I'm sorry."

A wash of moonlight blanches out the color in the room. It bathes us in a sea of grey, colorless as stone. It tries to siphon all of the hurt and drama from the moment, but its efforts prove impotent. Chloe has detonated herself in my world, and the fragments of evil she's unleashed are stabbing the life out of my relationship with Gage.

"Tell me." My voice shakes with a quiet rage. "If you love me you'll tell me."

He lies back on the pillow and gives into a long thoughtful blink.

"I just need a little time. I think I can get us out of this," he whispers up towards the canopy.

"What kind of time? Our entire junior—*senior* year? Chloe doesn't take no for an answer. Trust me, I'm well aware that she gets what she wants, but I'll be damned if she thinks she's getting you. This is one game I'm not playing. Tell me what's going on."

He leans up on one elbow and runs his fingers over the side of my face, tracing the outline of my lips before dropping down to my neck—the bare center of my chest.

Chloe. She is the black hole of destruction that sucks out all of the good things in my life and systematically takes them away. She stole my father, and now she's stealing Gage.

"This won't go away until she does," I whisper mostly to myself.

"She's indestructible with that protective hedge."

My hand floats up to the ring Gage gave me hanging from a thin thread of silver around my neck. I had it once, the protective hedge, and I was foolish enough to give it back. I'm sure all that babbling in her diary about a game of buried treasure had to do with just that. Chloe spent the last several weeks of her life securing her future, so that I couldn't kill her a second time.

Gage slips his hand into the hem of my robe just above my stomach.

"So what does she want from you?" This time it's me catching his wrist like a thief as I gently pluck him away from the warmth of my skin.

"To talk." He pulls me in, resting his head on my shoulder. "She's convinced the more time I spend with her, I'll actually want to be with her."

"Be with her," I mouth the words. Chloe was trying to land a kiss from Gage long before she knew she was terminal. I'm sure she wants something more than having him in her close proximity, like *being* with her in the literal sense. "So you think this will end soon?"

"It's never going to end with her. I just need to tactfully remove myself from the situation before she does something irrational."

"Does that irrational behavior involve me?" I already know the answer. Gage would die before he let one bad thing happen to me.

He pulls back, a direct stream of moonlight pours over his features. There's such a magnified splendor about Gage. Every piece of marble should ache to be carved into his likeness.

"It involves you." He gives a nod. "I'd let her set me on fire before I let her hurt you."

I nod into his words.

Chloe will never relent from her blackmail—I already know this. And Gage will never stop trying to protect me. He will end our relationship if he has to, I can already feel it. It's funny how this mirrors what happened to Logan and me, only I'd have to kill an entire faction of people to ever be with Logan—back when I wanted him—when I thought I knew who he was and what he stood for. But for Gage, only one person has to die, and it just so happens she can't.

Gage goes home at the crack of dawn, no thanks to my mother, who made it a point to bang on my door and offer to teach me how to look down the business end of a turkey—to which I unremorsefully declined.

It's a little after two in the afternoon, and I fully expect the Olivers any minute. I think Brielle and her mother are already downstairs because I can hear Mom exuding an unnatural level of glee that she reserves only for company. I shut my door and push the dresser over an inch.

"Holden?" I say his name a shade above a whisper. "Hello? Earth to Holden?"

Since we *are* having another sit down dinner, and he *does* seem to prefer an audience to embarrass me in front of, I thought I'd have a little tête-à-tête with my least favorite disembodied spirit. "Are you there?"

The dresser mirror splinters in a perfect spider web pattern.

I give a quick blink.

This is the exact kind of shit I'm trying to avoid.

"Look, I know you want a body. But destroying my life and embarrassing me isn't going to bring it to you any faster." Well really, nothing will, but that's beside the point. "It's Thanksgiving. That means there will be a ton of guests over, and I want to have a civil meal without the fear of my hand lobbing table scraps at people." Except maybe for Tad, but that's because he's an asshole and deserves to have table scraps lobbed at him, hey... "So, I've decided," rather spontaneously, "that if you want to earn your keep, you need to stay in line. That's not to say you can't be bad. I know you're a bad boy and some things never change, so I expressly give you permission to do whatever you like to my stepfather, Tad. In fact, I encourage you to unleash whatever the hell you feel like unleashing, just make sure there are no other casualties, and I play no part in it." I'd sic him on Chloe, but it's a mute point. "Got it?"

A bottle of red nail polish knocks over onto my desk.

"Good."

A fog of moisture starts to build on the window. It expands a foot in either direction then a line emerges—letters are being formed...*body.*

"Yes," I say backing out of the room. "You'll get your body."

Only he won't.

18

Give Thanks

The house is alive with the thick scent of turkey, intermingled with nutmeg and other spices that remain foreign to us the rest of the year. I sail downstairs just as my mother opens the door to the Olivers and Marshall.

Barron and Emma both greet us with such elegance I'm almost sorry for them to have to participate in the holiday at our house. But then again, the Olivers are a practical people, and they probably lowered their expectations as soon as my mother called to invite them.

"Dinner smells terrific!" Emma beams, leaning in to give Mom a quick hug.

"That's because of the hot date I had with Tom at five-thirty this morning." My mother laughs at her own joke. "I have an inkling we'll be spending a lot of holidays together from here on out. I have a really good feeling about your son and my daughter."

I walk over to Gage and Logan, still waiting to make their way inside, no thanks to the backlog my mother has created with her love affair with Emma.

"Happy Thanksgiving." I pull Gage in by the hand.

Marshall swoops in from out of the cold. Honestly, if it started to rain, I think we'd see snow.

Gorgeous per usual, Ms. Messenger. He hands me a blistering casserole dish.

wicked

"What's this?" It's firmly wrapped in ten layers of plastic, and I think all ten layers have melted together because it's so freaking hot.

"Sweet potatoes." He leans into my mother and engages in a lengthy embrace.

"Mr. Dudley said his sweet potatoes were heavenly." Mom gives a look as though she's craving more than just his sweet potatoes.

"I'm sure they are," I say, whisking the dish of molten lava to the kitchen.

Brielle and her mom, Darla, are already seated at the bar cackling with Tad about something. Probably laughing at the fact they're all Counts, and I'm a dumb little Celestra who doesn't know what the hell is going on.

Mom wastes no time in ushering everyone to their seats. Mia and Melissa made placeholders out of dried maple leaves with our names spelled out in thick magic marker. I frown at the fact that Logan and Gage will be on either side of me.

Mia comes over and leans in.

"I wasn't sure which one impregnated you," she whispers, "this way you can be close to both just in case." She gives a sly grin.

"You're so not funny."

I shoot a look up over at Marshall. He still thinks he's on the hook with Brielle. I wonder if this kind of info is worth anything to him? Perhaps a body for Holden in exchange for news of his newly demoted paternity status? It only seems fair.

Tad claps his hands together up over his head. It's so loud, for a second, I think he's firing shots into the crowd.

"Everybody in your seats. Whoop, whoop! Let's do this. Whoop, whoop!" he shouts.

Normally I'd be mortified by Tad's sudden need to replicate a dying train. I'd want the ground to open up and for it to swallow me—well—*him*, but not today. Just knowing Tad's a Count—that they all are—makes me feel slightly justified in my eye rolling endeavors that I'm prone to during moments like these.

Marshall lands across from me. Brielle and her mother have ended up at the opposite end of the elongated table. It takes up almost the entire length of the dining and living room, complete with hodge-podge seating ranging from kitchen stools to office chairs, which explains why Emma and Dr. Oliver are sitting about a foot taller than the rest of us.

I look down at the far end where Darla is adjusting her lipstick in the blade of a knife. She's been ogling Marshall openly since he walked into the room, and now she's rubbing her front teeth with her finger, asking him random questions at the same time. She seems to be lacking in common social graces. But I totally get it. Poor thing hasn't had much luck getting another boyfriend after I nearly stabbed the old one to death with a pair of kitchen scissors. Of course, I blame Chloe for that, too. Everything, good or bad, that's happened to me since my father died can be directly traced back to Chloe and the rerouting of my life.

I glance over at Gage who gives a comfortable smile in my direction. I think it's high time I start rerouting Chloe's life a little myself.

"Here we go!" Tad bellows as he hauls out a monster turkey the size of a baby giraffe and plunks it onto the table.

"Holy shit! Where did you get that thing?" Brielle's mother hoots into it as if it were the funniest thing she's ever seen. Forget social graces—Brielle's mom is flat out ripped. She

wicked

laughs so hard there's just air expelling from her lungs for a good thirty seconds.

"Mr. Dudley had it sent over yesterday," Mom offers. "It's from a rancher friend of his."

"It's certainly out of this world," Emma muses, saucer eyed.

I'm sure it's out of this world just like I'm sure the farmer was, too.

I glare over at Marshall for being so bizarre.

"That's right, it's a hybrid," Marshall offers. *Sort of like your ex.* He glances at me briefly.

Tad holds up two long, machete-looking knives in the air with all of the drama he can afford, then proceeds to rub the blades against one another in an attempt to sharpen them. Clearly Tad is savoring the fact he has a captive audience as evidenced by the methodical approach he's taking to serving up our dinner.

A tiny feeling of remorse comes over me for sicking Holden on him like some rabid celestial dog. That's pretty funny actually—Holden as my celestial bitch. I kind of like that. Maybe I can drag out this whole I'll-get-you-a-body thing for the rest of my life, or Tad's, whichever ends first.

"Speaking of overgrown birds," Tad says putting down one of the sabers he's through molesting. "Trapped a raven the size of a lawn chair out back today. Damn thing has been stalking us for days. Almost lost an eye to it last week."

Gage and I exchange glances. *Nev.* Shit. I need my bird back, safe, and in one piece.

"What did you do with it?" Dr. Oliver presses out a hesitant smile.

"I'm sure he humanely disposed of it." Marshall gives a smug look of satisfaction. He could care less if Nevermore were toast.

"I called animal services," Tad says, starting into the bird in front of him with long easy strokes.

I breathe a sigh of relief into Gage.

"But," Tad pauses in reflection, "they were closed because of the holiday, so I just got rid of the thing myself."

Double shit!

"I killed it and stuffed it in the turkey. Like that Mcduffen stuff they serve back East." He grins.

My entire body seizes.

"I think it's called turducken," Mom corrects.

"I don't want anything for dinner that starts with turd." Mia pushes back her plate.

"I jest," he says, continuing to saw away at the gargantuan creature. "I drove the damn thing down to the animal hospital."

I take Gage up by the hand.

Don't worry. We'll get him back. Gage nods as though he already knows this.

"Speaking of birds," my mother points with both hands over in our direction, "I think we've got ourselves a couple of lovebirds." Her entire face explodes a bright shade of pink as she continues to hack out a laugh. Obviously Darla wasn't the only one hitting the wine a little early.

"They're very nice together." Emma pinches a short-lived smile in my direction.

I thought she liked me once, but now I'm not so sure.

"What about these two?" Darla sloshes her glass in Drake and Brielle's direction until the wine dances right onto her plate. "Something tells me we'll be hearing wedding bells soon from this end of the table."

wicked

She's probably right, and for all the wrong reasons.

"Not my son." Tad doesn't bother looking up as he continues his meticulous excavation into the flesh of our dinner.

I swear I've seen trees grow faster.

"He's going to university," Tad continues, "studying medicine, internships will take about ten years, then he can consider all of the women he likes. But in the meantime, it's all about—" he raises his hand in an attempt to thump his finger against his temple and nearly slices his nose off in the process.

"Be careful!" Mom's hand rises to her chest in horror.

"Yes, do," Marshall interjects. "It would be awful to mar this wonderful day with tragedy." *You were rooting for it weren't you?* His lips curve just enough in my direction. "Shall we *count* our blessings while we wait for the master to dissect our dinner?" He over annunciates the word, count. *I have a feeling the corpse will decompose faster than we can eat it,* he adds.

I don't really care for Marshall referring to my dinner as a corpse, but I suppose he's right on both counts. And there's that word again.

Mia and Melissa volunteer the fact they are thankful for their new dog—who by the way, is holed up in their room, in an effort to barricade him from fornicating freely with our shoes. Darla says she's thankful for Brielle and spontaneously breaks out into tears. Tad pushes back his chair and stands in a dramatic fashion.

"I just want to say I'm thankful that *somebody*," he pauses to set down the overgrown knife he used to hack into our dinner with. He jumps a little, losing his footing as though something were trying to knock him off balance. "Whoa!" he shouts as he starts to fall forward. In an effort to stabilize himself, he knocks his wrist into the handle of the knife and falls forward onto the table embedding the blade directly into his stomach.

 Holy shit!

 I think I just killed Tad.

19

All For Nothing

Chaos and blood and screaming ensue.

Marshall gives a slow appraising glance in my direction as he helps Dr. Oliver quell Tad's fountain of bodily fluids. *Judging by Holden's artful expression of misfortune, I surmise you've arranged this fiasco yourself.*

My toes curl in my shoes as I cling onto to Gage. The last thing in the world I want is for Marshall to have a moment of misguided charity and call me out on delegating a near homicide.

Relax, Skyla, Marshall frowns disapprovingly. *Holden is still responsible. The only way you'll go to Justice Alliance is if he actually succeeds in killing him. I suppose we'll know in just a few short hours, won't we?*

Shit!

Everyone over eighteen evacuates the premises in an effort to rush Tad to the emergency room. I volunteer to stay home to calm both Mia and Melissa who started in on a choir of screams the moment Tad exposed us all to the long handled knife protruding from his abdomen. *God*—it almost went straight through.

I feel horrible. Like I've made a deal with the devil, but worse, because it's Holden. I should have known he was capable of anything. He tried assaulting me that night at the Falls. He tried to *kill* Gage, so of course he would be more than eager to provide a Thanksgiving stabbing. How could I have sicked him on another human being? But then again it's Tad, plus he's a Count, which sort of partially disqualifies him as a human. He's a hybrid of something sinister in and of itself—in fact, it seems everyone is a hybrid these days.

"Relax," I tell Mia and Melissa. "Go upstairs," I instruct. "Mom said she'd call as soon as she hears anything. And he's still breathing," I add to Melissa as a consolation. She starts in on a series of hyperventilating hiccups, and Mia leads her out of the room.

"What a mess," Drake says, trying to sop up the blood with a kitchen towel.

Drake doesn't seem all that freaked out that the only thing his dad ate for dinner was ten inches of stainless steel.

"I'll help," Brielle offers, walking over with a handful of paper towels. It takes three seconds before she starts retching into the mess, then embellishes it by adding a sea of foaming vomit.

I rush over to open the backslider. Can this day get any worse? First Nev, then Tad, and now Brielle yakking all over everything. "Brielle, are you OK? You wanna lie down?" I ask. "Get her upstairs." I motion to Drake.

"I don't want her puking in my room." He jumps back a good three feet.

Brielle rights herself and pulls over the bottom of the tablecloth in an effort to wipe off her face. I watch as a trail of dishes land on the stone floor one after the other breaking with a disturbingly even rhythm.

Drake and Brielle decide it's a good time to take my advice and head on up.

"Looks like a massacre took place," I mutter. I'm so pissed—it wasn't Holden who ruined Thanksgiving, it was me. I pick up a dish off the table and crash it onto the floor. It cracks into three equal parts with tiny slivers splintering everywhere.

wicked

Great. I'm sure I'll step on one barefoot later and end up in the ER myself.

Logan pulls a broom out of the side pantry and hands it Gage. He unspools a roll of paper towels and starts in on the bodily fluids. It takes us less than a half an hour to clean up the damage and scrub down the floors.

"Thanks for helping." I wanted to say, *I owe you one*, but I'm reserving that for later, when it's just Gage and me. I'm still upset over the fact Logan thinks it's a good idea to defect to the other side. It's probably just an excuse, like he hasn't been there all along.

My cell goes off, it's a text from Mom. He's going to be fine! Missed all vital organs. Dr. said it was a Thanksgiving miracle!

"Nice." I pan the phone over to Logan and Gage. "Looks like Holden went easy on him after all."

"Holden?" Logan inches back a notch.

"Yeah." I tell them about the stupid idea I implanted in Holden's long departed brain.

"Skyla," Logan looks genuinely shocked "you can't mess with spiritual beings like that. You're connecting yourself to him in ways you don't know."

"Oh, is that what they taught you, first day of Count 101?"

"I'm serious," he softens. "The more you interact with him the more power you give him."

"OK, so I won't interact with him anymore."

A slow gurgle starts up in the kitchen. We watch in horror as the two trash bags we sealed shut, split open and dislodge themselves in a wild rattle all over the kitchen and litter the floor with bloody towels, broken pottery, and vomit.

"Crap," I hiss.

Gage wraps an arm around my shoulders. "It's too late to ignore him, Skyla." He pushes his lips into mine. *But I think I have a way to get rid of him.*

✹ ✹ ✹

Gage refuses to let me in on his idea with Holden haunting the vicinity, not even telepathically is he willing to share the concept.

We clean up the area one more time, and I swear openly at Holden during the entire process, which drives Logan and Gage to alternately shake their heads at me.

Gage plucks his phone out of his pocket and stares down at it. "It's Chloe." He pulls a face.

"What does she want?" I've got a gut feeling—but I'm hoping for a second Thanksgiving miracle.

"Apparently, I'm taking her shopping." Gage tosses the phone up before catching it again.

"No." I'm dazed by his willingness to go. "It's a holiday. And might I remind you, you're not her boyfriend."

"And that I'll never be." He locks eyes with me driving home the point. He glances back down at his phone as though it were a pariah. "But, black Friday is upon us."

"More like blackmail Friday." I wrap my arms around his waist. "You're not going, right?"

"I'm going." He nods as though it weren't even a question. "Get some rest." He presses a kiss onto my lips. "I'll text you and let you know if I'll be back in time before you go to bed."

"I'll stay with her," Logan volunteers.

"No." I practically bite the air when I say it.

"Definitely, no." Gage says as he heads out the door in a hurry.

I walk over and watch as he gets into the car and speeds away. I can't believe this keeps happening. It's like a nightmare that circles on a loop.

"I guess you want me to leave, too," Logan rumbles from behind.

I glance back at the stairwell, Mia and Melissa have calmed down, and Brielle and Drake are probably *getting* down.

It seems like it's the right time.

"No, I don't want you to leave. In fact I want you to come with me."

"Anywhere," he says breathless.

"Good. Because we're going to see my father."

20

Light Drive

Early morning in L.A., a thin layer of orange smog lies over the city like a suspended vat of pollen. The sweet scent of Mom's roses dance in the balmy air as the sun warms over my shoulders like a friend I long to know again.

I made sure Mia and Melissa were apprised of the fact Logan and I were taking off before we left on our light drive.

"Should we still call it light driving? I mean now that I can't stand Chloe," I ask as we sit outside my old L.A. house waiting for Dad to come out for his early morning bike ride. I miss everything about L.A. even the plants skirting our property, the pale aloe plants that raise their powdered arms to God—the lavender verbena.

"She took so many things away from you." He squints into the sun. "I think it's the least you can take from her. Call it light driving and own it. In fact, own everything around Chloe—that ought to annoy the living hell out of her."

I give an impish grin. "I think it's my life's mission to annoy the living hell out of her." Also, to kill her twice, but I leave that part out.

My father bounces his bicycle out the door and pauses to examine the two of us.

"Skyla!" He lets his bike fall onto the lawn and pulls me into a tight embrace. "I miss you." He presses his nose deep into my hair, taking in the fragrance as though it were exotic incense.

wicked

I pull back and beam at him. He looks amazing. His hair is slicked, still dewy from the shower, hiding every stitch of grey. His eyes sparkle out at me, and it's only when he gives a few rapid blinks that I realize he's holding back tears.

"I'm right upstairs, how could you possibly miss me?" I was hoping I had impressed myself on him, and from the look of things, I have.

"I miss you knowing that I'm no longer with you." He circles over me with his somber eyes. "And look at you, you've grown into a beautiful young woman without my permission." He ruffles my hair on top. "Who's this? The lucky boyfriend I presume?" He turns to shake Logan's hand.

I take them in together, standing there—Logan and my father, and my intestines tether in knots. It's surreal to say the least. At one time, I thought I'd be with Logan forever, and for him to meet my father is beyond a dream.

For sure I thought now that Logan is a Count, I'd have an easier time seeing my life without him, but something deep inside still nags at me, sweeps me toward him, easy as dust with a broom.

"He's my boyfriend's, um…uncle, cousin—something," I swallow the last few words.

"Oh." Dad pulls back and examines him curiously. "Very well, you kids up for breakfast?"

༒ ༒ ༒

Dad piles us into the minivan, and we head out to a diner not too far down the road.

Logan and I sit together, so I can gaze over at my father without distraction. I love his effortless smile, the laughter that bubbles up unwarranted. I had almost forgotten what a joy he was to be around, how much jubilance he brought into my life.

We put in our orders then bask in the wonders of one another for the next several minutes.

"We're starved." I tell Dad about the entire Thanksgiving debacle as we wait for our food.

"Who's Tad?" The words amble out of him innocently.

Oh God.

I look to Logan for help.

"No, it's OK," Dad reaches over and touches my hand briefly. "You don't need to hide anything to protect my feelings. Is it someone your mother is seeing?" He blinks in surprise. "Has she remarried?"

Everything in me twists. I'd hate for my dad to suffer one ounce of pain over, of all things, Tad.

"He's not you. He doesn't even come close to being you." The words strangle out of my vocal cords.

A bus glides by the window followed by a steady stream of SUV's and overpriced luxury cars. I'd rather veg out watching L.A. traffic than break my father's heart over nothing. "He's crap," I eek the words out.

"Hey." He jiggles my wrist until I turn back to look at him. "Nobody's crap," he says softly. "I'm sure this Tad person has some redeeming qualities." His gaze drifts off to an invisible horizon behind me. "Wait a minute. It's not Tad-always-in-a-foul-mood-Landon, is it?"

"Yes." I pat my hands down on the table just as the food arrives. "He's constantly pissy and moaning about something, and he's a Count." I try not to shout the last few words.

Dad withdraws his perennial smile and drops his head down to his chest in thought.

"I want you to keep an extra eye on him," he says, still twisting his lips.

"I will." Then I let it all out. I tell him about school and Chloe coming back to life and to my birthday party minus the fact she contracted his death, and, of course, Logan being a Count. Logan who I thought I loved, but couldn't, and who I might be able to trust, but I'm still not sure.

"I'm sitting right here," Logan muses.

"I'm well aware," I say, rather annoyed.

"Can my daughter trust you?" Dad's eyes shine like twin globes. I miss those blue-green orbs more than I could ever know.

"Yes." Logan doesn't waver—doesn't break my father's heavy-handed stare.

"Don't worry, he's out of the picture." I'm still more than miffed by the fact he makes a habit of withholding pertinent information from me. It's like a character flaw. Deep inside I'm afraid to let Logan in again. He was so close to the rawest part of me—sometimes I think I'm going to break, or spontaneously combust from the pain of losing him. It's better this way with the impenetrable wall. You can't have your heart broken if there's a fort a mile wide around it. I've got mine encased in the fibers of Gage's vision. Ironically, it's that vision that hurts me most when it comes to Logan. When I accepted Gage's gift of knowing as the absolute truth—that was the moment I really lost Logan—that's when it hurt like hell to know I'd never have him no matter how many faction wars we won. "In fact my boyfriend, Gage, he's a Levatio," I continue absentmindedly, "and he's already told me we'll marry."

Dad blinks back with a look of both surprise and slight disgust. "I don't like the thought of you talking marriage so young." His cheek rises on the side, no smile. "And where is this Gage? Why didn't he come back here with you?"

I take a deep breath and tell him all about Chloe's blackmail Friday scheme, end with the story of how we exchanged left arms and how she slit my throat.

Dad reaches across the table and runs his fingertips over the scar across my neck.

"She did this to you?"

I don't dare tell him that she set him up to die, that I killed her in turn.

"Skyla." A look of despair disintegrates his features. "You've been through so much. I'm so sorry I'm not there to help you."

"Mom is. But she's not really my mother, is she?"

He studies the two of us from across the table. An uneasy feeling clots up the air, and I can tell he's searching for delicate ways to put things.

"No. She's not."

There are only a few true moments in life that define you, that make you aware of everything around you so acutely that you could remember the details right down to the cheesy 80's song playing over the speakers, and for me, this was one of them.

"I knew it." Something has always been missing, cluing me in to the abnormality of the situation. This insurmountable elephant that congested the distance between us, sucked the air right out of the room whenever she was around for too long. "Why the big secret?" I knew a half a dozen people back in L.A. who were the product of affairs, and all of them knew of their dubious conception. "Why don't I know anything about my real mother?"

My father draws back in his seat and takes in a full deep breath before expelling it in a sigh.

"It's because she's not human, Skyla."

21

Out of This World

The waitress comes by and refills our drinks. I try to relax, so I don't accidentally jump across the table in an effort to shake the truth out of Dad.

It's so weird. Here I thought Mom, well, Lizbeth, was my mother all along. I can't imagine belonging to anyone else. Sure I don't always get along with her, and ever since she married Tad things have been less than stellar, but at least I still have her in my life. I've always appreciated the consistency.

"Skyla," Dad leans into the table. "I realize things have been changing quickly for you, that you were thrown into this Nephilim world with no preparation, and I really am sorry for that." He takes a breath and examines me. "I had every intention of telling you once you came of age."

"Thirty? You were going to wait until I was thirty?" My mouth hangs open. That's like twelve lifetimes away.

"No," he gives a gentle laugh. "Eighteen, or so. I was going to wait until you graduated from high school. I thought that would give you just enough time to experience life as a normal teenager, and you'd be armed and ready to go to college. Obviously, I regret this."

"Please, don't regret anything." I can't bear the thought of my father losing sleep over this. "It's OK. Logan and Gage were nice enough to tell me what I needed to know." When they felt like it.

I shoot a look over to Logan.

I still don't get why Logan didn't rattle everything off at once like I would have.

"Now that we're here," Dad continues, "I want you to know you can come to me anytime and ask me anything. I want to help you. I'm on your side."

"Can you come to me sometime?" The thought of my father in Paragon thrills me.

There's something more than a forlorn look in his eye. He gives a passing glance at Logan and lingers there a moment before redirecting his solemn gaze.

"There would have been a way," he says through croaking sorrow. He clears his throat before pressing on. "Two things. Number one, it's not possible to travel into the future on your own. You need a supervising spirit. And, number two, you need to know where to go."

"I'll tell you where to go—heck, I'll take you," the offer speeds out of me.

"Neither of you belong in this world right now. You're time traveling, Skyla. The real you—the one that belongs here is at home oversleeping for school."

"If the Skyla oversleeping at home knew where to take you, could she?" I think I found my loophole.

"No. She would need a supervising spirit. And, besides that, she may not be able to because the influence is coming from a future source. The only thing you'd accomplish is filling yourself with psychological trauma." He gives a stern look. "You need to go through the events that have happened, Skyla. They'll mold and shape you, take you to the destiny that's been carved out for you since the beginning of time." He points a finger low against the table. "There is a reason these boundaries are in place, or else a Celestra would never die, we'd simply travel to a more convenient time to live. Promise me you won't try this."

"But if the Celestra knew he were going to die, and he had a supervising spirit then he could?" I ask.

"Yes." It comes out exasperated. "But let me make this very clear to you. If in any way you think letting Sleepy Skyla in on your plan won't change your destiny, think again. She can never know of you. Once you leave an impression on her," his hands slice through the air, "the world as you know it is forever altered. Promise me you will never do this."

My world will be forever altered? Probably in a good way. But I'll never convince him of that. I would be able to undo everything. I can go and kill Chloe in real time, well, probably get thrown into prison in real time, too.

I know full well I can't promise. If I made a promise to my father, I'd have to keep it.

"Promise?" He doesn't let up on the intensity.

I give a half nod. That's all he's getting from me.

"OK, start with my mother." I'm all for changing the subject.

"I met her in high school." He nods over to Logan and smiles.

My stomach clenches. It makes me want to drive the point home that there's nothing going on between Logan and me.

"Her name was Candy—Candace. We hit it off right away, and to be honest, I had a gut feeling right from the beginning that this was going to be the person I was going to spend the rest of my life with."

My entire body cinches. That's exactly how I felt when I met Logan. There wasn't an ounce of me that felt otherwise. It was like we had been bound together by some eternal cord right from the beginning. But if I'm going to be marrying Gage—

Gage who I absolutely do love, why didn't I feel that way towards him instead? Anyway, I do now, and that's all that matters.

"She was amazing." He shakes his head. "Whenever she walked into the room everybody knew it, and I'm not just talking looks, there was something different about her."

"Like Skyla," Logan interjects.

My father appraises him quickly.

"Do I look like her?"

"Mostly. You have quite a bit of me in you, too." He winks.

"Mia looks like me," I add. She does now more than ever.

"How is she?"

"She's good." I don't dare tell him she's converting to Landonhood. I know for a fact she's supposed to go to the courthouse in a few weeks to start the process of changing her last name.

"I think when I get married I'll keep my last name," it comes out sad, uncalled for.

"Messenger-Oliver," Logan's cheeks flush with color.

"That's a mouthful." My father raises his brows as he sloshes the ice in his glass. "Don't feel obligated because of me. You'll always be my daughter, and I'll always be your dad."

"My mother—did she burn?"

"She did." He pushes out a hard breath. "You were three months old, and your grandmother was watching you. I was at work—had just finished grad school and so had Candy, she was interning at a lab doing genetic research, and there was a fire. She was in a high-rise on the twenty-fourth floor, the windows were stationary, and the only exit was blocked from debris that fell during the explosion."

"Explosion?" I take in a breath.

"Natural gas, something to do with a pipe that was left on."

"Oh my, God." My hand flattens over my chest. "So, you think it was the Counts?"

"I know it was the Counts."

"So, she was a pure Celestra, and so are you." I say it as a fact.

He shakes his head.

"I'm not pure, not by a long shot. I'm Celestra with a lot of human mixing."

"Then how can I be pure?"

"I wasn't kidding when I said she wasn't human. She's something called a Caelestis."

"Oh, I know what that is!" A serious flashback of my trip to Sectorville with Marshall rips through my mind. "They sit on the decision council."

"You do know." He straightens. "How do you know?"

"She's involved with a Sector," Logan is quick to dispense.

"What?" Dad's eyes flare with worry.

"It's not a big deal." I'm going to strangle Logan for even mentioning Marshall. Didn't he notice that I artfully left out certain details earlier when I was filling my dad in on *everything*? Like the fact my faux mother, too, is a Count.

"Sectors are a huge deal," Dad scolds, "I don't want you near one, got it?"

"Got it." I can still feel Marshall's greedy tongue massaging out my tonsils. I don't really know how to defend him. "Um, he's really kind of nice, and he's super smart, and he could easily be a model." For a second I envision Marshall sprawled out in his underwear on one of those huge framed posters in Abercrombie, then Logan, then Gage. It's strange how the mind works. According to Marshall, Gage spends most

wicked

of his time imagining me without my underwear, and I keep wondering what he looks like with them on. I hope to solve that mystery soon.

"Skyla," my father leans over takes up my hand, "you have to know he wants something."

I wonder if it's Gage or Marshall he's referring to.

"Like the Caelestis wanted something from you?" I ask.

He doesn't answer. Just gives a sly smile like I pinned it right on the nose.

22

Give a Little

Logan and I return to the butterfly room near four-thirty in the morning.

"Thanks for coming with me." I rub the palms of my hands against my jeans. Just holding his hands to get back here made me explode with heat. The sooner he leaves, the better.

"Will you return the favor sometime?" he asks.

"Where you going? Some big Count convention? You wanna present me yourself?" I'm only half kidding.

"Yeah, something like that." His eyes avert. "I'm going to see my parents. I'd love for you to meet them. I'm going to ask about my lineage, and I was thinking it might be a good way for you to get the answers you're looking for."

"I'm not looking for answers, Logan. I already know you have Count blood. And, yes, I realize that Dr. Oliver said you were close to pure but not like me. What does it really matter? You've already made it clear you're going to renounce yourself as a Celestra to glean info out of their playbook. It doesn't change the fact I can't trust you, does it?"

"Why shouldn't you?" he asks softly as though he were truly puzzled.

"I don't appreciate people keeping things from me."

"Gage is keeping something from you."

"That's different. It's not his fault, it's Chloe's, and besides, I'm going to get to the bottom of this very quickly. She's having her I'm-not-dead-after-all party on Saturday, and I have a few methods of extracting information from her."

wicked

"Whatever you're planning, please don't do it." He's got that look on his face that suggests everything I put my hands on turns to disaster.

"I'm going to implement anything and everything to get my boyfriend back." A spiral of heat spears through my stomach.

His stony gaze drops to the floor as he considers this.

"I'll be there if you need me," he looks uneasy as though he were struggling with something. "I want to prove my loyalty. Gage said there were five remaining Counts that need retribution for the Celestra that were killed."

"Yes. Gage and I are going after them."

"You don't have to."

"We don't need you coming with us." I like the thought of a getaway with Gage—murderous as it might be.

"Then let me do it alone."

"No." The thought of Logan going rogue freaks me out a little. A Count on a killing spree is never a good thing.

"Then it looks like we'll be doing it together," he says.

I don't say anything, just match his determination—observe his strong jaw-line as it flexes with anticipation.

"Then it looks like we are."

✺ ✼ ✺

I text Gage as soon I wake up, but too bad for me because I don't wake up until well after three in the afternoon, and Chloe's already tightened the leash. I pull a face as I stare down at his text.

Mall crawl. B over soon as I can shake her.

I give a huff of a laugh. He wants to shake her. I wonder how Chloe would feel if she knew how much Gage loathed her for this. Doesn't matter. I plan on beating the crap out of her tomorrow night until she fesses up whatever it is she's threatening him with, or better yet, until she leaves my boyfriend the hell alone. I should cut out a thousand black butterflies and cram them into her locker with a note that reads her days are numbered— that she doesn't get another cocoon.

There's a light knock at the door, and Mia steps in.

Her hair's pulled back, and I notice for the first time that she's grown a little to where we're just about the same height. I look over her features in a new light. She wears my father's face like a mask, and now that I survey her bone structure a little better, her mother is present, too.

I wanted to ask Dad more about my biological mother, like why she came to earth to begin with. Still so much I want to know, but there's great comfort in the fact I can go back anytime I want, even if he can never come here. I'm pretty sure he has no clue old mom—Mia's mom, is a Count.

"What's up?" I ask stretching like a cat.

"I guess growing another person makes you really sleepy." She circles around my desk and eyes the broken mirror on the vanity. I cut a look over to the window to see if the word *body* is still visible. A dense coat of fog presses against the glass as though it were fighting its way in. I run my fingers over the window in an effort to deface Holden's efforts at communication.

"I wouldn't know. I'm not pregnant."

"You got rid of it?" She swoops over to me with a mixture of amusement and horror.

"What? No." I could never do that to Gage's baby. An image of a tiny newborn with bright blue eyes and an infectious dimpled smile washes through my mind.

God, we're going to have the cutest kids on the entire freaking planet. I hope they all look exactly like Gage—well, maybe not the girls.

"So do you know who the father is?"

"Shut up." Leave it to Mia to snap me out of my baby-loving fantasy. "I'm not having a baby."

"You can deny it all you want, but I found these under your bathroom sink." She holds out a huge white bottle that I hadn't noticed she was carrying.

I snatch it from her and examine it. Prenatal vitamins. It's like Brielle's trying to frame me or something.

"They're not mine."

"Save it, sister." Her lips draw out in a line. "I hear you got a car for your birthday, and I've got places to go."

"I don't have my license, and I gave the car back."

"Well then, you're stupider than you look." Her entire person slouches as she perfects a hardened glare.

"It's like looking in a mirror." I turn around and start riffling through my drawers hoping she'll get the hint and disappear.

"You're going to get that car back and your license all in the same day if you're smart, or your little secret won't stay a secret for long. I'll give you one week." She leans into me as if to finalize the threat.

"Look, I'm really not having a baby. I don't care how many clues you stumble upon—you're a horrible detective. Nancy Drew you are not."

"When Mom and Dad find out that you're multiplying behind their back, you're gonna be in big trouble. You're going to wish you listened to me."

There's no way in hell I'm going to be threatened by my little baby Count of a sister.

"Besides," she leans in, "I'll tell Gage I saw you kissing that teacher." She spears me with a hard look.

Crap.

"No." She can't tell Gage. She's going to ruin everything. "You're like, pure evil." I spin her around and shove her into the hall.

"One week, Skyla!"

I slam the door behind her.

"You'll be sorry!" she shouts.

If she tells Gage, she'll be the one who's sorry.

23

Count Me In

That evening, I call Brielle and ask her to come over. Mom is staying another night at the hospital with Tad, and Gage said he wouldn't be here until after he showered and changed. At least I know he's not with Chloe, unless, of course, she's has him showering with her now. God, the thought of Chloe seeing Gage in his underwear, stabs me with jealousy.

"What's going on?" Brielle breezes in. Her hair looks muted, darker, and her eyes are slightly glazed over. She crashes on the bed without giving it a second thought.

"You." I rattle the bottle of vitamins in front of her.

"Oh, thanks, you got a soda lying around?" She takes them from me and unscrews the cap.

"Are you kidding? Mia thinks they're mine. She thinks *I'm* the one having a baby."

"Are you?" She eyes me up and down.

"No. I'm not you. I'm holding out." Not really, but it sounds better than Gage won't let me.

"Gee thanks. You really know how to kick someone when they're down." She pops a giant orange horse pill and knocks back her head in hopes it'll go down.

I pick up a half full water bottle that's been rolling around my floor for weeks and hand it to her.

"Sorry. I didn't mean for it to come out that way. It's just the idea of Mia thinking I'm knocked up makes me insane. Besides, Gage and I haven't done anything exciting yet," I exude all the necessary disappointment as I flop down next to her.

She downs the water bottle before tossing it over near my shoes.

"That could easily be remedied. Just take control of the situation. Gage is a guy, and he's not blind, I mean look at you. He's got one hot girlfriend. I think all you have to do is light the match. Once that fire gets going, it tends to get out of control real quick."

Light the match. I make a mental note. It practically goes hand in hand with my mother's advice of handing out the invitation. Maybe I'll combine the two?

"So you going to Chloe's party?" she asks, rubbing her hand over her stomach.

"For sure. And you?"

"I'll probably be too busy puking my ass off." She closes her eyes in exhaustion. "That's what I do now. Besides, I can't freaking stand her."

"Really?" I'm not sure I believe this. I'm not sure I believe anything Brielle says.

"Really," she assures. "So what happened with you and Gage? He's like her right hand man ever since she got back."

"She's blackmailing him."

Her head ticks to the side. "No surprise there."

"So are you going to tell Dudley it's not his baby?" I ask.

"And ruin an easy A? I think not."

"Brielle! Are you still working for him?"

"Are you kidding? I couldn't make it five minutes without gagging from the stench of all that horse crap. I'm back at the bowling alley, kicking my feet up and texting, where I belong. Plus, Logan can care less if all I do is hang out in the bathroom. He thinks I'm cleaning it."

"Nice."

Chloe mentioned in her diary that she set in place one perfect BFF. It's got to be Brielle. I shouldn't have her in my room, or my life.

"Well?" Her voice spikes in frustration. "What's she blackmailing him with?"

Brielle's hair is spilled out on the pillow like a series of thick crimson snakes. Her eyes glint out like a broken green bottle, and her skin's bled free of all color.

"I shouldn't have asked you here," I whisper mostly to myself. Her not liking Chloe is probably just a lie. "Sometimes I wonder why you and I are friends." An unexpected swell of emotion rattles the last few words out of me as I hold back the urge to cry.

"Skyla." She sits up. "What the hell's going on? Come here," her voice softens as she pulls me into a hug. "You're insane if you think we shouldn't be friends. We're better than friends. I think of you like a sister." She pulls away still holding me at the shoulders. "And I'm going to have your brother's baby." She pats her stomach. "See? We're practically family."

"Does Drake know?"

She shakes her head. "I'm telling him tomorrow night. But, anyway, why are you going to Chloe's party if she's trying to snatch Gage away from you?"

"I'm going to try and kill her." I watch Brielle's face for the slightest trace of loyalty.

"You might have to kill Michelle, Emily and Lexy to get to her. She's in the bitch's protection program."

"I don't mind offing the bitch squad." I narrow in on her. "In fact, I plan on racking up quite a body *count*." I spit the last word in her face.

An electrical storm brews outside leaving a sizzle of brilliant white light crackling through our world every few seconds. The electricity went out an hour ago, and both Mia and Melissa went to bed with flashlights. I can't stop thinking about Brielle, and how trustworthy she might be. Logan sprouts up in my mind like a weed. Should any Count be trusted no matter how much evil he has flowing through his bloodstream?

A shadow emerges by the bathroom door, and I jump back into the corner of my bed.

"It's me," Gage whispers as he strides on over.

He slips off his shoes and crawls in next to me.

I don't bother with words—words might lead to Logan or Chloe—and I plan on taking care of Chloe myself tomorrow night. Instead, I press in with a welcoming kiss and wrangle him closer until it feels as though I'm going to push right through him. I plan on lighting that match to see if I could start an unquenchable fire.

"I missed you." I snuggle into him, taking in his clean soapy scent.

"I missed you, too." He circles my neck with kisses, and it lights me up from the inside.

"So tell me how to get rid of you-know-who," I whisper directly into his ear in the event Holden is lingering around like the perv he is.

I thought we could ask my dad for the next viable corpse. Give him the body of some 90 year-old man with a grenade for a heart. He twitches his brows, impressed with his own solution.

"Would your dad go for that?"

We'll see.

wicked

"OK." I track my finger along the inside lip of his jeans.

"So I talked to Chloe today," he says it low as though he wished he didn't.

I let out a sigh. A rumble of thunder explodes overhead and shakes the window so violently I fully expect it to explode into the room.

I don't want to talk about Chloe, not now, not ever.

"So, what happened?" I pull up on my elbows and take him in. Gage is made up entirely of shadows, drawn in by charcoal lines, hair that lends itself to the night, eyes that explode with glitter like a freshly shaken snow globe each time they move.

"I drew some boundaries. Let her know I wasn't going to touch her, hold her hand."

"Nice." I lean in and reward him with a kiss.

"She's got Nevermore."

"What?"

"I guess Tad turned him over to an animal shelter, and the Bishops had a leg band put on years ago in the event something like this happened."

"Is she giving him back?"

"What do you think?" He gives a bleak smile. "She put him in a giant cage and locked him up in her room."

"Crap. She's stealing everything from me."

"Funny. She said the same thing about you."

My blood boils just thinking about it, so I change the subject. "Mia thinks I'm having your baby." I stray far away from the subject of me clawing Chloe's eyes out tomorrow night.

"Oooh," he moans with a smile. His dimples ignite like two black dots, and his teeth flash through the night like lanterns.

"It's not me who's pregnant. It's Brielle."

The smile fades off his face.

"It's not mine," he teases. "That's pretty wild."

"Are we going to have babies, Gage? You know, one day?" I lean into his arm like a pillow. I like feeling his warm flesh beneath me, feel his blood flow through his thick cord-like veins right under my temple.

His head comes down next to mine, and we sit and listen to the night detonate like a series of cannons igniting—echoing above us.

"I think life should surprise you that way."

"So you know? You've seen them?"

Lightning flexes in and out of the room like an electrical current gone wild.

Gage answers with a searing kiss that never seems to end.

That night, I dream in kisses. I dream of Gage, and a perfect brood of identical little boys with black hair and cobalt eyes in a line that goes on forever. I turn around and standing behind me is another line of little boys, each one a doppelganger of Logan. They call out to me, pull at my clothes—my hair. I try to tell the blonde boys I can never be their mother, that I have another destiny, but they tell me I'm wrong. They tell me that deep inside my soul I know it's true.

24

Debt Threats

In the morning, I hold out a lock of hair and brush it over and over as I veg out in front of the fragmented mirror. That dream tunneled into my brain and has been replaying itself over and over like a horror movie. First of all, I don't plan on having two hundred boys. Second of all, I'm never letting Logan near my baby making station, so it doesn't seem fair that his evil Count spawn are harassing me in my sleep. I pause and put down the brush. There's got to be a way to pull him out of my heart, extract every fiber of Logan Oliver from my being. It's not fair to me, and it's not fair to Gage, to have him haunting me in my dreams—my waking hours.

Gage. He's driving me to Chloe's resurrection party tonight. Once I pluck Chloe bald and cull her eyes out, we should totally go out and celebrate after.

"Dad's here!" I hear Melissa squeal from the hall.

A rash of thumps and screams erupt as Mia and Melissa run down to welcome Tad home.

It is sort of my fault he almost committed harry kerry in front of his own children, so I head on out.

I see Drake coming out of the center bathroom sniffing at his hand.

"Gross," I mutter.

He motions for me to come into his bedroom. It's loaded with rumpled clothes all over the floor and a musky odor that I try not to inhale all the way.

"What?" I'd flop on the bed, but I know what goes on there.

"I'm gonna break up with Brielle tonight."

"*What?*" My eyes spring open. "You can't break up with her."

"Yes I can. She's always cranky and bitching and moaning like everything that's wrong is all my fault."

"Well maybe it is." It *so* is.

"It's not. And she's got like this viral stomach flu and she keeps coming over when I asked her not to. I hate puking. It's like she wants to get me sick on purpose. Who does that?"

"Right." Stomach flu. "Well make sure you listen to anything she wants to tell you first. You know, in case she wants to break up with *you* or something. She did mention there was something important she wanted to say tonight."

"Cool." Drake nods into this, looking more than mildly pleased with my line of thinking. "Thanks for the heads up," he high fives me. "It'll be way easier than me doing the dumping, plus she won't care that I've already got Emily lined up to replace her."

"What?" I'm like my own echo.

"Yeah, and she won't think I was cheating."

"Lovely."

🦋🦋🦋

Drake and I amble downstairs where Mom has already laid Tad out on the sofa, limp as a paper bag. "It could take weeks to heal," my mother moans as she puts a tray of his favorite foods together in the kitchen.

"Months," Tad corrects sounding more than all right. "I'll have to go from crutches to a cane just to keep the pressure off my insides." He plucks a two-liter bottle of soda off the floor and takes a swig right out of the container.

"We'll have to put off baby making a few weeks," my mother confides to everyone within earshot.

Really? Must we go on like this?

Sprinkles speeds in, and runs a series of wild laps, barking the entire time to keep us apprised of his exact location.

"Someone catch that hairless rat." Tad cranes his neck to get a better look. "I'm having the animal shelter pick him up in the morning."

"You are not." Melissa snatches him up in her arms.

"He ran right underneath me, and I almost carved my initials into my heart on my way out of this planet. He's a menace and a medical trauma waiting to happen."

"He was up in my room the entire time," Melissa drops a kiss between his ears.

"Nice cover up 'lissa," Tad balks, "glad to see your older sister has been rubbing off on you."

"What's that supposed to mean?" I want to say, it's nice to see him back to his own hateful self, but that would probably just prove his point.

"See, Lizbeth? Bad behavior spreads like a contagion. The next thing you know, they'll be sneaking off with their boyfriends and staying out all night in a *barn* of all places."

"Oh, so we're back to that again," I fold my arms. I can't wait to see his face when Drake produces his mini me in exactly six months.

"Yes, we're back to that again." He flicks on the TV.

"You're wrong. I happen to be a great role model." OK, so maybe that was a teensy little lie.

Tad struggles to turn in my direction. "Girls, whatever you see Skyla doing, do the opposite. That oughta keep you safe."

A choking sound emits from my throat.

Mia cuts me a sly grin. "So," she starts in slow, "if Skyla is such a bad influence..." She walks over to the center of the room where both Tad and Mom can see her. "Maybe there should be an incentive program for those of us who have some dirt on her."

"What?" I'm really beginning to dislike that word, almost as much as I'm beginning to dislike Mia. She's seriously gunning to dethrone Chloe as bitch of the century.

"That's ridiculous," Mom carries over a tray loaded up with triple bypass written all over it. Hey, maybe its Tad, Mom's trying to kill with her cooking?

"I kind of like this," he adjusts himself to a sitting position. Not even a wince of pain, it's like he's faking it, only I saw the blade go in myself. "I say we toss out an award and field what comes our way."

"What about Drake?" I ask indignantly.

"Turnabout's fair play," Mom chides.

"Only, I'm clean as a whistle," Drake says before pouring the milk straight into his mouth waterfall style.

He wishes.

"Fifty bucks if the info's valid and punishment worthy." Tad pops open a bag of chips. "Our kids are going to police themselves."

I look over at Mia who's smiling like a lunatic, and yet I know she's impotent.

Drake gargles in the background with white foaming bubbles shooting out of his mouth. And he's going to wish he were impotent, very, very soon.

It would be so easy to sell him out for fifty dollars, but I'd hate to set another one of my bad examples. I glare openly at Mia from across the room.

"Skyla?" My mother shakes her head in disbelief. "Just keep out of trouble, and you won't have problems with anybody ratting you out."

Right.

Tad unfolds his newspaper. "Something tells me I'll be out fifty bucks by the time the weekend's over." He looks back at me. "Isn't that right?"

I turn around and leave the room.

I'll have to speak to Holden about working on his aim.

25

Odd but True

A light drizzle escorts Gage and I all the way down to Emily Morgan's house. It is one seamless grey night, devoid of color and shadow, just a continuous stretch of two-dimensional gloom that castrates the life out of the world.

A huge square box sits upon a lonely hill covered with uneven paneling and a crooked smokestack chimney. A hint of apricot light glows through the oversized paned windows—half of them are broken on the second story.

"Did you forget to mention something? Like the fact Emily lives in a haunted house?" I watch as a scarf of fog trails along the periphery, dancing in and out of the crevices in long rippling waves.

"Looks like it, right?"

Tons of cars are parked cockeyed all over the front lawn and zigzag up and down the street.

"You know," he reaches over and takes up my hand as we get out of the car, "we still haven't had our birthday date."

"Birthday date?" I like where this is going.

"Snorkeling." He rattles my hand. "You up for it tomorrow?"

"Yeah, right after the typhoon we're scheduled to have, or better yet, let's go during. Who knows what sea creatures are lurking in those twenty foot swells?" I pull him into a sweet kiss. "Besides, I had something far more intimate in mind."

"I'm thinking I like your idea better." He breaks out into a killer grin. Nobody smiles like Gage.

Of course Chloe wants him—any girl would have to be insane not to.

"You're gorgeous. You know that?" It comes out breathless. "In fact, why wait until tomorrow? I say we start this party tonight."

He pushes a kiss into me with a grin, and his teeth graze lightly against mine.

"OK, we can start tonight." His hand slips up my shirt and warms my back.

"Are you?" I bite down on my lip before I can finish the sentence. "Are you sending me an invitation?"

"Oh, I'm definitely sending you an invitation." His lids sink low over his cobalt spheres.

"I accept," I say dreamily.

He leads me up the creaky steps to Emily's house of horrors.

I'm so dazed it feels like I'm floating on air. I can't believe Gage sent me the invitation.

I can't believe I'm going to have sex with Gage tonight!

✺ ✺ ✺

Logan stands by the door like a bouncer and manages to completely suck the feeling of euphoria right out of me. It's like I can practically see his doppelganger children drifting in and out of the shadows like a bunch of mini poltergeists. It's bad enough to have one dislodged spirit asking for a body, let alone two hundred. Besides, I'm never going to have Logan's babies, ever.

A pang of sorrow spears through me and suddenly I'm pulled down by longing and sadness. I find myself more pissed off at Logan than I was to begin with.

"Gage?" I spin into him. His eyes shine like indigo floodlights in this dark environment. A riotous thump of music streams from somewhere deep in the house. "Maybe we should just go home. You know, start our own party." I twirl my hair into him.

A hand clamps over my shoulder, digs into my flesh with its razor like fingernails.

"I thought you'd never get here," Chloe says, stepping into Gage.

Her hair falls in dark waves midway to her back. She looks polished and holds the scent of new clothes mixed with expensive perfume that tries too hard.

"We're here." Gage doesn't bother hiding the fact he's more than slightly perturbed.

I'm glad he shows it.

"Brody's here, floating around somewhere," she practically sings the words.

Gage shrugs as though it means nothing to him.

"Come," she pulls him over by the hand. "I'll take you to him."

Gage takes his hand back and leans into my ear.

"I'll go say hi and come back," he whispers.

She whisks him off into the crowd, right through a darkened corridor until I can't see them anymore.

"Can you believe that?" I take a few steps deeper into the house with Logan following close behind.

A soft glow illuminates the entire downstairs with bodies filling in every free space.

A glass cupboard greets us dead ahead filled with nothing but metal and ceramic dragons—every shape and size. I pause to take them in—weird glowing eyes, long split tongues lashing out, wild.

Freaky.

I head into a huge cavernous room divided with couches and tables. Right above the fireplace, glowing in silver glints are two crossed swords speared through a giant coat of arms. The face of a menacing dragon is etched in gold with inlaid ruby eyes that sparkle a deep crimson.

"Creepy," I whisper.

"Tell me about it." Logan leans in until our shoulders are touching. "You should meet her parents. They've got some serious issues."

"Let me guess, you dated her, too?" Logan seems to have made the rounds when it comes to Paragon Island girls. It really makes me feel less like his one true love and more like I took a turn.

"Nope." His hands flex in defense. He points up behind me, and I turn around.

A giant canvas stretches across the entire breadth of the room just behind the dining room table. In this dim light I can make out a field—horses and warriors in the heat of battle. I walk over to it and hold onto the back of a chair as I examine the piece in detail.

"The horses," Logan begins to narrate, "behind them there's a row of men with assault rifles. In the far corner, there's an angel with his arms stretched out, supervising the event."

My mouth falls open as I walk over to the far end of the picture—that face, those eyes.

"Oh my, God," I breathe the words. "It's him."

"Him?" Logan struggles to see what I'm looking at.

"Marshall." His name hisses out in a breathless whisper.

"Holy shit." Logan stares at the image spellbound.

"I've seen this war," I say, speeding across the room trying to take in as much as I can.

"What do mean, you've seen this war?"

I dart a quick look at him. I don't recall ever telling Logan and Gage about me kissing Marshall to glimpse into the future. As much as I'd love to tell Logan just to watch his stomach churn, I don't dare say a word. I'd never forgive myself if I hurt Gage that way.

I point over to the background figures and the bodies running near the horses. They look soaked, fatigued, some of them carrying large overgrown guns. "I saw us. You and Gage were with me. I think I had on wings." I circle the painting for clues—for more faces I might recognize. "What do you think it means?"

"It means whoever painted this saw the same thing you did."

"It's our war." Something in me ignites when I say it. I turn to face him fully, gaze into those glowing amber eyes that watch me with animated suspense. "We're going to fight. We're going to live that picture, you and me and Gage."

"How did you see this war, Skyla?" His features sharpen with concern.

I shake my head.

"Can you find out more about this? That might be the upper hand we'll need."

I take a deep breath and imagine Marshall lashing around my mouth, hot with desire.

"I can, but I don't want to."

"You have to, Skyla. It might be the only way we'll win."

26

The Budding Artist

"Hey," Ellis pops up next to me. His hair is slightly tousled, and his eyes glow an eerie wash of pink. "What's up with you and Gage?"

I walk him away from the painting as though my vision might accidentally rub off on him—or in the event he looks up and suddenly recognizes Marshall. Even though Ellis was in the ethereal plane when we watched Gage wrestling a lion, as far as I know, Marshall was only visible to me. I've almost hung myself more than once by blowing his Sector-based cover, the last thing I need is Ellis cinching the noose.

"Nothing's the matter with Gage. We're perfectly fine. In fact, I think we're going to leave now and have a little party of our own." I scan the crowd. I'll put off scratching Chloe's eyes out for another time. I can't believe Gage sent *me* the invitation. This is going to be epic, it's going to be write-a-poem worthy or—

"Did you hear me? She's all over him." Ellis looks confused by the situation.

"Where are they?" It sounds like Chloe just bumped herself back up on my to-do list.

Ellis leads me by the hand through a thicket of bodies, entire tangles of flesh create one large mass of humanity, laughing and yelling. A thin veil of smoke fills a covered patio out back, and I pause when I see them. Gage looks stern as though he's telling her something. Chloe sloshes around him with one hand holding up a red plastic cup and the other riding up and down his chest like a serpent. And to add insult to injury, she's feeling up my boyfriend with *my* freaking hand.

"Wait," Logan appears. He holds me back by the shoulder just as I'm about to bolt. "Gage said he had a very good reason for going along with this. I swear to you, Skyla, he would never do anything to hurt you."

Michelle drifts behind Logan, pecking at something on the floor, jutting her neck out in odd thrusts as though she were poultry. Something about her looks different—something about her hair. It's either the world's sloppiest ponytail with short wisps sticking out in every direction or—

She turns around and exposes a bald spot just above her left temple.

My mouth falls open.

It's freaking short. It's scalp hugging. She's freaking *bald* in like ten different places!

Michelle moves in a slow circle mumbling into thin air, to anyone who happens to pass by while sporting the world's most horrific home haircut. Choppy and jagged on every side, cut way up high by her ears.

"Who do you think did that to her?" Logan marvels.

"There's a good chance she did."

I walk over and rattle her by the shoulder to see if I can shake her out of the stupor she's in.

"Are you drunk?" I ask.

"Naw, I see them, they—" She babbles on about flying—points up to the sky.

"Who cut your hair?" I ask accusingly.

"I cut hair." She twitches in irritation and shoots off a dirty look before stammering into her shoes.

It's the rose. Marshall has no idea how insane she's become.

wicked

Of course, I can't really stand Michelle. I don't mind too much that she cut her hair to look like she was attacked by a flock of angry bats, especially since I let her get away with all that torment she inflicted upon me a few weeks back when I thought she was with child. But a part of me feels sorry for her.

Without putting too much thought into it I reach up and unhitch the clasp. I'm surprised with what ease it slides into my hands as though the necklace itself were far too willing.

Michelle slaps the back of her neck as if a mosquito had landed before shuffling off into the house. I let the blackened rose slip off the chain and into my palm—examine it in a platinum beam of moonlight. It's like holding a little piece of hell, a hotbed of evil Fems ready to unleash their most horrific endeavors on whoever it comes in contact with, and at this particular moment it's coming in contact with me.

"What's that?" Logan leans in to inspect it.

For a moment I consider my options.

"It's my welcome back gift for Chloe."

"If it's from you, she'll never put it on."

"I'm not expecting her to." Now ingesting it is a whole different story.

I push my way through the crowd, over to where Chloe clings to Gage like a skintight sweater.

"Hey? You mind if I spend some time with my new BFF?" I try to sound light as I lean into Gage. It doesn't take much for him to gently push her in my direction.

"Hi Sky!" She cackles. "You mind if I call you, *Sky*?" Her tan skin looks smooth, hard as bronze in this disorienting light. Her lips shine as she draws out a pink cellophane smile, and for a second, I consider shoving the rose deep inside her throat right here in front of a thousand people.

I hear Logan's voice rumble behind me, and I turn to see him talking to Carly Foster. Next to her, stands a tall brick house of a guy with dark hair and a face that happens to be the male version of Chloe—must be Brody. I look at him for a moment, he's menacing in size. If I attack his sister he might tackle me, or worse, eat me as a snack.

"Let's go inside." I tick my head towards the door and see if she'll take the bait.

Gage circles around, and just as I think he's about to wrap an arm around my waist or stand shoulder to shoulder with me, he goes over to Logan and Ellis instead.

An unexpected warm breeze picks up as an explosion of lightning electrifies the night. A series of seizure like flashes go off as though someone up in space were flicking on and off the lights. Just speaking to Chloe inspires a power surge of celestial proportions.

"Follow me." She takes me by the wrist, and we head down a stairwell that leads to the yard below. A roar of thunder detonates overhead, shakes the earth as she pulls me into a hazy room full of people smoking and playing pool. We dart through a slim door near the back, into a dark corridor. She kneels down and takes me with her. I can feel her patting around in the dark. Smells like mold in here, a combination of air that hasn't been circulated in months and old mothballs. She lifts a latch, and light comes from out of the floor. It's a cellar. A stairwell leads deep underground, and I'm not really too fond of these kinds of places.

"Follow me," she whispers, carefully holding onto the wall as she makes it down the steep flight of stairs.

Behind my shoulder, the game room illuminates a thin seam of light from beneath the door. No sign of Logan or Gage, but I sense them nearby and this makes me feel safe.

wicked

"Are you coming?" She shouts from the bottom.

I clutch the rose in my hand and head on down. Chloe may have her intentions, but I certainly have mine.

A series of exposed light bulbs run across the ceiling of the cavernous space that seems to run the entire length and width of the house. Then I see them—racks and racks of canvasses that take up most of the space in the interim. Running against one wall is a cluttered counter filled with tubes of paint, plastic cups with brushes sprouting from the tops. The thick scent of linseed oil clots up the air.

"So who's the artist?" I ask, examining the vast display.

"Em." She looks at me with a dare in her eyes, as if she's already in on the fact that these aren't just paintings. "Aren't they amazing?" She doesn't take her eyes off me. It's like she's trying to hypnotize me, sway me to do her bidding with her enveloping magnetic stare.

"Why are you with Gage?" I ask point blank.

"Because he's rightfully mine."

My jaw goes slack from the sheer audacity.

"You don't own people." I walk over to a group of canvasses laid out to dry on a rack marked *touch and die*.

More battle scenes. I'm mesmerized. One is of a group of bloodied men lying in a pile, one of a horse that looks as though it sparkles. Foot soldiers trekking on a mountain with angels intermixed—so strange. But it's the last one that stops me in my tracks, it makes me take in a sharp breath and forget to let it go.

It's a girl. Huge angel wings, a dirty shade of blue, expand across the canvas. Long flowing hair painted pale shimmering gold. A radiating light, so bright emanates from behind her, I wonder if it's an explosion—looks almost nuclear. But it's her profile that loosens me. I recognize her so completely.

I'm the girl.

It's me.

27

The Kill Zone

"Emily did these?" I go over to the one painted in my likeness and wave my hand over the girl in the picture fully expecting her to wake up and speak to me.

"She has a gift." Chloe sounds bored as though it means nothing.

"What kind of gift is this? Is she one of us?"

"She's something." Chloe comes up besides me, and stares down at her work. "I thought you might like these."

"Shit," I pant as I walk along and take in the brutal scenes one after another—nothing but blood and carnage—outright butchery. One with a dry riverbed, it looks calm. Everything in it lost in shades of sepia—another one with my effigy. There's a marked wound on my left shoulder blade just above the wing. "This is going to happen," I say to myself.

"Yeah, well, I'd really love to sit around and go over Emily's psychotic finger paints, but I have a party to get back to."

I spear her with a look. Doesn't she realize it's me in the picture? I have a hard time believing Chloe has no idea what these paintings mean.

"I've got news for you, Chloe. Party's over for you and Gage." I take a step towards her.

She huffs a laugh. "Oh, Skyla. You have no idea how to keep a guy, or a secret to yourself."

Before I can register what's happening I'm flying backwards into a stack of upright canvases as tall as my father.

I land hard and take them all down with me accidentally dislodging the rose from my hand in the process.

"It looks to me, Skyla, you're the one without Gage." She stands over me with her feet set in defiance, a mocking smile teeters on her lips.

I sweep her feet out from under her just the way Logan taught me, and she lands hard on her side.

"You bitch." She crawls over to a giant blue bucket and tosses it in my direction, nailing me right in the nose—milky water sloshes all over my clothes and shoes.

I let out a sharp moan.

Before I can recover, I feel something slither down off the top of my head and run my hand over it to find a slick of bright red gloss adhering to my fingers.

Chloe stands above me squeezing the life out of a large tube of paint.

"Death made me faster, stronger. I've been meaning to thank you for making things so perfectly easy," she grits her teeth, expressing the remaining contents from the tube.

I knock her over like a bowling pin and smear the thick glob of paint off my fingers and onto her face.

"You should be dead," I struggle to snatch her by the wrists while scanning the area for the pendant. My eyes sweep the floor until I snag on it, crouching like a spider over by the stairs. I inch over on my knees, dragging Chloe with me as she writhes and bites the hand I wear courtesy of her own spare parts.

"Go ahead," I grunt through the pain. "Chew it off, I never did like that arm anyway."

I let go of her briefly and dive onto the rose, embedding it into the palm of my hand as I slap down on top of it.

A horrible burning pain erupts over my back. I scrape the rose along the concrete and shove it in my mouth for safekeeping.

I'm going to kill Chloe. I'm going to skin her and paint a beautiful picture with a brush soaked in her blood.

I roll her off my back only to see her pinching a rusted out razor with blood rising on the sides.

Shit!

I struggle to take it from her. Arms flail, the ceiling and the floor make repeated revolutions, with me on top of Chloe, Chloe on top of me. Bottles of solvent rain down on us like gasoline. Chloe presses the razor into my neck ready to reopen the wound that's barely managed to heal.

A burst of rattling noises explode from the top of the stairs. This quiet strangulating hatred we've engrossed ourselves in so completely is now disrupted with the rustle of bodies, our names being called out of turn.

Chloe's head jerks toward the stairwell as bodies thunder down the stairs. She's blocking my view, cutting off my air supply as she sits with her knees on top of my chest. The razor twitches over my face, splits open the left side of my cheek in a quick clean slice.

She pushes her face into mine. "That's from Logan."

A pair of arms appear over her and attempt to pluck her off.

"Let go of me!" She shrieks bouncing hard on my chest as she struggles.

The sheer heft of Chloe's weight propels the rose to shoot out of my mouth. She plunges her hand over my face in an effort to stand—sending the rose to the back of my throat.

And it happens.

This is one of those seismic moments.

I absorb the fact that Gage is standing over me offering his hand, that Logan is rattling Chloe against the wall—Ellis and his dirty grey sneakers tapping down the stairs. The three of them look on in horror as I try to strangle myself, writhing on the floor gagging from my efforts.

Chloe did it.

She made me swallow the rose.

Oh fuck.

28

The Dark Rose

Chloe ambles up the stairs leaving patchy fingerprints of paint on the creamy white walls. It looks like a trail of blood—I wish it were.

Gage hoists me up in a sudden burst.

"Are you choking?"

"I swallowed," I bring my hands up around my neck, "Michelle's demonic rose."

Ellis pulls in closer as if he expects to see something.

"I'm going to dream Fems," it comes out a broken whisper.

"Can you breathe OK?" Logan takes off his t-shirt and presses it against the cut on my face.

"Yes." I shake my head in disbelief at what this might mean. "This place is loaded with paintings," I tell him. "Can you and Ellis take pictures with your phones?"

Logan drags Ellis off without hesitating.

"Let's get you to my dad." Gage gently wipes my face with the back of his hand as though he were wiping away tears.

"I can't. You have to take me to Marshall's. It's that rose of a thousand nightmares he gave her, and right now it's making itself at home in my stomach."

His eyes close briefly, and he shakes his head just enough to let me know he's against the idea. "Are you sure?"

"I need to be there now," I say pleading. "Teleport me."

Gage pulls me in, and I wait for everything to fade away and the room to transform, but nothing changes.

"Looks like it's not going to happen," he says looking around the vicinity.

"What's not going to happen?"

"I can't take you. There's a binding spirit here." He appraises the room in this new light. "Come on, we'll see if we can do this outside."

※ ※ ※

Gage and I appear right outside Marshall's door, and I explode over it with my fists until the porch light cuts through the night in one volatile clap.

"What the hell's going on?" Gage asks trying to calm me.

"The rose, it's a training ground for Fems. It gives you night terrors and all kinds of terrible things." And apparently really bad hair days for a long time to come.

The door swings open and Marshall stands there bare-chested with nothing but a pair of boxers on, looking as though he's opening his eyes to the world for the very first time.

"What is it?" He squints into me. "Dear God. Get in here." He swiftly shuts the door on Gage.

Gage opens the door and strides on in.

"I need to talk to you," I say.

Marshall looks over at Gage. "Go home and get some rest. I'll handle things from here." He walks over and picks up a pair of jeans lying at the base of the stairs and jumps into them. There's a shirt hanging from the chandelier in the entry, and I don't even want to know why Marshall has his clothes lying strewn about in odd places.

Gage walks over and whispers in my ear. "I'm going to pick up my car and drive back." He walks out the door and lets it slam like a gunshot.

wicked

"Looks like both your boy toys have a disdain for me. I'll settle the score come finals." He swipes his hand over the top of my head and sniffs at the red gloss on his fingertips.

"It's paint," I offer.

"That slick running down the side of your face is not." His eyes flicker with questions.

I grab him by the shoulders and pull him in.

"I swallowed the rose you gave Michelle." The words draw out in a haunting refrain. I can feel the warmth of his skin, the electric current he emits strums through me—soothing and pleasurable.

His eyes remain fixed on mine—his entire person frozen and unmovable.

I've never seen Marshall without his shirt on. Everything about him is perfect, every muscle defined and at attention. His lips twist as he takes a breath.

"Did you try to extricate it?" His affect doesn't change. He remains staunchly fixated, unmoved by what I've just told him.

"Extricate it?" That's probably like an exorcism, or a fish hook he sends down my throat to yank it out, or a—

"Vomit."

I jump back.

"No." I rise my hands up to my ears. "I can't stand throwing up. I'd rather die than throw up."

"You might have to." He comes towards me with a determined gait.

"What are you doing?" I back up cautiously until I hit the wall. A shiver of pain explodes between my shoulder blades. I let out a groan as I slip further into the room and away from Marshall.

"I'm going to help you." He wags a finger in the air.

"No!" I point over at his stupid finger and its vomitous insinuation. "You do not have my permission to *help* me."

"I'm afraid I don't need your permission love. You have something boiling in your stomach acids that's extremely valuable to me."

I duck behind the sofa as Marshall flexes his knees and elbows as though he's ready to attack.

"Marshall!" I drag myself carefully over to the next sofa.

A smile blooms on his face. He hops onto the couch and bounces across the cushions.

I linger a moment, watching him a good two feet taller perched up like a god. I would do anything to get this rose out of me, to stop Chloe from threatening Gage into her life, to not vomit all over Marshall's soft leather sofas.

"Take me, bind me, I'll be your wife." The words speed out of me in a frenzy.

A smile slides up the side of his cheek, and he hops down from the couch with a thump. "We'll negotiate terms later. It doesn't change the fact I need that rose back."

And with that he sparks a well-orchestrated chase—me with my arms flailing in every direction, Marshall with his uproarious barks of laughter—the slow circular dance that ensues around the piano—the backwards shuffle that pins me so perfectly against the window.

I can feel the cool of the night emanating through my sweater, something cold, something wet, and for the first time I realize my back is raw from bleeding no thanks to Chloe and her razor happy hands.

I let out a short-lived breath as Marshall presses into me. He picks up my hands and spreads my arms high over my head.

"You're going to thank me in the morning."

"I bet you've already used that line tonight."

A tremor of laughter gets caught in his chest. His features glimmer with the slightest hint of perspiration, and I'm vexed by his rugged good looks.

"You only think you know me," he rasps.

Marshall swoops me up in his arms and charges us to the kitchen. He doubles me over the sink and inserts his middle finger down my throat so far until I'm retching and kicking, and trying to gurgle out a scream.

"Don't fight it, Skyla," he demands as he probes over and over—but nothing.

It takes a full five minutes of Marshall poking at my uvula before he calmly extricates his hand and pumps it full of soap.

"It's not going to work," he says, lathering himself in a frenzy.

"What's going to happen?"

"Do you scare easily?" He switches off the faucet and wipes his hands.

"Yes," I can hardly squeeze the word from my vocal cords.

"Well, then, you won't like the next few days."

"You mean," I look down briefly.

"That's right. It'll all come out in the end. Make sure you flush twice—you don't want vitriol like that getting locked in the pipes. You'll be subject to house terrors, and that's a bit more complicated to deal with."

I head to the refrigerator and ransack it for anything potentially capable of inducing a quick bout of incontinence.

"Logic dictates correctly," he starts, "but you're failing to realize that it could prolong your misery. If you don't mind me saying, it's best things bind naturally to ensure a safe arrival." He gives a long tired blink. "Now, if you'll excuse me, I have a guest that needs tending to."

I slam the fridge shut and stomp over to him.

"I very much *do* mind." I slap my hands flat against his chest to push him away, but don't. Instead, I relax into his soothing rhythm, let him wash over me in flowing waves of determined bliss. I glide my hands over his bare chest, smooth as velvet. "I'm not going home Marshall." A tight knot locks down my vocal cords. "Tell her to go," I whisper.

"So it's true. You'll be my wife?" A hint of delight plays on his lips.

I take in a deep exhausting breath.

"Hey." A soft voice drifts from the kitchen entry. Gage strides in with his brows drawn together. "Everything all right?" He looks at Marshall good and pissed.

"Take her home." Marshall places my hands back down at my sides. "If you need me," he plucks my cell out of my jeans and speeds into it with his thumb, "call." He hands the phone over, before settling his fiery eyes back on me. *Be mine, Skyla.*

"No," I give a fearful whisper.

"You'll regret this." It comes out sharp—threatening.

I already do.

29

A Stitch in Time

Gage drives us to his house, where I find myself seated in the kitchen with a weary looking Dr. Oliver examining me from above.

"Identical to Logan's," he muses, pulling a strand of invisible filament between his fingers. "I've been apprised of the situation with Chloe. I want to sincerely apologize for the part I played in creating this nightmare for you."

"No, please, never apologize. You've been nothing but kind." It kills me to hear the strain in his voice. If anything I'm the burden.

Emma walks over and surveys the damage.

"I'm sorry about Thanksgiving, too," I add.

"I had a feeling dinner was a long shot," Emma quips.

"Sorry," I whisper again. Of course, Emma hates me. In fact, once I do marry Gage, she'll probably never look forward to sharing a single meal with us.

I tell them about cutting a deal with Holden's ghost. "So you think we could get a—" I don't dare say the word, body. Instead, I look around the room for signs of my least favorite apparition. "You know, recreate the Chloe thing only with someone else?"

"Mmm," he shakes his head. "I'm afraid I can't help you with that one. I'm stepping down from the resurrection business. Not for me." He starts in on the stitches. I can feel the tugging and pulling. It hurts so bad you'd think he was pouring battery acid all over it. Where the hell is Marshall when you really need his feel good vibrations?

Gage takes up my hand and kneels besides me—Gage who actually offered to *gift* himself to me tonight. I sniff back tears. Now look at us. I'm being sewn back together by a mortician while a herd of rabid Fems wait patiently for me to fall asleep, so they can scare the crap out of me for practice—*practice*. I could have been raking my body against Gage right now if I had only listened to Logan and not gone down there with Chloe. I roll my eyes at the thought.

I squeeze Gage by the hand until Dr. Oliver gives one last snip and hands me a mirror.

"Crap." I look ghastly. There's not a scarf in the world that will hide this incision, not one way to keep this from the Counts who parade around as my parents. "My blood is back to normal, so I can heal faster," I say, trying to convince myself.

"If you get the proper rest you could have them out by morning. Little to no scarring at that," Dr. Oliver affirms.

A small noise emits from my throat as I press my lips together in fear.

"What's the matter, Skyla?" Dr. Oliver pauses from closing his bag midflight.

"I think," Gage interjects, "she's afraid she won't be able to get much rest tonight."

That's a morbid understatement.

※ ※ ※

Logan walks in just as Emma and Dr. Oliver head up to bed.

He wags his phone over at the two of us. "I'll be going over these pictures with great interest. I'll let you know what I find."

"Are you sure you're not going to withhold valuable information?" My stitches pull as I say it. "Email them to me, and I'll have Ellis do the same. And please Logan, send them all," I say, irritated. I'm dying to study Emily's apocalyptic artwork in detail.

"Done." Logan rubs his thumb over his phone before replacing it in his pocket. "Are you OK?"

I look over at Gage. "As long as you're with me tonight, I'll be OK."

Gage winces at the thought. He looks uneasy before blowing out a breath. "Chloe has this crazy idea I'm spending the night with you."

"What?" I don't like where this is going. Of course, Gage is spending the night with me, but what business is it of hers? "Where'd she get that idea?"

"Me." His dimples depress as he pulls a face. "I'm sorry. I accidently told her I wasn't giving up any of the time I was spending with you. And when she asked if I'd spend the night with her instead of you I said that's where I draw the line."

"That's a good thing," I say relieved.

"She agreed." He shakes his head. "But under one condition. I spend just one night at the Bishop's, and she'll leave my nights alone forever. I'll be on the floor far, far away from her I swear."

"You can't go," I say, wild with fury.

"I have to." He gives a tired blink. "Last time, and it'll never happened again. She promised."

"She operates under a backwards code of ethics," I nod into him thoroughly annoyed. I cut a look over to Logan. "Just like the Counts."

Gage does the unimaginable and leaves to spend the night with Chloe. Logan takes me home and settles in at my desk uploading the pictures right onto my computer.

I look in the bathroom mirror, and the first frightening thing I see with that rose tucked safely in my esophagus is myself. The hair on the top of my head is crusted over with dried red paint. My entire face is smeared with blood and pigment, and my white sweater looks as though I leaned up against a bloody carcass of hanging meat.

Shit.

I swat at the sink with a wet hand towel.

I absolutely hate Chloe. Tonight was the night Gage and I were supposed to be together, and she blew it.

I cock my head into the mirror and groan. Honestly, if I were Gage, I would make up a million excuses to get away from me, too. I'm hideous. But I'm not Gage. Gage would have loved me exactly the way I am. He's beyond normal like that.

I take the world's longest hot shower and toss on my cheetah print robe before plopping on the bed. Everything in me aches, and I'm exhausted beyond recovery.

"Hey," Logan comes over and gives me a gentle shake. "Wake up, sleepy head."

"No," I moan pushing him away.

"You told me to keep you awake, or you'd rip my balls off, remember?" I can feel his warm breath wash over me in spurts as he gives a gentle laugh.

"I can't do this. I can't stay awake." My eyes feel dry as a chalkboard.

"Come on," he pulls me into a sitting position. The full weight of my head rolls over my neck, and at this point I could care less if it rolls right off. "I'm going to take you somewhere."

wicked

He lands on the bed next to me with his fingers secured over mine.

"Where we going?" I fight to keep my lids open. "Back to the party? To the part where I stupidly took the necklace off Michelle?"

His teeth blink on and off like a flashlight. "You can't change the past, Skyla."

"Then where?" I ask weary and with great disinterest.

"To meet my parents."

30

Meet the Parents

I had no idea that Logan's parents once lived on the mainland before moving to Paragon and buying the bowling alley. In fact, I'm stunned to be standing on a pumpkin farm in Oregon in the freezing cold of winter in anticipation of the door opening. But it does, and a young couple who look only mildly older than us, stand back and examine first Logan, then me.

"Honey!" A beautiful blonde with her hair in a slick French knot gives Logan an all-encompassing hug. "What happened to your face?" She pulls back before washing over me with a smile. "You must be Skyla, I've heard so much about you!" She takes up my hand and leads me into the house without giving me a chance to say hello.

His father looks a lot like Dr. Oliver, strikingly so. In fact it takes everything in me not to ask if they're twins because I happen to know they're not. This is Barron's father, too, which in and of itself is difficult to wrap my head around.

"Jack—and this is Julia," he says extending his hand.

The Olivers—these Olivers—live in a spacious country home with Americana décor scattered all around. Two mustard velour sofas sit in the middle of the living room and Logan and I take seats opposite his parents.

"Tell us everything that's happened. Have you graduated?" His father looks relaxed, not at all concerned that he might turn around and combust into flames at any moment. Honestly, if I had my children visiting me from the future, and I knew I was soon to be a human candle, I'd walk around with a fire extinguisher twenty-four seven. Hell, I'd live in the bathtub.

"Nope, still a junior." He looks over to me sheepishly for a second. "I'm really glad that you were both able to meet Skyla. She means a lot to me."

"We're honored to have met you," his mother smiles. "I hope you'll visit often, and please, when the time comes, bring the children." She leans in with excitement as tears well up in her eyes.

She looks so young, hardly a candidate for grandchildren. Then it hits me, Logan might be bringing her grandchildren someday—it just won't be with me. A pang of jealousy heavy as an anchor settles in my chest. And suddenly I'm hating this new person who's yet to enter Logan's life.

"Actually," Logan starts.

I clasp his hand and pull it over to my lap.

You don't have to tell them about us, I say.

No, it's OK, he reassures.

"Skyla and I have decided to just be friends."

"For now," I add trying to soften the blow.

So there's still hope? A flash of optimism flares within him. He's ready to interpret the smallest hint I'm willing to give.

I don't think so. And even that was generous.

"These things happen." His mother fans a smile. "We broke up and got back together so many times I lost count."

Gosh, she practically sounds like a teenager, too. This is fascinating—young Dr. Oliver and some hot blonde chick. It's like we're on a double date with friends.

"So tell us about your face? You're both cut. Were you in an accident?" His father inspects us from a distance.

"Actually, no, it was a battle." Logan nods.

Thank you. I give his hand a squeeze.

"Anyway," he gives a depressed smile before continuing, "the purpose of my visit is to let you know that through reliable sources, I've discovered something about myself. For years I was content knowing I had near perfect Celestra blood," Logan pauses.

They shift in their seats and exchange uncomfortable glances. I bet they totally know.

"But, it turns out, I'm part Countenance." The words come out baritone, and seem to echo unnaturally.

The thought of Logan as anything but Celestra shocks me, but a Count? I still can't digest that. Any other faction I would have embraced without hesitating. It would never have had the power to tip the scale of my mistrust for him. A small part of me would trust Logan if he wanted to lead me right off Devil's Peak—a very small and foolish part. I hate that she still exists.

"So you do know." His father relaxes as though he could rest easy now, as though he could finally breathe. "Your grandmother was mixed."

"My side," his mother pats her chest. "I've got some Levatio mixed in as well—Barron is abundant with the Levatio bloodline, but Liam is like you. The degree of Countenance in me isn't a secret, just nothing we advertise. Is this presenting a problem?" Her eyes widen. "Is that why?" She points between the two of us.

"No," I say, trying to save face.

Some strategy of his—bring me to meet his parents and make me feel like a total ass.

Logan gives a gentle tug. *That's not why you're here, I promise.*

Oh, right, the hand. Funny how I'm not so quick to shake him loose. I refuse to do it in front of his parents.

"It played into the equation," Logan admits. "I did, however, want to let you know I'm going to renounce my Celestra status."

"What?" His mother throws her hands up to her ears. She reminds me a lot of myself actually.

"No, absolutely not. I can't agree to this." His father twitches as though Logan were considering manslaughter—as though he were going to turn the bowling alley into a giant bonfire in a fit of insanity.

"I'm not asking permission." Logan doesn't shift or break his gaze from his father.

Damn—Logan is hot when he's defying his parents.

He looks over and I blush.

"I'm doing this because I want to help a friend," he rattles my hand in the air in the event there's any misconception. "And, I think it's going to give us the advantage we need in the faction war."

"How's that going?" His father asks with deep concern.

"They've killed sixteen Celestra. The faction council decided the Counts are posturing," Logan pauses.

"So they'll do nothing." His mother looks pissed.

That's the exact reaction I had. God, I really love her.

"Someone," he looks over at me, "decided to take matters into her own hands."

"I would have done the same." It speeds out of her.

I give a satisfied smile.

"It was Skyla and Gage." He nods as though confirming more things than one.

"There are still five left, and Logan's going to help me with those." I don't mention Demetri. I want the man Chloe sanctioned to kill my father all on my own. Perhaps my dad will come with me? What kind of irony would that be?

"Logan," his father shakes his head, "don't defy the faction council, and for God's sake don't turn on your people."

"I'm not turning on anybody."

"They'll make you pledge over to them," he continues, "you'll have to prove your loyalty. They could kill you if they think you're a liability, and the justice alliance wouldn't hold it against them. You wouldn't be a war hero, or a martyr—you'd be a turncoat."

"I'm not a turncoat. My alliance lies with Celestra." He rubs his thumb against my hand when he says it. "I want this war over quickly, and the power shift to revert back to where it belongs. I'll die if I have to."

All movement ceases in the room. It's as though a verbal bomb just detonated. His parents tunnel into him with an intensity that speaks louder than actions or words.

I lose myself looking at the boy to my left. The damage to his perfect features inflicted by my own unwavering anger. I would have carved his heart out that night if I could have. I shake my head as though offering an apology.

"You'll be a hero then." His father admits quietly as though it were a sad reality just waiting to transpire.

"He already is," I say.

🦋 🦋 🦋

After the visit—after shocking the hell out of his parents and leaving them in a depressed stupor—Logan takes me out back, and we walk through damp open fields peppered with miles of twisted yellow and brown vines.

He takes up my hand, and I let him. We *are* still light driving and terrible things could happen, we could get separated, I could altogether lose him, or Fems could sprout

out of the ground. But really, I think this might be the only time-space dimension possible I might ever get to do this.

So how is it that you and Liam are mostly Celestra, well, and part Count, but Barron is Levatio? I ask, trying to wrap my head around all of this.

Mostly, Levatio, he corrects. *It's works like a blood type. That, and the fact when you're old enough you naturally hone your powers in whatever faction you're destined to be in.*

So does that mean Gage is a Count? The thought prevents me from taking another step.

I'm betting he doesn't have a drop. Our luck seems to run in opposite directions. He compresses a sigh. *Season's over.* He points over to an old weathered barn with misshapen pumpkins trickling out of it. *Whatever they couldn't sell stays there until they can figure out what to do with it.*

I'm sorry. It's so sad to think they're gone now. That those people in the house who are probably consoling one another over the fact their son is about to pledge allegiance to the Counts, are actually long dead, just like my father.

Don't be. We're so lucky to visit our parents. In fact, we can go and visit your dad again, find out more about your mother, if you want.

I do, I pause as the sun melts into the horizon over a patch of maple trees. A few spare leaves hang onto brittle branches and light up the sky with their auburn glory. *Maybe tomorrow night.* Since I don't plan on sleeping again, like ever.

OK, it's a da— He stops shy of using the word date.

A date with a friend. Like we haven't already ambled into major awkward territory.

"So how are things with Gage?" He says it out loud as though he wants to put it out there for the sky and the earth to hear.

"Great." I seem to lack the proper enthusiasm. "Except for, you know, Chloe." I'm so pissed I could nail her through a wall. "I have no idea what's going on."

"I do." Logan's quick to interrupt. "Holden the not so friendly ghost ring a bell?"

"Crap!" I take in a sharp breath. "She said she wanted to high five me and that she couldn't believe it was me who killed him. I did this, and now she's probably threatening him with going to the police." I shake my head in disbelief. "But she killed Emerson." A surge of adrenaline spikes through me as though Emerson's death were just the kind of ray of light I needed.

"Then we need to prove she did it," Logan nods into my line of thinking.

I'm going to beat that little witch at her own game. Then Gage and I can get to the business of exchanging our gifts—each other.

Logan stares into me with that deer in the headlights look.

Our hands drop, and we exchange sad horrified expressions.

The wind picks up. A bird calls out, and it reminds me of Nev trapped in Chloe's bedroom lacking the fresh air and sunshine he so desperately needs. That's how it feels with Logan. Our love suffocated without the freedom, the wingspan it needed, and now here we are contemplating the reality of me being with Gage in a very real way.

"I think we should go home now," I whisper.

And we do.

31

Roll Over

Logan and I managed to stay out until morning.

As soon as the sun illuminates the perennial grey shield that covers Paragon, we hear Mom and Tad shuffle out of their bedroom, so I thank Logan and tell him to go home and get some sleep.

But no sleep for Fem infested me. Instead, I rush downstairs to get some coffee. Lots of caffeine will totally douse the feeling I have to pass out on the stairs. No wonder Michelle tossed herself off Devil's Peak. It's starting to sound like a darn good idea right about now. No sleep, equals pure torture.

Valuable—I balk at the word Marshall used to describe the piece of metal lodged in my intestines. I hope he's got a spare lying around. I have a feeling I'm really going to regret giving Michelle a well-needed vacay. Hey, maybe I could get him to outfit the entire bitch squad with one of those haunted blooms? Except it would probably take twelve pendants to have any real effect on Chloe, she's so full of evil herself.

In the family room, Mom helps Tad get settled onto the couch.

"Well look who's just getting in?" Tad sneers as I pass them by.

"Tell me it's not so, Skyla," Mom's eyes round out as she gawks at my boots and jeans.

"Nope, just up early. Couldn't sleep." Part of that was the truth.

I stare out the back window where the world looks groggy, half-awake itself. A blue-grey morning struggles to open its lids and stretch into life.

"So, Skyla, how did it go last night?" She shores up his covers before he motions over to his legs. She raises his feet and manually stuffs a sofa pillow underneath his thick black socks.

Note to self, never use the sofa pillows *ever*—not even disinfectant can save them.

"It went well." I swallowed an entire legion of Fem riddled demons. Now I just have to keep myself regular in order to ensure my sanity doesn't erode faster than it already has. "Real freaking well," I whisper, opening the fridge.

"So, what did Gage give you for your birthday? If you don't mind me asking." She sweeps over—biting down on her lip as though she were expecting me to expose a diamond-laden engagement ring. Funny, because I did receive a ring, only it was from the wrong Oliver. A heavy feeling of sadness drapes over me.

"Gage and I haven't exchanged gifts yet. I'm hoping for tonight."

"Hope for something a little more realistic," Tad shoots from across the room. "It's a school night."

"Right. I meant early this evening. Maybe we'll go out for a bite or something." A bite of each other. I stop myself from breaking out in an awkward giggle. I'm completely slaphappy from a severe lack of sleep.

A clear image of Gage without his shirt on pops in my mind. His steel cut abs, that triangular shape just below his stomach that dips down to his thighs. I swear you can see the outline of every single muscle on that boy. I plan on making it my goal tonight to trace each one out with my tongue. "What a body," I mouth the words as I pull out a mug and pour myself a cup of coffee.

"What the?" Tad mutters from the couch. He swats himself as though an angry swarm of bees were attacking him.

I smirk over at him.

Everyday should begin with Tad kicking his own ass.

"What?" Mom fans him with a magazine before jumping on the coffee table and drilling out a scream.

It's probably a mouse, or a fly, or a gnat for that matter, she has the same knee jerk reaction to anything under three inches. It's no wonder she's not pregnant by now.

I dart over. "What is it?" I'd love a pet mouse. They're so cute and sweet and—oh—holy freaking shit!

An entire army of long black spiders crawl all over him at top speed. He lets out a series of low guttural moans that make it sound as though a cow is being brutally assaulted in the middle of the living room.

"Black widows!" My mother's lungs blow out the words at Mach five, and within ten seconds a thunderclap of footsteps rumble down the stairs.

Tad spirals off the couch and onto the carpet like a man on fire. He rolls and screams as Mom smacks him hard and fast with a magazine in each hand.

If one didn't know what was transpiring, one might be prone to believe that my mother was beating the crap out Tad. Say, someone like Melissa, who either A. got up on the wrong side of the bed, perhaps four hours too early, or B. is in the middle of a raging bloody period and feels the need to expel her wrath by way of a fist fight.

"You *bitch*!" Melissa gives a high pitch wail that could serve as a worldwide communication method for Counts—

probably does. She pulls Mom back by the hair and pushes into her chest.

"Melissa!" My mother shrieks forming a shield with the magazines.

The chandelier over the dining room table starts to move in violent rocking heaves before it twists and spins like a top.

Holden.

It's like the word *body* is a calling card for all kinds of craptastic things to happen, well, to Tad anyway. And now we've got a circus you could sell tickets to, complete with spousal abuse, black widows, and sideways stepmother bitch slaps.

As soon as the ruckus dies down, Mom yells for Drake to help load Tad into the minivan. Tad's face is bloated twice its normal size, and he's dazed from the thorough pummeling he's just endured.

Not one spider remains. I lift a sofa cushion with caution. Nothing.

"Nice show, Holden," I say under my breath.

I only hope he didn't kill Tad for real this time.

✼ ✼ ✼

That night—fourteen cups of coffee later, I'm so pumped that Gage is actually coming over I can't stop shaking from excitement. Well, OK, the caffeine may have played a tiny part, but that's not how I want to remember this.

Mom is spending the night at the hospital with Tad. Turns out he's got a touch of the blood poisoning, and they want to pump him full of antibiotics so he can live to see another day. Wouldn't that be just weird if the body I gave Holden was Tad's? That would be a disaster of monumental proportions.

Then I'd really have to kill Tad to keep him away from my mother or else, God forbid, we'd have mini Kraggers running around the house. I shake the thought out of my mind.

"Hey beautiful." Gage appears near the doorway holding a round birthday cake with a lit candle pressed in the center.

Gage is beyond gorgeous tonight. He's completely godlike with the glow of the candlelight warming his features.

"You look flawless," I say hypnotically. I want to forget the cake, put out the candle and start our own blaze.

I motion him over to the comforter stretched out on the floor.

We're totally on the same wavelength because I've got three votive candles sitting up on the window seat filling the room with magical flashes of light.

"I saw Nevermore," he says placing the cake between us. "He says hello. I've trained him to say, *happy birthday, Skyla*."

"I bet Chloe liked that." I hate that he was in Chloe's room—that he spent the night. That's about as appetizing as finding hair in my food.

"She wasn't thrilled," he whispers, taking up my hands. "You'd better make a wish." He gives me a feverish kiss on the mouth.

I can feel the heat from the flame rising up around my neck, exploding over me as we linger, not wanting this perfect moment to end. It feels good kissing Gage, being alone with him. Although I hate to admit it, but it also feels good to have my eyes closed longer than two seconds—damn good actually.

We pull back, and I just gaze at him—take in his iconic beauty. "I officially dub you the keep Skyla the hell awake committee. Are you up for the challenge?" I annunciate the word *up* as though it were provocative, but instead it just sounds vague.

"I'm up." He tilts his head at me. "Make a wish before we accidentally set your room on fire."

"Oh right," I stare down at the smooth orange blaze elongating itself into the night.

Wishes—I'd like for the faction war to end, but in a way, I don't. It seems like that will only complicate things, and I sort of like having Gage, with no pressure to choose Logan. Not like I could ever choose Logan anyway, he lies, he broke my heart—he's a Count.

I look across at Gage—so soulful, so sweet with those melted glacier eyes. "I already have everything I want right here." I blow out the candle, and a plume of smoke rises between us, spirals up soft as a dream.

I get on my knees and scoop a layer of frosting off with my finger. I make my way onto his lap and smear it over the side of his neck, pushing my lips up to it. It is unadulterated bliss kissing him through the sugary frosting—an intense glorious pleasure to clean it off his person. Kissing Gage—massaging my lips up and down his neck in one sweeping motion is by far more sexually intense and relaxing than ever kissing Marshall or Logan for that matter. There's something pure about our love, in every way sublime, just like Gage himself.

I feel myself drifting. Gage rocks us back onto the floor, and the room starts to fade. His flesh gives way beneath me, and I'm floating, unmoored from the world, sailing into a pure heavenly sleep.

The room quakes. My eyes spring open to find a dark figure lying next to me. It stirs and turns, exposing an unnatural grimace that spans half its shadowed face, large yellow eyes, and severe wrinkles covering the entire mass of its flesh. My mouth falls open in a scream, but nothing comes. I'm paralyzed, unable to move or breathe from fear.

wicked

Then something loosens, and it takes less than a second before I hop on both feet ready to eject myself from the vicinity.

Squatting by the door is another creature with unnatural folds and depressions in its charred flesh that makes it look more animal-like than human. Its clawed fingers pat steady over a long slender drum. The rhythm fills my ears with a horrible thump that vibrates my entire being with its nagging beat.

"I gotta get out of here," I struggle to make it to the window, but it grabs me and shakes me.

"Skyla!" Gage hisses in my ear.

"What?" I pant, soaking with perspiration.

"You were having a nightmare. Are you OK?"

"I think so." No—definitely I'm not OK. I just sit there, dazed. It takes all of my strength to keep my eyes open, but the thought of that eerie grimace, that *thing* touching me, freaks the hell out of me. "Keep me awake," it comes out weak—feeble. "Are you ready to exchange kisses?" I look over at him blankly.

He gives a gentle smile. "Kisses?" He pushes in a quick one. "Do you mean gifts?"

"Yes," I give a hard blink in frustration. "I totally meant kisses—gifts." I did it again.

"You go first," he says with a smoky look in his eyes.

God, Gage is effortlessly hot, and that is gift enough.

"OK." I pull off my t-shirt and toss it to the floor. "That's just a sneak preview," the words puff out with sheer exhaustion. "I'll let you unwrap the rest. I run my thumbs on the inside of my bra-straps trying to look sexy, but it feels so comfortable I just leave them hitched there, awkwardly, like a farmer in overalls.

He tilts his head thoughtfully, examining me, not sure what to make of my sneak preview. He traces the top of my bra with his finger. "The cake is part of my gift since I made it just for you."

"You did not!" My mouth falls open with surprise.

"Did to. And I only set the smoke alarm off once, which is a new record for me."

"I love you," I say dreamily.

He pulls a piece of paper from his pocket and wands it in front of me.

"Is that what I think it is?" I draw a breath in anticipation. Gage once wrote the sweetest poem, I hope it's another one just like it.

"I thought I'd share my feelings for you," he says it low. The words string out like musical notes and dance through the air.

"Read it to me."

He shakes his head. "I can't see in the dark."

"It's not dark." I flick a finger in the direction of the candles.

"How about I read it to you later." He leans over and puts it on my nightstand. "Maybe you could tell me a little more about my gift right now." A wicked grin spreads across his face.

"First, I want to thank you for sending the invitation." I'm so tired. I sway to my left until I hit the bed. "I thought I was going to have to send it myself. I'm pretty relieved I didn't have to—guess I'm a little old fashion that way." I give way to a gentle string of laughter.

"What invitation?" He rolls me over on top of him.

"You know, the body invite." Oh shit. I just said the magic word, and now Holden is going to show up and turn everything to crap. I hold my breath to see if a giant spider is going to crawl out of my shirt, or if the window and mirror are going to explode simultaneously, but nothing.

"Body invite?" he repeats.

Perfect. In the event Holden didn't hear *me*, there's always Gage.

I try to ignore it. "So did you bring protection?"

"Against what?" Gage seems genuinely perplexed.

"Do I have to draw a picture?" I try to sound light, but I just sound annoyed.

Something twitches to the left.

I draw in a sharp breath and hide my face in his chest. It's that creature, that thing, watching us from the corner.

Something tells me it's going to be a very long night.

32

What in the Hell

Gage and I take our time getting to know one another on a far more physical level than ever before, but really it was nothing like I had envisioned. We spent the night clothed and highly supervised by an army of creepy Fems, which Gage kept trying to assure me only existed in my imagination.

It's probably a good thing nothing major happened. I'd hate to have the embedded memory of wrinkled Fems with bat-shit crazy grins as a part of the experience.

The next morning, I catch a ride to school with Drake and Brielle.

Brielle sits humming along to the radio as though everything were normal. She seems completely unfazed by any drama, if there is any drama, going on between the two of them. I can't tell whether or not they're together, or broken up, or if Drake is aware of the fact he'll be a father soon.

I drift off to sleep on several occasions on the way over to West, the only thing jolting me awake from time to time is the pothole-riddled road. Each time the tires sink, I smack my head into the window.

As soon as we park, Brielle and Drake take off for first, each slamming their door as they stomp off in separate directions, so there's that.

I rest my head on the seat in front of me as I grab my backpack off the floor. It beckons me to stay awhile in this strange, yet amazingly comfortable position, so I give, and my eyes seal shut.

Dreams wait for me in the dangerous world behind my lids. I'm dressed in white, with my arms and legs spread out, spinning on a large grey stone. Brielle comes over and sits down next to me. A giant goat crawls out from under her shirt, and she smiles over at me, tells me it's her baby. A tunnel emerges. I walk for miles down darkened corridors—so many doors to choose from. If I choose the wrong door I'll be lost, banished forever. But if I choose the right door, I become eternal and get to live with Logan and Gage.

A hard knock explodes on the window of Drake's car, and I spike up in my seat.

It's Gage. He's got the face of an eagle, and he's bare-chested. I get out of the car and follow him to class. I don't think twice about the dramatic change in his features, just admire the way his feathers band in layers, the nobility they bring to him.

"I can't keep my eyes open," I tell him.

"I'll be here for you," he says without moving his beak.

I miss old Gage.

I miss the way things were before Chloe.

ʬ ʬ ʬ

The sky rolls back exposing long red gashes in the sky. Clouds like bruises fill in the periphery, and a brilliant band of striated tissue leaks a puddle of blood onto the senior lawn at West Paragon.

I walk into Marshall's class feeling far more dazed than I was during first. My muscles ache as though I just swam a mile through wet cement to get here.

Marshall looks arresting, standing there chatting with a student.

You never know with Marshall and his Sector ways if you can trust him. He has a mind technique he uses on the entire lot of us, and today I'm acutely aware of it. I can see him for the spatial creature he is, an errant nodule sent to moderate us, confuse our minds with stories from heaven.

Marshall wants to marry me, but it's Gage I'm going to be with.

I look over across the room at Gage. He looks regal sitting there with Chloe. His feathers all neatly arranged in rows by color—first the snowcap above his shoulders, then short brindle feathers, and then a strip of gold. But it's his beak that drives home his nobility, makes his strength known to everyone around.

Ellis turns to face me, he's shirtless, and wears the face of an ox. I marvel at the flesh on his chest, rubbery, like a crash test dummy.

I laugh right at him, and he gives a goofy grin back.

"What's so funny?"

"You're funny," I say. "You look real scary. I bet your mom's proud, though." I don't know why I add that last bit, I just do.

"I need to go back and get my stash." He nods over and over as though he's keeping a beat to some private song.

"I don't think so," I say flatly. The bell rings and interrupts me. All I can focus on is how painfully wide his nose looks. He should put a ring in it. He looks menacing, and if I didn't know it was Ellis I'd probably run away. Then I remember what I was about to say. "We can't go back—ever." I look across the room and see Chloe speaking to Gage. My Gage. She's got my damn bird, and now she wants another one. She'll imprison him behind bars, and I'll never see him again. I pound my hands flat against the desk.

wicked

"It's because of her!" I shout the words to ensure everyone in the room can hear. I stand and point over to Chloe the witch. "I killed her, and she wouldn't stay dead." My voice cuts through time, you could hear it all the way back in the forest that night after homecoming.

"Ms. Messenger?" Marshall moves like a ninja and pulls me outside by the elbow. "Get a grip on yourself. Have you had any rest?"

"No. I can't sleep." I take in his radiant beauty. Marshall glows in colors that I've never seen before. They dance around his face like a rainbow of exotic flowers, sparkle like cut glass. I slip my finger inside the collar of his shirt. "Do you shave your chest?" The words thump out of me.

"Clearly you are in no condition to remain on the premises. Take your things and leave."

"Skuce," I don't recognize the word. I think I'm just making them up now, because having a private language is reasonable and necessary. I take a step back.

"Go to the restroom and douse yourself back to reality. I suggest you see me later if you haven't imploded before then."

His shoes create a hollow echo as he walks back into class. They code a message to me that lets me know we've been invaded. I bolt down the stairs slipping and falling. Holden helps me up as we venture outside.

The dark sky yawns, and a patter of rain begins its harsh assault. It's the first clue that the faction war has come to Paragon. Holden and I need to fight to bring down the Countenance.

We lie in wait as an entire infantry of Counts head in our direction—each in their own brilliant color cleverly disguised to throw us off course. We wait until they're right in front of us then jump them one by one. I twist arms and legs, tear out patches of hair with my bare hands. Holden laughs and cheers. We are unstoppable.

Time pulls apart. It shreds easy as wet paper, further and further away from me. I find myself on a field in the sun. A girl with hair the color of rust, dead eyes, comes to me. She speaks her native tongue of lies, but I scratch and claw at her, spin her over my arm and toss her in the sky like a dinner plate. I don't wait for her to land. I just run.

Days melt into weeks, and the wind blows through my hair wild and untamed, the earth twists under my feet as it moves me closer to my destiny. I come to a clearing and see Logan and Gage—Logan with the face of a donkey. He looks so regal, destined to be mine, but the world says I can't have him.

"Here." He tosses me a long black gun, cool to the touch. I hold it up to my cheek and let the metal sooth me from the blistering heat.

"Right here, right now!" Logan shouts, and we rain fire upon the enemy. They look so human, so afraid of the three of us. We slaughter them all in a hail of gunfire.

The sky grumbles overhead. God approves of the bloodshed. I always knew he would.

"I did this for us all," I say.

"We did it," Logan smiles with his strange bucked teeth. "Now you have to choose, Skyla. It's either me or Gage." His ears peak over his eyes.

"You can't have us both," Gage doesn't move his beak when he says it, and this makes me wonder about him.

I run.

I run under the shadow of an ash-covered sky. My clothes adhere to my body, my shoes fill with water, and I don't stop moving until I hit the cemetery.

I want to find Emerson and tell her the good news, but it's too dark, there's too much rain.

A hole in the ground with a huge granite slab abandoned beside it waits for me.

If I lie in there I'll be safe. No one will find me, and I won't have to choose. I can rest and sleep in peace—a lasting slumber that wraps its arms around me strong as death.

I crawl inside and let the dark embrace me. Pierce follows me in.

It feels safe now that Pierce is here with me.

"Will you stay?" I ask.

"I will," he says.

He grazes his teeth against my lips, my neck. I can feel the blood drawing out of me. It brings me closer to Pierce, and I don't want him to ever let go.

My final thought before I sleep is this—how strange to die in a cemetery.

33

Here

My eyes feel like chalk, my muscles too heavy to move. I let out a groan. It feels good to struggle to wake from this ceaseless slumber.

"Skyla," Gage whispers in my ear.

My lids flutter open—two, three times before he comes into focus. I see his beautiful black hair freshly swept back with the track marks from the comb still in it, eyes like brilliant sapphires.

"You're going to be OK." His lips land soft on my cheek.

"The faction war." I try to sit up but can't. My hands and feet are tied down with miniature leather belts. "Oh God." I know exactly where I am and suddenly I'm one thousand percent awake, and I want to get the hell out of here.

"Relax. If you get too agitated they'll come in."

"I'm in the psych ward?"

"Yes."

"Tad did this," I say accusingly.

"Dr. Booth did this. You've been out of your mind."

"What?"

"You freaked out at school then went missing. Your mom is under the impression you were kidnapped and given psychedelic drugs then dumped off at the cemetery." His eyes pull across my face with sadness. "You had another run in with Pierce."

"Pierce?" I lay my head back against the hard bed as tears pool in my eyes. "What happened?"

He lets out a breath. "He hurt you."

"Was I…" The words damn up in my throat and constrict my breathing.

"No, no, it was nothing like that."

I'm afraid to ask how he knows this as a fact.

"He bit your neck. Actually he scratched you down like a cat sharpening its claws. It was pretty bad."

"What do you mean *was*?"

"You were able to heal pretty well. The doctors are amazed at how quickly your scars disappeared."

"How do you know it was Pierce?"

"My dad saw the same puncture wounds you had after homecoming. The doctors think you were mauled by a wild animal while you were in the sarcophagus."

"The sar-what-agus? Oh my God, a grave?" I close my eyes and press my lips together. "What else happened?"

"At school, before you left, you took down a few people on their way to gym."

"Oh no." Freaking out doesn't begin to explain the emotions running through me right now.

"It's OK, no one's dead. It happened so fast they thought they were jumped by a bunch of guys from East." He gives a little laugh. "Just a few broken bones."

"Broken bones?" My eyes dart across the ceiling in a panic.

"Nat's expected to recover."

"Nat? I beat up Nat?" I'm horrified.

"Her, you almost killed. She's here on the fourth floor." Gage grafts those blue eyes onto my skin. I can feel the pain as he tries to pull them away. "She knows it was you, Skyla."

"Oh shit." I give a hard blink.

"Yes." He breathes a sigh of relief. "I'm just glad you're doing better. I really missed you."

"You missed me? How long was I out of it?" It could be senior year for all I know.

"One week."

About an hour later, Dr. Booth has the restraints taken off and escorts me into a square box of a room at the end of the hall. It feels as though my legs haven't been used in a year. It feels as though an entire decade has passed, and I'm afraid of everything that's transpired around me in the interim.

"Well Skyla," he says, pursing his lips to one side. "Gage filled me in on what really happened. Has he told you the cover up?"

I shake my head. I think he did, but I wouldn't be surprised if my brain somehow muddled the facts, and everything I thought I heard was somehow null and void.

"An unidentified person attacked you, bound you, left you for dead at the cemetery." The hard commas engraved on either side of his face emphasize his age. "The perpetrator is also most likely responsible for the attacks on the other nine students."

"Nine?" It croaks from my throat. My threadbare sanity won't allow me to believe this.

"The police will want to speak with you. They'll ask if you remember any details about the attacker."

"Nat remembers hers." I spit out the words.

He nods. "I hear she has an abusive boyfriend." Dr. Booth is deadly serious. I know in my heart what he's implying. I know how it will all go down if I even remotely go in that direction.

"And if I don't name my attacker?"

"I may have heard a rumor from the chief of police. They hope to arrest Natalie's attacker and look for DNA evidence on the boys that were injured. You could be a danger to yourself and others for a very long time to come." His dark eyes laser through me.

It's me or Pierce. One of us will go to jail, amass a juvenile record, become infamous on this very small island.

"I'm suddenly remembering every single detail."

The police are kind enough to come into my hospital room along with Mom and Tad.

I snuggle into Gage as he sits besides me.

"I can't believe that lunatic is free right at this moment," Mom scratches at her head before hastily pushing back her bangs. "We need him arrested tonight."

If I wasn't so groggy, so weak, in this impotent state of evaluation I would swear she loves me.

"We're going to need lawyers to pull this off," Tad looks at her as though she's lost her mind. "Let the state take care of this. I'm staying out of it."

"She was nearly killed! You saw her throat when it happened. He left her there for rats to gnaw at her like she was...she was..." Her hands flail as she struggles to formulate a sentence.

"Come on, those rats are down there every night chewing on a smorgasbord of corpses."

"Excuse me?" Gage looks indignant at the fact Tad's demonizing his father's facility. "The cemetery is free of vermin

I can assure you." It's clear by the looks on their faces no one seems to believe him. "Do you mind if I drive Skyla home?"

"Yes, we mind," Tad barks. "And you, by the way, can stay the hell away from her if you don't mind."

"I agree," my mother says coldly.

"What is going on?" I fasten myself to Gage for protection. Clearly the demonic rose has had its side effects with the family as well.

The rose! I must have...come to think of it, I do feel better.

Then it all comes back to me. Gage, Logan, Ellis, all with strange animal heads. Oh my God—I *did* beat those people. I threw Nat in the air like a ragdoll. Pierce...I finger my throat.

"Pierce Kragger did this to me," I say out loud. "I want him arrested."

34

Now

I'm finally able to convince Mom and Tad that it would be very healthy for me to go out and have a nice hot meal with Gage as soon as they discharge me from the hospital.

"What the heck are they so pissed about?" I ask as we step into the Oliver's house with our fast food bags.

"No clue. They turned on me mid week. One day your mom was nice as can be, and the next, you would have thought I was caught filling her tires with razors."

I run my fingers through his hair as we place down the bags. He pulls me into a tight embrace, buries his face in my neck and just breathes. I push him back an inch, surprised by the quick bite of pain.

"I'm sorry, did I hurt you?"

"No, it's OK." I go over to the oven door and appraise myself in the glass. I look completely normal from what I can tell. The scar on the side of my face is a thin seam of flesh, not a stitch in sight.

"She lives." Logan walks over and scoops me into a hug without hesitating. He presses a quick kiss onto the top of my head. *I love you.* It comes out horrifically somber, and I wonder if he meant for me to hear that after all.

"I'm OK," I say, pulling away. His stitches have come out on the side of his face, and there's just the thin trace of a line left to remind me of what I did. "I named Pierce as my attacker."

"I know." He looks from me to Gage. "I had a friend hook me up with a Glock 19."

"What's a Glock 19?" It sounds dangerous, and I'm afraid it is.

"It's a gun, Skyla. I've got the names of the five remaining Counts on your hit list, and I'm going to track them down and finish the job."

"Hit list?" He makes me sound like some maniacal killer. OK, so maybe I am, but still. "We don't need guns, Logan. We can use the spirit swords, or—"

He shakes his head and interjects, "We need something faster for what I have in mind."

I pin him with an isolated stare. It takes all of my energy to look at Logan, and I know for certain that there's no way in hell I'll have the energy to chase someone around the room with a knife.

"OK, you shoot, but I'm coming with you," I say.

"I'll go with him." Gage offers, wrapping an arm around my waist.

"We can all go," I shrug over at Logan. I know he wanted this to play out like some kind of romantic death date. Like we were suddenly going to morph into a futuristic version of Bonnie and Clyde, that maybe it would be the binding cord we needed to solidify my trust for him, but he needs to face facts, Gage is, and always will be a part of my equation.

I can feel myself floating into Gage, relaxing for the very first time since I've been awake. A week—I lost a week of my life. I shake my head at the thought.

"I dreamed the faction war was over," I say.

Logan's cheek rises and pushes in his newfound dimple.

"I hope you want it to be."

wicked

✖ ✖ ✖

Gage drives me home.

"I get my truck back tomorrow," he says as we head into the house.

"Are you serious?" Now it feels like I've been gone a million years.

"Yup." He lights up with a smile. "I'll take you for a drive if you want."

"I want. I always want to be with you." Why can't we get married now? I'm so sick of pretending to be Tad and Mom's daughter. It's all a parade of lies, and I'd rather be with Gage every day—every night, in a real bed, doing real things.

I stand on my toes and give him an urgent kiss in the entry.

"There you go!" Tad bellows. "She's home for two seconds, and they've already conjoined faces. Lizbeth?" He heads back into the kitchen.

I lead Gage into the family room with caution. Everyone is sitting around watching TV, or doing homework at the table.

"We're having this out right now." Tad ambles over to Mom and takes a defiant stance at her side.

They look unimaginably pissed.

"Mia." Tad holds his hand out until she deposits her cell. Tad manipulates the buttons then shoves the screen into our faces. "See this? This is what's been going on while you were lying at death's door, Skyla." Tad wiggles the phone uncontrollably, and I can't make out what he's talking about, so I take it from him.

Oh crap.

It's a picture of Gage and Chloe—her arm is linked through his, and she's looking up at him adoringly. They look like a couple.

Great.

An unexpected wave of sadness comes over me, and tears start to break through. I blink them back and hand Gage the phone.

"Did you get fifty dollars for that?" I ask Mia.

Her vellum eyes widen in horror. She shrinks back as I fast approach.

"You think it's funny accusing my boyfriend of cheating on me?" I shower my anger over her in one hot breath.

"I'm sorry, but he was with her, and I thought you'd want to know."

"So you embarrass me in front of the family and Drake and Gage? Good going, sis, I'll be sure to remember that and keep an eye out for ways to bring you to your knees in humiliation."

"Why are you mad at me? He's the one that did it!" She points at Gage.

Mia's right. The only reason I'm shouting at her is because Gage was caught. It has nothing whatsoever to do with her. In fact, had he really been cheating on me, I would have thanked her, and the only thing I'd be bringing my knees to would have been his balls.

"Sorry," I say to Mia.

I turn to look at him.

"I swear she's just a friend." His chest pulsates as though this were real—as though I didn't know deep in my heart that Chloe is gunning for something way more than friendship and handholding.

"I believe you."

wicked

"Oh my, God." Tad throws his hands up in disbelief. "See that girls? File that under never believe your boyfriend when there's photographic evidence. He obviously took up with this girl while you were gone. Lizbeth?" He shakes his head at her.

"Gage," my mother comes over, "I really like you. I really, really do, but please, if there is anything in you that is interested in someone else, just come clean with Skyla, and gently let her go."

It's like some nightmare that keeps unfolding, this thing called my life.

"I'd like to talk to you outside a moment," I say to Gage as I swiftly drag him out the front door.

The cool night air licks at my neck. For the first time this evening I'm acutely aware of the fact my skin feels raw as a sunburn.

"Tell me what's going on with Chloe." Tears blur my vision. I think the emotional toll of Chloe's blackmail scheme has finally taken effect, and an entire river of damned up tears is waiting to fall.

"Nothing's changed."

"She still threatening you?"

He doesn't say anything. "I said, is she still threatening you?" I drill the words into the night—rattle the leaves on the trees with my anger.

His eyes close momentarily.

"She was never threatening me," he looks away when he says it.

"What?"

"She was threatening you."

"It was Holden," I say. "It's because I killed him." The words come out inaudible. "But we know she killed Emerson." I pull his hands down and hold them. "We can fix this."

He shakes his head. "It's not because of Holden."

"Then what?"

"I gotta go. Get some rest, and I'll be back in two hours, I swear."

"Where you going?"

"Ellis is having some people over."

"You're meeting her there, aren't you?" I'm beside myself at the thought.

Gage presses out a sigh, and the night lights up with his vaporous sadness.

"Tell me right now. If you want me to be your girlfriend, if you love me like you say you do. Tell me what in the hell has you acting like a trained butler monkey."

His eyes widen at the inevitable collision we both knew was coming.

"No." He says it clean, simple as though telling me the truth were never an option. "I love you. And right now that means protecting you."

"Dammit if you don't tell me—I swear I'm breaking up with you. You promised me you'd never keep anything from me. You *promised!*" I shriek into the night. I don't care if Tad or Mom or an entire choir of celestial angels can hear me. I want to know exactly what he knows. I'm so *sick* of the way the Olivers prefer to keep me deaf, dumb, and blind, for my own safety.

He doesn't say anything. A whole ocean of time sails by. He penetrates me with that hypnotic cobalt gaze and makes me want to forget everything I've just said, take him up to my room and have my way with him. They could all watch at the door, I really don't care.

He leans in and kisses me gently on the lips.

"Sorry, Skyla," he says before walking down the driveway.

35

Tonight

I acquiesce to Tad and Mom's request and get up to bed early. Mom brings me a cup of hot chocolate and takes a seat besides me.

I wonder if this is the right time to bring up the fact I know she's not my mother? That I know she's a Count—that I just saw my father last week, but don't. I sit up and take a sip of the warm creamy liquid and trace the burn as it singes its way down my throat.

"If you really believe Gage is innocent, then I do, too." She strokes back my hair.

My mother would acquit him of my own murder—she's that in love with Gage. Then again, so am I.

"I do." I'd hate for there to be weirdness around us next time he comes over. Plus I'm going to be connected with Gage for the rest of my life. The thought warms me and yet saddens me for Logan.

"You know, your father and I weren't always perfect." She hitches her long bangs behind her ears. "Don't get me wrong, there was never infidelity involved," her hand flares in protest, "but we loved each other very much." She stares out the window reaching for him in the recesses of her memory. "He had this way of cocking his head to the side and looking at me with his eyes kind of like this..." She demonstrates by looking seductive and puzzled at the same time. "He used to drive me crazy with hogging the remote and leaving the cap off the toothpaste, but once he was gone I missed everything about him—I wanted all of it back." She gives a hard sniffle. "Anyway—don't throw Gage away because of something that was probably innocent. He really does seem like a nice kid." Her glassy eyes sparkle with affection. "Sort of like you." She tousles my hair making me feel all of about twelve. "You haven't sent any invitations out have you?" Her voice is low and garbled as though it was the last thing in the world she wanted to ask.

"No," I say sharply. Although, I thought I had one sent to me.

"Good." She slaps my leg. "I was worried for a second. Sometimes sex can change things." She glances over to the broken mirror. "And try not to destroy things when you're angry at your boyfriend."

She gets up and says goodnight before closing the door.

I can't imagine sex changing things between Gage and me, not in a bad way at least.

I settle back into my pillow and think about it. Think about what it might be like afterwards, like the next day, or at school after we've totally gifted ourselves to one another. A part of me thinks it would only make us feel closer, take our relationship to some magical nirvana-like level. Another part of me wonders if it'll be strange and awkward. Will we feel pressured to do it all the time, and what if we don't? What if I'm not enough for Gage, and he wishes he could leave me and be with someone else? I don't really believe that last part. If anything is true in this world it's that Gage will love me to the grave and beyond.

The piece of paper he gave me as a birthday gift still lies folded next to my alarm clock. I reach over and snatch it up. I wish Gage were here to read it to me. I would love to soak in his smooth voice, watch the words tumble from his lips as he expressed exactly how he feels.

I unfold it and take in the familiar penmanship that strokes across the page. Gage wrote this with his own hand. I trace the words with the pads of my fingertips.

Skyla,
Farther down the road I see you,
a heart that measures in time with mine.
We breathe the air of a world forgiven.
Spin on this planet, once thought divine.
I'll stand beside you until I am driven,
into the light so brilliant—into the light sublime.

I read it five times without stopping. It brings tears to my eyes. In six short lines, Gage managed to encapsulate the span of our entire lives together. *A heart that measures in time with mine*—that verse burns itself into my memory, sears my soul with my love for him. Moment's that haven't even happened yet, he's defined so eloquently, so full of beauty and grace.

How stupid am I to sit here welling up with tears while Chloe is out pawing all over my man?

I snatch off the covers and head to the closet for a quick change.

There's no way in hell I'm going to let Chloe have Gage another minute.

He's the love of my life, and neither Chloe, nor her threats, are going to keep me away from him.

36

We Belong

Ellis Harrison's house is thumping in the night. Literally you could see the sound waves echoing into the mist as they create a rainbow of vibration into the deep purple sky. A dark impression of the moon hangs curiously low as a fine dust of fog moves over the island like a shroud.

I asked Logan to pick me up and drive me over without saying a word to Gage. I want to surprise him. Truthfully, I thought Gage might say something to Chloe and ruin operation kick Chloe's ass, or drown Chloe in the pool, or hang Chloe by the ankles from the balcony—all of the above.

Logan parks in his driveway and heads inside to get something while I duck across the street.

It's dark in Ellis' house, save for the powerful flaming tongues that emit from the fireplace. It's strange how I feel so comfortable here, so much more at home than at the Landon house, which feels like a prison, like another wing of Ezrina's lair.

"Hey you!" Brielle screams in my ear while landing on my foot.

I yank myself free from under her heel.

"Are you better? Who the hell kidnapped you? I heard they arrested Pierce."

"Yes," I say rather dazed at her nonchalant attitude. "It was Pierce. He's sick. He almost killed all those people, and I heard he really messed up Nat." I throw in those last few things for good measure. "I guess she was confused and thought it was

wicked

me," I shrug, "she's probably covering for him. That's like your typical abusive relationship," I say, panning the area for Gage who happens to be abusing me at the moment by dating Chloe for my supposed own good. It's like dating other people to keep me safe is a new kind of pox in my life.

"Oh totally." Brielle buys everything I'm selling.

"So, how'd it go with Drake?" I ask, calling off the search party for a moment.

"It went." She shrugs. "He's totally in denial. He says he needs a break."

I gasp. "I'm sorry."

"Don't be. He just needs to wrap his head around it." She blows a bubble like it doesn't really matter.

I catch a glimpse of Drake in the corner wrapping his head around Emily, and I suddenly have the urge to spear him with the poker from the fireplace.

"You wanna get out of here?" I know I risked my ass coming down here to kick Chloe's, but I'd sacrifice a good bitch slap to take Brielle to get a burger and shake. That is, if she drove. It really does suck not having a car. I might just ask Logan if I can buy his dad's car off of him, so I can have my own ride. Just because I don't entirely trust him doesn't mean I can't buy something off of him—work for him—love him.

"What? No. This is where all the action's at, baby." She thumps me hard in the hip before taking off dancing into a crowd of bodies.

Why can't I be more like Brielle and less like me? Her boyfriend—the father of her child is doing something far worse than Gage, and she's having a great time at the party, hell, she *is* the party.

I scour the vicinity for signs of Chloe or Gage and run into Logan instead. He's carrying a white folder, and it looks like he wants to pass me notes from English class, only we don't have English together, or any other class for that matter.

"What's this?" I take it from him and step outside under the porch light.

It's the pictures from Emily's house. The paintings.

"I printed them out and tried to put them in some kind of order. They're fascinating. The details she picks up are amazing. Skyla, that one she did of you was beautiful. I'm ready to offer serious cash just to hang it in my room."

I give a wry smile still flipping through pages and pages of pictures. The faction war. It's laid out before me in detail right here in my hands, part of it anyway. She doesn't use a lot of color. In fact, the entire palate seems to be bathed in light and shadows.

"You ask her about these?" I'm curious whether he ventured out on his own after my not so rosy mishap.

"I tried asking if she was into art and stuff, and she said not really."

"That's weird. Did Gage tell you there was a binding spirit in the cellar?"

He nods. "He thinks it may be in the entire house. Definitely something is going on there. I've always thought that family was odd."

"Are they Counts?"

"No," he's quick to answer.

"Not that you'd tell me." I don't bother hiding my resentment.

"I'd tell you."

"In your own time." I can't hide the hurt. It's late, and I'm exhausted. And who knows how many pints of blood Pierce managed to siphon. "I gotta find Gage," I say, handing the book back to him. "Can I borrow this sometime?"

"Sure."

I look at him standing there, sweetly washed in a scarf of pale light emanating from above. His entire person is bathed in gold, and somehow I find this fitting. I run my hand along the side of his face and rub my thumb gently over the hard line of skin that's not ready to forgive me by way of disappearing.

"I'm sorry."

He catches my wrist and kisses my open palm.

"You don't ever have to apologize to me."

༺ ༻ ༺

Logan and I wander out to the back where we find Michelle and Lexy cackling into the night with a group of girls from East.

Funny how when I first arrived on Paragon I once classified them as the source of my misery, and now they're inconsequential, just irritating fleas on the existence of my being.

The air is crisp with no breeze. The pool glows a soft arid blue in contrast to the tall black forest that surrounds the property. It blocks out any light that might have come from the night sky—offers an ebony hug instead. It makes me miss Nev, his slate colored wings perched high in the branches—his pensive stare, he comforted me.

Then I see her.

Chloe.

Her hair is down, long and straight with a mirror shine reflecting the shimmer from the pool. Gage sits by her side disinterested in whatever it is she's filling his head with. I wonder if her strategy could work? Force someone to be with you twenty-four seven in the event they might like you—fall in love with you out of convenience.

"What are you going to do?" Logan brushes up against my shoulder. The soft scent of his musky cologne wraps around me like a memory.

"I'm going to put a stop to this. I can't let this just go on forever, and Gage cares about me too much to rock the boat with whatever it is she's threatening him with." Me. She's threatening me, but I don't feel like getting into semantics.

"Messenger—" It's Ellis. "I see you eyeing her like a lion stalking its prey. If you plan on dying each other red, or stabbing each other in the back, take it someplace else. The last thing I need is cops at the door."

"Nobody ever calls the cops on you, Ellis." I don't take my eyes off Chloe.

"Yeah, well, I can feel it coming. It's sort of a gift." Ellis knocks back his drink.

"I've got a gift, too." And I'll never be able to give it to Gage at the rate we're going. And I'm definitely not in the mood to give it to him while he's carting Chloe around like a charity.

I walk over just as the two of them stand.

"Leaving?" I ask, wrapping an arm around Gage.

"What are you doing here? Are you feeling OK?" he asks, ripe with concern.

Chloe blinks into me. "I hear you're angry with him."

My cheeks flush with heat. How could Gage tell her the intimate details of our relationship? Was he venting? Obviously he doesn't hate her as much as I do.

"You should understand how much he really does care about you," Chloe gives a crooked smile. "I do too, Skyla."

"Bullshit. The only person you care about is you. Are you happy to be back again? Happy to be inviting yourself into my

wicked

life just hoping my boyfriend will give you half the attention he does me?"

A powerful slap burns across my face.

"Shit." Gage pulls me in. "Are you OK?"

I look up to see Chloe standing there alone, unattended.

"Are you surprised it's me he's comforting?" I say, making my way back over to her. "He doesn't want to be with you, he never has. Do you know how desperate it makes you look to have him glued to your side when Logan, Ellis, Brielle, Drake and I all know it's because you're blackmailing him?" OK, so maybe only half of those people are aware of the situation, but still, I would have read a phone book of names out loud to hurt her if I could. "And, by the way, what are you holding over him? If it's about me, I think I have a right to know."

Her skin blotches out unnaturally. Her eyes glaze over with quiet rage as she takes a step forward.

"I'm ready to tell you, Skyla. Are you sure you want to know what only Gage and I are privy to?"

"Yes." I step forward loosening the hold Gage has on me. I want her to tell me, make me understand what could possibly create such a stronghold over my boyfriend that he would break a promise to me and not utter a word—how he could be faithful to Chloe in that respect and not me.

Chloe pulls me in by the waist and walks me towards the deep end of the pool. I watch as a steady rise of steam softens the ripples on the water, how it looks so inviting, already I know we're going in.

She walks me backwards towards the very edge, holding me in a tight embrace until my shoes are hanging halfway off the concrete. She presses her lips to my ear as though she were about to kiss me—maybe she is. Her perfume fills my nostrils.

Its aggressive scent wipes clean the palate of Logan's gentle reminders.

We fall backwards into the warm waters as I stare up at a crisp navy sky. Chloe anchors her legs around mine, and we sink like lead. We burrow down towards the bottom until my feet connect with plaster.

She speaks right into my ear even though I hear her thoughts long before she says anything. The words come out so terrifyingly clear. I look up in fear that the bubbles will rise to the surface and let everyone in on my secret.

Chloe pushes off and swims away.

But I linger as long as my breath with allow.

And now I wish I never knew.

37

Dirty Little Secret

I float up to the top and catch Chloe talking in an animated fashion to the bitch squad, accusing me of pushing her in. Typical.

Ellis launches himself into the pool with a cannonball landing a good two feet away from me.

"Gee thanks," I say wiping down my face, still trying to catch my breath. Bodies start falling in, one after another until the water jags up and down like a tempest.

Logan pencil dives next to me and pops up like a cork.

"And I thought we'd never swim together," he says with a smile.

"I'm not in the mood for swimming." I pull my arms over the lip of the pool and rest my chin on my hands.

"What'd she say?" Logan's hair is plastered back as his t-shirt floats up around his chin.

"Maybe we should grab Chloe and drown her while everyone's in the pool?" I put it out there like it's a viable option.

He shakes his head and places his hand gently against the small of my back.

It's killing me Skyla. Tell me what she's holding over you. I really do want to help. Logan looks boldly into my eyes, burns a hole into my heart with the tenderness of his words.

She knows Marshall's a Sector. I shiver as the thought sails through me.

The expression bleeds from him as he goes under then reemerges. "She won't win. We won't let her."

She has Gage. She's already won.

His hand slides off my back.

I always forget Logan is listening.

Gage gives Chloe a hard look as she heads toward the gate. He speeds over to me and squats down near the waterline.

"I'm going to take her home," he says reaching down and rubbing his thumb over my cheeks. "She says you know."

"We both do." I glance over at Logan.

"I'll come over later and tell you what she's thinking."

I shake my head over at her. "The last thing I want to discuss is Chloe's next move."

"Then let's talk about ours. We're going to come up with something. I promise." He presses in a quick kiss to my cheek before bolting towards the exit.

There's that promise again.

I glare openly at Chloe as she wrings the water out of her hair. Chloe has us so twisted around her finger, it's going to be like hostage negotiations just trying to see Gage.

"Can I have a ride home?" I ask Logan.

"No." A playful smile teeters on his lips. "I want you to come with me to shoot off my new gun."

"Can we use Chloe as target practice?"

He shakes his head.

"Where we going to do this?" I ask.

"Faction meeting in Belize."

wicked

It's dark under the shadow of a nonexistent moon. The air is thick with humidity, and there's a breeze that wraps us in the perfumed scent of night-blooming jasmine.

"So light driving, huh?" I say as Logan leads me down a quiet narrow street with tall archaic buildings on either side. His hair is grey at the temples, the skin around his eyes is more textured, worn with time, and I wonder if it's because that's his true age, but don't ask.

He pauses and pulls me in gently by the elbows. Half his face is locked in the shadows, the other half illuminated by a streetlamp—ironic because that's how I see him now, half Celestra, half Count—half good, half evil.

"Light driving as a mode of transportation is only good for emergencies." He gives a gentle smile. "This just happens to be one." Logan holds a paternal quality that I find irresistible.

"I've been meaning to ask if I could buy that car off you," I say to relieve the tension in the air.

"It's yours," he says with little interest as he pulls the black and green gun from out of his jeans and starts plucking at it.

"It looks fake. Like something you'd see in the arcade."

"I assure you it's very much real." His eyes widen then retract. "Skyla," he says pleading, "let me do this alone. Stay here or let me take you home."

"No." Nicodemus something or other was one of the names of faction leaders who cleared the way for the death of a Celestra. "Might I remind you, while the faction leaders banded together and decided they were fine with the Celestra deaths that occurred en mass, I wasn't."

"It's going to get ugly," he warns. "Stay here. I'll get you when I'm through."

"There's no way I'm leaving you," I hiss.

He takes me by the hand and doesn't debate the issue. Instead he leads me towards a brick building, and we ascend a stairwell off the back. We float up the stairs like ghosts, without one sound, or one breath that could possibly give us away.

A triangular window affords us a peek inside a well-lit room. A small circle of eight to ten men sit knit together passing papers back and forth.

Logan presses his back against the wall. I can feel his warm breath as he pants unsteady.

There is no one else I would do this for. Not one soul on the planet. I love you, Skyla. He pushes his lips to my cheek with a fiery passion as though he were kissing me for the very last time.

Logan storms into the room.

I don't hear questions, or voices, just rapid-fire explosions stemming from his hands.

Logan rushes out. Over his shoulder, I see blood splattered up against the walls as a horrible groan emits from deep inside the room.

Then we disappear.

🦋 🦋 🦋

An evening in Sri Lanka stirs of exotic breezes—spices with names I can't pronounce and saffron colored robes that filter through the streets. I pull in close to Logan. I miss home, Gage, and the old Skyla and Logan who didn't run around the world offing people with bullets.

You killed too many, I say.

They're planning to annihilate the remaining Celestra. He raises his chin into the night and takes a deep breath.

You know this? I ask.

Logan, who has always been steeped in mystery, seems to know a little too much about everything.

He nods. *The Counts are getting ready to graft me in as one of their own.*

And you think this is a good idea because? I already know what he's going to say.

I do and so does your father. Logan pushes me in with a tight embrace.

"My dad?" I pull back and ask out loud.

"Yes," he circles into a nod. "He's a great guy, he's been mentoring me."

"What?" I have to agree with him about my dad being great, but mentoring Logan?

"So he thinks infiltrating the Counts is a brilliant idea? How do I know you're not playing both me *and* my dad? How do I know *you're* not Demetri Edinger in disguise?" God, I've never even entertained the idea. Talk about coming out of left field.

Logan recoils at the thought.

"Come on," he whispers, leading us through a seaside villa that glows a soft vanilla.

How are we hitting these faction meetings at the right time? I ask out of curiosity. Logan is obviously and undeniably in the know.

The Counts hold New Moon festivals. The leaders have a meeting beforehand to officiate it. We're traveling back further and further into the evening, so by the time they realize what's happened, it'll be too late to stop us. Logan pulls his cheek back with pride.

Can't they go back and meet up with us? I'm no genius, but if they can, we could be walking into a bloodbath.

They'd need a treble to pull that off, and they'd need a supervising spirit to give them one.

Why does that sound familiar? Oh that's right, my dad talked about it. What exactly is a supervising spirit? More crap I don't know. Great. Aren't I locked in a treble with freaking Ellis? And what supervising spirit approves of pot laced light drives?

A Sector, Fem, he glances over me with reservation, *a Caelestis, or another higher order.*

Chloe traveled into the future to slit my throat. That means she must have one.

That means she has one for sure. Logan nods into this before pausing at the door.

I take in a deep breath as we head towards the entrance.

Logan dives in and shoots up the room in a series of explosions.

He ejects himself and lands on top of me, his lips hitting mine hot and wet as we quiver back to another time.

38

Rome if You Want To

It happened again in England. The hint of a sickle-shaped moon bared witness to the carnage of Logan's wrath. I stand nearby, afraid, watchful of what the beautiful blonde boy that lies buried in my heart is capable of. All along I thought trust was the issue with Logan, now I wonder if the problem was sanity and his seemingly short supply.

Logan is exterminating Counts at record pace—their blood on his hands. In mere hours, he's transformed himself into a perfunctory killing machine. Nothing will ever be the same after this night. And it makes me wonder if this night is our last of peace.

"You don't have to worry about killing them," Logan says changing out his clip, "They're less human than you think they are."

I think of Ellis and suddenly doubt that.

"Where are we?" I ask, staring at the thick cobbled roads. An entire millennia of foot traffic has worn a slick patina over the walk.

"Welcome to Rome." He pulls a kiss off my lips and peels a layer of my soul off with it.

"Don't do that," I say breathless. "I'm with Gage."

Logan swallows hard as though he had forgotten, or at least hoped that I did. I can feel the drought of our love emanating from him in this fractured moment of time.

"I'm sorry." He leads me by the hand up towards an intersection, then I see it— grand and pious. It eats up the night in one monolithic fit of glory. The Colosseum.

"In there?" I ask.

"No. In there." He points to a building across the street from the ancient structure. We take a seat on a nearby bench so we can take in all of the beauty of what lies in front of us. "I wish it were under different circumstances." He wraps an arm around my shoulder. It feels genuinely platonic, so I leave it there.

"I wish everything was under different circumstances. Especially the fact Chloe managed to worm her way back to life." I hate that the entire Chloe debacle happened because she played off my stupidity.

"Loyalty," he corrects. "Chloe redefines manipulative. She's a harmless looking spark that can turn a forest to cinder with her pinky."

"You got that right," I say. She charred the landscape of my world the instant she showed up at the party.

"So, you wanna tell me about what happened that day you took down half the student body and ran into Pierce?" Three deep lines crease just under his left eye as he gives a gentle smile. It feels as though I'm here with a much older man. I like this aged version of Logan. Something about him curbs my anger, erases some of the hurt caused by the teenage version.

"I thought we took down the Countenance. You and me, even Holden was helping. Pierce," my hand rises involuntarily, "was a friendly face when I saw him." I shake my head. I was so lost. "Um, Gage, he had the head of an eagle, and Ellis, he had the head of an ox." My gaze drifts up towards the thousands of stars watching over us in a spectacular blaze.

"And what kind of face did I have?" He rounds his hand over my knee natural as breathing.

"You had the face of an ass," I say politely removing his now roving hand.

"Figures." His expression sours. "I would do anything to regain your trust."

A swell of emotion envelops us like a membrane. I can't break free from his steely gaze. It's so hypnotic, so comfortable to get lost in Logan's eyes.

"Is that all you want from me?" My heart jumps in and out of rhythm.

"I want everything you're willing to give me."

We exchange an entire season of sorrowful sighs before heading over to a rectangular building with mirrored windows. But it's the Colosseum that captures my attention. It looks straight out of the pages of a history book, so unearthly old, so foreign, you would think it were some unbelievable movie prop, a cheesy bad replica, but here it is. It stands erect in the night broken and beautiful, lit up like a jewel.

Logan walks us in through the side of the seemingly docile building. He leads us down a long stairwell that narrows to an opening at an underground level.

I'm not sure we should be killing people like this. Maybe this one we should let slide? You know let bygones be bygones? I suggest.

You want to let your father's killer slide? I can guarantee more Celestra deaths. What we're doing is going to save lives. He pauses tenderly examining me in the stale thread of light.

I pull him further along, not wanting to get caught up in the moment. If anyone would have told me months ago I'd be going to Rome with Logan one day, I would have envisioned a far off honeymoon. I would have had stars in my eyes over sharing something so special with him. Bullets and blood, and racking up a body count would have been nowhere near the list of things I expected.

"Honeymoon?" He pulls me in, enamored by the thought. "I'll remember that."

I'm not sure if he means because it's a nice thought or because he thinks it's still an option, either way it was a fleeting fantasy, and that's all it'll ever be.

"Skyla." My name depresses from his lungs lower than a whisper. He closes his eyes, and a seam of tears ignites over his lashes.

Then he galvanizes. Something fires him up like an engine. He roars to life and charges us down a football field worth of corridors. Voices emit freely from an opening to our left, and Logan jumps inside, all hellfire and fury, then a strange eerie silence.

A hand reaches out and pulls me inside.

"Logan!" It speeds out of me in a panic.

Logan's hands are restrained behind his back, his lips bound with duck tape.

Looks like they found their treble.

39

Gone Wrong

Four well built men, surround us like a garrison. I'm assuming they're all Counts and they've somehow become aware of the fact that new moon faction councils are turning into a hell of a lot of bloody fun for a couple of young Celestra—well, one Celestra anyway. For the record, I'm not having any freaking fun.

They push Logan into me hard, and we smack into the wall behind us.

Don't move. Logan rubs the side of his face up against mine, our twin scars meet for the very first time. It feels intimate, passionate, and the armed thugs waiting to pump some serious metal into us are the morbid witnesses to our necrotic brand of love.

We have to fight. Remember what I taught you? He moans in order to stall.

Yes. Sweeping out their feet, the chokehold, wrestle them to ground, and break their arms—the ball buster.

That's the one. Logan bends over and hikes his leg up behind him in the air at record speed. My brain registers this as though it were all happening in slow motion. He knocks down two of the men to his right with his ballerina-ninja-like move producing a shower of teeth and blood.

All four men rush him. They catapult on top of him with their bodies as though they were dousing a fire.

I try to harness my strength by way of anger. I think of Chloe and the way she's bound me with her knowledge. The way she stole Gage right from under me, and now I'm powerless against her emotional bondage. She could blackmail Gage all the way to altar if she wanted. Maybe Gage's vision of me marrying him doesn't even take place until we're all senior citizens—or worse he's confused me with Chloe.

I pluck two of the men off Logan and toss them behind me with unnatural ease. Logan loosens up enough to kick his way up off the floor—grunting, panting—nothing but a tangle of questionable limbs. The first two return and restrain my arms leaving my legs in prime position to kick one square in the nuts, so I do.

He lets out a horrific *oof.* Back home, it would have probably sounded more like an ugh, or a ooh, but it's funny how even amidst great pain the recipient of my punishment remains true to his foreign roots.

Why is everything so quiet? Why is everyone looking at me like I've just committed the most heinous atrocity? Oh right, they've all got a pair—

I turn and knee the man to my left, then the one to my right. It happens so fast, almost simultaneously. It's as though I had psychologically immobilized them, and now they're all victims to the bionic groin throbs I've doled out.

A lone man struggles with Logan. He sees me fast approaching and runs out the door.

Logan pulls out his pistol and points it down at the three men writhing in pain. Logan is doing this for me. I've encased his heart in permafrost and reduced him to nothing more than an executioner.

"No," I say placing my hand over his. "We're leaving."

wicked

We return to the butterfly room. It feels so good to be back to my normal life as I take in the colorful specks lining the walls. I lie down and soak in the peace and beauty of the butterflies as they watch over us with hushed appraisal.

"I'm sorry if it was too much for you," Logan lands on his stomach next to me.

"It was my idea." I never said I had any good ones. "What's going to happen next?"

"They'll find a way to make us pay for this." His face offers no apologies whatsoever. "You were right though, it was necessary."

I reach up and run my fingers through his hair. It's courser than I remember. So is Logan.

"Do you know this because—"

He cuts me off, "My conversion? Yes." He adjusts himself onto his elbows. "Trust me, what we did tonight was a public service."

"I do," I breathe the words.

His face angles towards me, and he gives a humble smile for the first time in a long while.

"You do?" There's a boyish quality about him when he says it.

I lean up and circle him by the waist in an awkward embrace that's neither platonic, nor romantic.

"Yes, Logan, I do."

🦋 🦋 🦋

Gage texts me in the morning and offers a ride to church. Not only is he going to look great to my mother, but I get to spend the whole entire day with *Gage*.

I head downstairs and find Tad and Mom hunched over a stack of papers at the kitchen table.

"Watcha looking at?" I ask, pouring myself a bowl of cereal and hopping next to Drake at the bar.

"Well, look who's up?" My mother beams at me as though I were eight. "Are you feeling better?"

"I feel fine." Truth is I'm wrecked both physically and emotionally, but globetrotting and murder will do that to you.

"So what's with the forest worth of paperwork?" I reiterate. Probably renewing their membership to Counts International.

Mom and Tad exchange glances.

"If you must know..." Tad is clearly irritated with the inquisition.

Wow. I should reward myself for riling him up at this early hour. Then again, it seems right on schedule for me.

"Your mother and I," he continues, "are getting ready to visit a fertility clinic in Seattle."

"State of the art facility." Mom leans in confidentially.

Sorry I asked. I think I would rather they were renewing their memberships to the slaughter Skyla committee—just about anywhere other than a freaking fertility clinic.

"So," Tad continues, "looks like we'll be using any monies that might have been allocated for your college educations and pilfering them in an attempt to bring forth yet another child into this world we're ill equip to provide for."

Drake scoffs as he inhales his last spoonful.

"Your father's teasing," Mom insists. "He wants this child as much as I do, if not more. I'm secretly hoping for twins."

"Twins?" Tad balks.

Two Tad juniors? I'm just as shocked as Tad at the idea.

"Relax. It's very common to have five or six embryos take when undergoing this procedure."

"Five or six?" His face lights up a strange shade of purple.

"Well, we wouldn't have to do any of this if you were able to hold up your end of the bargain." She eyes him below the waist.

I guess Tad's not the sperminator after all, looks like Drake holds that title—the sperminator—the *impregnator*—same difference.

Drake drops his spoon on the way to the sink and bends over to pick it up. His shirt rises midway up his back exposing a sea of navy ink, and Emily's signature scrawled out in huge flowery letters.

Oh. My. God.

I abandon my cereal and follow Drake upstairs.

40

Ink

"Where the heck you going?" Drake asks as I file past him into his bedroom.

"Let me see your tattoo." I'm giddy over the idea he's inked up his back. I'm pretty sure it will piss Tad off spectacularly and put a fifty-dollar bill right in my pocket. That could be the first payment for my new car. Heck, I could finance the car *and* insurance on Drake's bad behavior alone. I should get a bonus of like a thousand dollars for the fact he knocked up Brielle. Only, that's probably the one thing I'll never tell.

"I don't have a tattoo. So get the hell out."

"Irritable much? I'm talking about the Sharpie chicken scratch on your back."

"Oh that." He takes off his shirt, exposing a thick tangle of underarm hairs that make me rethink breakfast and perhaps every other meal of the day.

"Check it out." He turns around.

The images stare out at me, and I let out a little shriek.

"Pretty cool, huh?"

"Holy freaking shit!"

"I know, right?"

He's really digging my reaction, only I'm not really digging his body art.

Three tall figures are displayed on Drake's back—all three with the effigy of a man, shirtless, one with the face of an eagle, the other with the face of an ox, and the third with the face of a lion.

"What is this?" I mutter. I told both Logan and Gage about my weird hallucination, nobody else on the planet knows about it other than the three of us, and sure as hell not Emily-the-haunted-artist-Morgan. And why the lion and not the donkey? Did she have it wrong, or did I? "So, did you tell her what to draw? And what did she do it with, a marker?" I stop just shy of touching his back.

"We were in her room. Things started to get freaky, and she asked if I wanted my back done. I had no idea she was going to whip out a bottle of India ink and start diagramming hieroglyphics and shit, but it's pretty cool."

"India ink? That's like ten times more permanent than a tattoo," I tease.

"Shut up." He pulls back on his t-shirt. "I saw you talking to Brielle, she say anything about me?"

"Yes, she's still totally into you. How can you be with Emily when she's having your baby?"

"Shh!" He walks over and opens the door an inch to scout the hall before shutting and locking it. "She's not freaking pregnant, OK? She's psycho. She's trying every trick in the book to keep me hanging around."

"She *is* having a baby," and she's always been a touch psychotic, but I omit that fact. "She really likes you." I don't know why. "Besides, I still have the positive pregnancy test floating around in my bathroom, plus a bottle of growth pellets for that spawn of yours she's lugging around." I kept that gross stick in the event Brielle wanted it for a keepsake. I don't even know if it's the type of thing pregnant women keep—a stick full of pee, but if it were mine and it meant Gage and I were about to have a baby, I think I would. Logan races through my mind, and I shake him away.

Drake studies me, walks around in a slow suspicious circle as though I were keeping something from him.

"I think Mia's right." He folds his arms at his conclusion. "You went and got yourself knocked up, and now Brielle is using your catastrophe to try and get me back. It's a twofer. You lock yourself up with whoever, and she shackles herself to me. *And,* had I played along, how much do you wanna bet she'd magically lose the baby before she balloons out? My mom used to watch those cheesy soaps all the time. Trust me, I know the mind of a woman."

Drake's expert level of stupidity leaves me breathless.

"You're a moron," is all I can manage.

"And you'll soon be the reason I'll be collecting some serious Benjamins. You're a magnet of irresponsibility, and thanks to you, I'll have an entire stack of dead presidents by the time the New Year rolls around."

"Grant—not Franklin, is on the fifty dollar bill," I say indignantly. "You will never have a stack of dead presidents with Benjamins, because Benjamin Franklin was never a president."

He shakes his head. "Who cares? You get the point. So who's the daddy?"

"You are," I say without thinking.

Drake pulls a serious face of disgust just before his cell goes off.

"It's her. Great. I got my own personal stalker." He glares into the phone.

"Aren't you going to answer it? You should at least talk to her."

He spins me towards the door.

wicked

"Wait, what made Emily draw those figures?" I say trying to slow myself down from being firmly ejected.

"Wouldn't you like to know." He launches me into the hall and slams the door behind him.

Yes, I would.

🦋 🦋 🦋

Gage picks me up at nine in his *truck*. I'm so glad to see it, I actually throw my arms over the hood and give it a kiss.

"How about one for me?" His dimples ignite on either side without trying.

Gage comes over and wraps his arms around my waist, cleanses me with his touch.

"I really missed you," he whispers.

"I really missed *you*," I say before indulging in the hot of his mouth.

"Holy Christmas!" Tad shouts. "Are you on the way to church or a motel?"

"I don't think the neighbors heard," I mutter hopping into the truck.

Gage and I quickly pullout and head onto the road so we won't have the Landon Counts tailgating us all the way down.

"Logan told me about your little adventure," he says, padding over the steering wheel with the palm of his hand.

I'd hardly call the slaughter we took part in an adventure.

"I guess we pretty much avenged those Celestra deaths," it comes out quiet, sad.

"Not according to Logan. He says you have one left in Rome and still have Demetri Edinger to get to."

"Yeah, well, I'd rather off Chloe any day of the week. Speaking of which, what are we going to do about her?" I can't help feeling like it's game over for me. Here I thought we were going to take down the Counts, stop them from killing any more innocent Celestra—hell, from *eradicating* Celestra then Chloe steps in and effortlessly becomes the new millstone around my neck.

"What exactly did Dudley say when he told you not to tell? Do you remember his exact words?"

"Not really. He basically said I couldn't tell anyone he was a Sector or he'd be bound, and if it came to me or him, he would always choose him."

"Great." He stares out at the road depleted. "Maybe he just needs a pure Celestra to turn in? Maybe if Chloe were to tell him she knew he was a Sector, he could turn *her* over to the Counts. The Counts only wanted you because you were pure, I don't see the difference."

"I hope you're onto something. I'm getting the feeling the only real thing holding Marshall back from handing me over is the fact he wants to marry me." Have my partially human children and hold dominion. I'm sure that entails lots of great perks like him morphing into Logan or Gage on demand, but I'm not interested. "I'm not going to marry Marshall am I?" It seems like a stupid question to be asking Gage, who has already assured me he's seen us take that mad dash down the alter.

He tilts his head thoughtfully to the side as though seriously considering this.

"I don't know."

"What?" I jump a little in my seat.

"I don't know. I know that we get married, but I don't know at what point, or what the circumstances are."

"What do you mean circumstances? People get married because they're in love, not because of circumstances. What did you see in the vision that made you think we were getting married? Was it a big wedding?"

That would be sort of awesome if he could fill me in on all the decor and colors and bridesmaid dresses and stuff because I'm not really creative in that way. I could plan the whole thing backwards—sort of reverse engineer the entire event.

"I never saw a wedding," Gage glances over and gives a mischievous half-smile.

I reach over and run my fingers through his thick damp hair.

"Well, well, aren't you a dirty little liar."

41

The Art of War

Paragon Presbyterian erects itself like an ancient relic of mass and marble into the dull grey sky. It's carved of stone with etchings and statues molded right into the infrastructure. A wash of fog stretches over the building and escorts us inside as it seeps into the foyer.

I'm half expecting the walls to tremble, or the floor to open up and drop me into Ezrina's lair as some after effect of hosting the rose of a thousand demons inside my intestinal track, but nothing.

I turn around to tell Gage and bump right into Michelle Miller who's still sporting her run-in with pinking shears. It looks a little more refined, like it's the scalp clenching salon version. Surprisingly it doesn't look bad on her. I bet it's totally easy to wash and style in the morning and—oh freaking shit!

The rose gleams off her neck like it never skipped a beat.

"Where'd you get that?" I shriek.

Gage pulls me a step back.

Michelle looks dazed—stoned. Heck, Ellis Harrison looks more lucid any day of the week with an entire marijuana field clouding his brain.

"It fell in Dudley's room. He gave it back to me," her voice sounds distant, wholly removed from her person, and suddenly I'm wondering if *she* should be in the facility with that thing on. And speaking of which, it's not the exact same pendant I swallowed, is it?

She picks the rose up puts it into her mouth as though it were a habit.

I push my face into Gage's chest in disgust.

"Excuse us," he says escorting me in.

We take seats near the back with a group of the kids from West. East keeps to itself a few pews in front of us.

Pierce! I recognize his freakishly wide shoulders that look as though he's wearing football padding beneath his jacket—and *Nat*.

I shrink a little in the pew.

"Relax," Logan whispers, "he can't do anything. He's out on bail, he has to behave."

"The reason there's bail to begin with is because of me," I whisper back.

Gage secures his arm around me and pulls me in tight. I don't know if it's some kind of signal to get Logan to stop talking to me or if he wants to make me feel safe, but either way it's working on both points.

Pierce turns around and glares right at me as though some sixth sense alerted him to my presence. He bites over his lower lip exposing his sharpened canines then retracts them slowly into his mouth.

"Did you see that?" I hiss. "He just threatened me."

"Won't hold up in court," Logan points out.

Nat turns around—her eyes still blotchy and swollen, her nose distinctly broken. She looks as though she were in a major car wreck even though the only thing she collided with was a delusional version of me.

She gives me the finger and turns back around.

"Did you see *that*?" I flinch at the gesture. "That is completely illegal in here." I push into Gage a little deeper.

"She always did have class," Gage whispers.

This isn't going well. In fact, I can't imagine the rest of my days going well ever again.

Marshall walks in as if on cue.

Ms. Messenger, he says, striding past our pew, landing on the other side near Tad and Mom.

It really is a wonder this entire place doesn't ignite. It's a tinderbox of assholes, well, not that Marshall's one of them, but sometimes he is.

The worship music starts up. My eyes wander towards the art along the walls. I've never really taken an interest in art, before Emily and her cryptic compositions injected themselves in my life.

Just your run of the mill poster sized paintings of angels, here. White robes, wings, nothing out of the ordinary. After a while my eyes trail up towards the pulpit. Something white and glazed harnesses my attention on the front of the pulpit itself. I straighten in my seat to get a better look. The bust of four figures carved in creamy marble stare back at me, one of a man, one of an ox, an eagle, and a lion.

Maybe Logan was supposed to be a lion, and I made him an ass? I give a wry smile.

I look over at Marshall who stares studiously ahead. I'll have to ask him what all this means. Am I the man—the *woman*?

From behind Marshall the curve of dark hair emerges. Chloe gouges me with a hate-filled stare. She eyes both Gage and I as though we just ate her firstborn. She cuts her gaze to Marshall, then me again, and gives the hint of a smile.

Crap.

The microphone crackles, and I redirect my gaze.

"Spiritual warfare," the man at the pulpit clears his throat. "Wars—they happen just about everyplace." He gives a little smile as though the idea he was about to present was absurd. "The book of Revelation reads, 'And there was a war in heaven. And Michael and his angels fought against the dragon, and the dragon and his angels fought back.'"

Marshall turns his face ever so slightly in my direction.

A war in heaven—can you believe that, Skyla? He glances over at me, serene as the ocean before a typhoon. *You should— because you, my love, play a very crucial role.*

42

Wild Abandon

After the service, Gage informs me he's taking me on a top-secret date.

"So you're stealing me away?"

"Consider yourself kidnapped." He gives a sly smile.

We pull into a quiet emerald cove marked Rockaway Point that sports a sandy beach the color of charcoal. We get out and I scoop up a handful, watch the ebony dust run from my fingers in a shower of sparkles.

"This is amazing. I can't believe how beautiful this place is," I say.

A row of pelicans jet out over the horizon, their bills give a history lesson on prehistoric birds all on their own.

He holds me with one hand while carrying a fast food bag and a soda in the other.

"Now that you're here it doesn't look so beautiful. You outshine the best nature has to offer." He gives a playful bite to my earlobe, and my stomach erupts in one hot bite.

I swill the ice in my oversized drink and look up at him. Gage looks sublime against the heavily charred sky.

"I can't believe Chloe gave you the afternoon off." I examine him for clues. His cheek rises on one side when I say it. "So what's the deal? Is Sunday really the day of rest?"

He stares out into the rugged whitecaps. They cycle in and out with a recklessness that leaves you in awe.

"I worked out a deal with her." His jaw clenches.

"Oh. I don't think I want to know." Whatever it is I'm sure it isn't anything to do a cartwheel over. The last thing I want is for Chloe to ruin my moment with Gage. She's already ruined so many. "I officially ban Chloe and Pierce and Tad from our conversation for the rest of the afternoon—make that all day."

Gage spreads a thick plaid blanket under the umbrella shade of a coral tree. Its bright red flowers dot the plain fat leaves like miniature trumpets. It feels like a cavern of privacy right here in open nature. I'm pretty sure we've officially found our spot. I hope something momentous happens to confirm this.

"And what about Logan? Is he banned?" His cheeks flex with disappointment.

I wonder if Logan played up the boyfriend angle while telling him about our trip? If he told him how he stole that kiss, stretching the truth to make it sound as though I had initiated it—*wanted* it.

"We can leave him out for sure."

The waves crash on the shore in an explosive roar as though somehow Logan himself had intervened with nature and was disputing his absence from our conversation.

"I think he was supposed to be a lion," I say as we grab our burgers and start in on lunch. I take a sip of my soda and lose myself watching the boiling sea thrash over and over.

"Who?"

"Logan."

Gage dips his head.

"Sorry." I give a quick shrug. "So tell me about our wedding vision."

Gage played coy after I grilled him on what exactly it was he saw, and he promised he'd tell me later.

He sucks into his straw examining me with great intensity as though somehow I had liquefied, and he was drinking me down deeply.

"I saw us together," he reaches over and picks up my hand, "we were facing the judge and he said, I now pronounce you man and wife."

"Did you see my face?" My heart thumps unnaturally. What if this is the caveat? What if it was a misunderstanding right from the beginning?

He nods. "When you turned to kiss me. You whispered I love you." The apples of his cheeks darken.

I scoot in and lay my head in his lap.

"So it is you." I smile up at him. "A judge, huh?" Sounds like a quickie to me, but really I don't care. I'd run to the courthouse today if he'd let me—if my heart didn't demand I fight a faction war and give Logan an official big fat no. My stomach tightens in knots. It feels so official—Logan and I over forever.

"I love you," I say it out of guilt for letting Logan steal another minute of our time.

He scoops me up and gives a soft lingering kiss, laced with the sweet taste of soda.

I dip my hand up his t-shirt and feel his warm flesh underneath.

"I love you with an eternal passion," Gage breathes the words hot into my ear.

My mouth falls open at the thought of eternal love.

"You have an amazing way with words." I dig my fingers into his hair at the base of his neck, soft slick tendrils, so unnaturally dark it gives off the slightest hint of blue. "Loved the poem. I wish you'd write one for me everyday."

"Maybe I am. Maybe I'm just saving them all to give to you one day."

He gives a gentle rumble of laughter lying besides me, sliding his hands up the back of my sweater. His warm fingers push under my bra and curve their way over stopping shy of my chest. I watch as his eyes shut just barely, as they roll back in ecstasy when I draw a line down his chest. It's so easy like this with Gage. Everything about it feels right.

"Were we at the beach our first time?" I wash over his neck in kisses.

His hands slip down into the back of my jeans in one quick motion.

"Hotel." His chest quivers with inaudible laughter and jostles me.

I sigh into him. Forever now I'll be eyeing the hotels on Paragon, counting them out, wondering which one we'll be in, which room, not that either of those things matter right now. Gage has the patience of a saint, something of which I seem to be sorely lacking.

"We can practice," I say taking off his shirt. Then without hesitation I whip off my sweater and roll us in the blanket, engulfing us in enough privacy to practice just about anything.

His eyes light up in the shadows like brilliant blue stars as he rolls on top of me. I can feel his stomach over mine his chest just cresting, afraid he'll crush me with his full weight. I reach back and unhook my bra, yank it off in one stealth move. I toss it into the bushes, pressing the small of his back into my bare flesh until I can feel him covering me completely.

I wonder how many man-hours it will take before we get it right.

43

The Muse

Monday, I manage to avoid Chloe for the better part of the afternoon as I bask in the false impression of a reprieve, but come sixth period I can tell by the haughty look in her eyes she's still hell-bent on controlling my life. Who knew that words I once whispered to her about Marshall would give her such jurisdiction, allow her to dismantle my relationship with Gage—turn me over to the Counts on a whim if she wanted.

"OK, team," she shouts into the wind. "We have the all state competition coming up in April, and we need to bring it home. How did you do last year?" She holds her hand to her ear.

A low mumble of *we lost*, groans from among us.

"And why did you lose?" She looks genuinely pissed as she aggregates us with an eternal hatred. "Because there was no leadership," she barks it out while pegging Michelle with her venom.

Technically I wasn't here either, but I don't offer up that information.

"So," she continues, "with the help of Ms. Richards, we are going to catapult this team to the number one slot, you got it?"

We give a dismal *yes* in unison. Michelle is so out of it, plucking away at grass blades, to even care if we're all in uniform let alone if there's some altruistic level of unity. Really someone should do an intervention.

I tune out Chloe's barking and look over at Ms. Richards sitting on a bench in the distance, referring to her clipboard now and again. I still can't believe she's related to Ezrina. Creepy. Now that I know, I can see traces of her great, great grandmother in her. Same wild shag of copper hair, eyes too large for her face—there's always been something unnerving about her perennial high-strung behavior, always restless and jittery, just like her predecessor.

Chloe covers me with her shadow.

"Well, Messenger?" She hollers with her hands wrapped around her mouth like a megaphone.

All of the other girls have paired off, Emily and Michelle, Nat and Kate, Brielle with Lexy, so I guess that leaves me and—

Chloe gives a swift kick to the back of my thigh.

"Up!" she barks.

I spring to my feet and wrap my hand around her wrist.

Do that again, I beg of you. See how far you can push me, I glare into her.

I believe you're angry, Skyla. Angry enough to kick my ass everyday of the week, her face lights up with dark pleasure. *But it's Gage who you're really fighting for, not some hurt feelings over a little bruise.*

Isn't that funny how we're both fighting over Gage, and yet you can never really have him? I ask.

I have more of him now than you do, she reminds me. *All of West thinks we're together.* She ticks her head when she says, together.

I hate to break it to you, but most of us operate in this little thing called reality. The reality I know says Gage loves me—and hates you.

A fiery slap ignites across my face. The sound of its fury lies buried in the wind.

Try me Skyla, she warns. *Say it one more time, and see how fast I hunt down Dudley.*

The sun breaks free for a moment, illuminates us with its spotlight as though we were on stage. Chloe's rage gleams like a jewel. It places the thorny crown of indignation on her head, and my presence alone is enough to press it in—make her bleed.

Chloe has gone feral, all because of her outright obsession with Gage. I can't say I blame her. I would go mad without him, too. But he's mine, and he always will be.

I think we both know that.

And we both know it will never change.

※ ※ ※

That evening Mom drives me and my sisters over to Marshall's house for our math, slash, horseback riding lessons.

Paragon is lit up like a Christmas tree, literally. Giant colorful bulbs dance across rooflines. Trees are wrapped in twinkle lights up and down the island. You would think the city issued a mandate, stipulating it a public service to decorate everything on or around your property line. I watch as mangers and giant cartoon cutouts of Santa Claus spike, lawn after lawn. Some people have completely lost their minds with elaborate light shows that coordinate with music, one with a merry-go-round in their front yard and a miniature Ferris wheel with stuffed animals riding along as passengers. Another house has a bonafide single passenger airplane out front with Santa at the helm.

I don't remember Christmas in L.A. being so impregnated into our world. Tad is making us wait until later this week to decorate. Mom had to talk him into bumping up the festivities from Christmas Eve. What's the point of decorating twelve hours before the big event anyway? When my dad was alive, we started singing Christmas carols right after Halloween.

Mom pulls into the huge circular drive and takes off as soon as we file out of the car.

Melissa circles around back while Mia hangs around an extra second to vex me.

"So you gonna make out with your teacher again?" She stands almost eye to eye with me now, and somehow I find this irritating.

I take in a quick agitated breath before answering. "No, Mia. I'm with Gage. All making out takes place with him, nobody else. I swear." I hold up two fingers like a girl scout.

She cocks her head to the side. "Does he know about the baby?"

"No," I hiss like an irate cat. I'm not sure if she means Gage or Marshall.

"You're going to have to tell eventually." She shoves her purse under her shirt and wags her tongue out the side of her mouth.

"There's nothing to tell. I'm not having a baby." And if Gage keeps arresting me like a criminal before any real action happens, I never will.

"How's the car coming?"

"I take the driver's test Friday." The first test I'm actually looking forward to. I think I'll celebrate by taking Gage out after—ironic since technically it's Logan's car I'll be taking him out in. I think about being with Gage in the backseat of my new car, and my stomach explodes with excitement. Then my ridiculous brain flops the situation, and I see Logan and I going at it like two wild beasts, me in a ball gown with the skirt hiked up around my waist, him lying naked on top of me. We fog up the windows and there's a hand pressed against the glass just like in that one movie.

My fingers fly to my lips. Logan? A ball gown—really?

"I've got a date Saturday night," Mia says snapping me back to reality.

"You can't date, you're like seven."

"Thirteen and a half. I got my braces off last Tuesday, thanks for noticing. Oh, that's right, you don't notice anything unless it involves you."

"Mia." My mouth hangs open.

She takes off around the back.

※ ※ ※

After a series of hard knocks, I let myself into Marshall's palatial estate and find him in the living room untangling Christmas lights straight out of the box.

"Can't you do some Sector magic and have the best darn tree that ever was?" I say plugging in the lights he's lassoed himself with.

Marshall glows beneath the pointed crystal bulbs.

"Pretty," I say walking over and helping him out.

"Yes, you are." He throws them in the air, and they land perfectly around the fifteen-foot pine standing erect in the middle of the room.

"I think you should put it in the corner."

"As the woman of the house, I'll gladly let you supervise." He maneuvers it back a good three feet near the piano.

"Perfect," I say. "So, my father gave me an interesting piece of news." It feels like a million years ago that I saw my dad. I can't believe Logan went back without me, something about that doesn't sit well with me.

wicked

"Which is?"

"My real mom is a Caelestis. Her name is Candy. I'm sure you know all this," I say plucking a box of apple red ornaments from out of a shopping bag.

"Candace," he corrects, "and, yes, we've met."

"God," I pause in horror, "you're not my father are you?"

"What kind of pervert do you think I am?" Even in his utter disgust Marshall is cuttingly attractive.

"Sick enough for it to be true on some level. How well do you know her?"

"She's an acquaintance."

"I'd like for her to be an acquaintance of *mine*. Can you arrange that?"

"I can arrange lots of things." His finger twirls in the air. "Next time you come in, leave your poltergeist at the door. That spook of yours is running around the celestial sphere bragging about this body you're supplying him with." Marshall looks annoyed at the thought. "I could remedy this you know."

"By giving him Chloe's body?" I think it's a stroke of genius.

"Getting to you already, is she?" He attaches a gold ball to the boughs of a lower branch.

"You don't know the half of it. And Holden's been his raucous self with the exception I thought he helped me win the faction war." I tell him about my hallucination. "And now that rose has mysteriously ended up around Michelle's neck again," I say accusingly.

"Sounds like a Christmas miracle," he gives an impish grin.

"Nice work. No details please."

"What can I say—the Fems were restless."

"What exactly is a Fem? I remember Logan tried to explain it to me once. He said they were nothing but balls of air."

"Do they look like balls of air?" He motions me over to the tree, and I get to work.

"No." Anything but.

"You're a ball of air, I'm a ball of air, we're all a ball of air, but we reside in temporal bodies, don't we?" Marshall eyes me critically as though my answer were of some importance.

"Don't tell me I'm going to be a ball of air in the afterlife." First of all, balls of air seem to be exempt from all physical activity, which slightly downgrades Gage's offer to love me for all eternity, at least the way I want.

"For a time, then you'll be back in full working order, new body intact—this I promise."

That vision of Logan and me steaming up the backseat of the Mustang spikes up uninvited, and I try to shake away the thought.

Marshall gives a Cheshire cat grin as though he knows what I'm thinking.

I suck in a lungful of air. "You do know!" Obviously I've dumbed down to a mere mortal after Pierce tried to suck the lifeblood out of me.

"Relax, it's not quite as bad as it seems. You've piddled down to your boyfriend's status. When your mind goes to mush I can see through it like a window. And the evening gown would have looked spectacular on you, had you not been horizontal."

"OK, I gotta go." I try to bolt for the door, but he snatches me back by the elbow.

"Come here, love," he says it sweetly, "I'll try to arrange a meeting with your mother. Consider it an early Christmas gift. She, however, has a mind of her own, and I make no promises."

wicked

I remember the last time Marshall gave me a present, and I found out my entire family, including Logan, were Counts. Not sure he knows how the whole gift-giving thing is supposed to work.

"OK," I'm almost afraid to accept.

"I'll answer your question about Fems, but first I have to express my utter disdain with your recent actions concerning high powered weaponry and the pretty Oliver, whom, by the way, I suggest you steer clear of."

I swallow hard.

"That's right, Ms. Messenger. I've been apprised of your erratic and, might I add, violent behavior." He points hard to the spirit sword hanging innocently above his fireplace. "You have authority to use it. Not that one, the one that lies in your possession. You do not have authority to blow people's brains out for sport. You've upped the ante. You have no idea who these people are or how they operate. I implore you to cease and desist your murderous spree at once."

"So if I killed them with the sword, we wouldn't be having this conversation?"

"Perhaps not." He looks at me sharply. "And to answer your question, Fems are a lower order of celestial beings," he hesitates a moment, "they've sided with Countenance."

"Sided with the Counts?" I examine him in earnest. "Sided against what?"

"They're trying to incite a reversal of power. As it stands now, Sectors rule supreme."

"Sectors rule and Fems drool?" I'm only half joking.

"Haven't you learned to never slander a celestial being? Be wise, Skyla, that sword in your mouth wields more power than you know. And try not to have such lewd thoughts around me regarding the pretty one. It's infuriating to see my wife engage in carnal relations with someone other than myself."

I'm finding Marshall's rapid-fire admonishing worrisome and amusing all at the same time.

"So you're in a war with the Fems?" I ask, ignoring the rest of his babble.

"They're posturing." He places a bulb on the tree and wraps his arms around my waist, admiring his work.

A part of me knows I should push him away, then again, a part of me knows I might get more of Marshall's truths if I don't.

"So you're about to have a battle with Fems? What kind of payment are they taking from the Counts to do their dirty work?" All I know is that Fems are shape shifters that torment innocent people like me at the Count's bidding.

"The Counts have aligned with Fems. So when the battle commences, and they try to overthrow Sectors, they'll have two planes of dominance as will the Counts."

"I thought you trained Fems? Don't you control them?"

"Does the word coup ring a bell? Has there never been a government overthrown on this planet before? It's happened once before in the ethereal plane, the Fems taking down the Sectors, but over time we reverted back to power."

"And now they think it's their turn," I nod, getting it for the first time. "What happens to the rest of us if the Fems and Counts take over?"

"Ever hear of the dark ages? The bubonic plague? Horrific oppression—disaster, that's what happens. They rather enjoy winnowing the masses."

"Why is that?" My eyes sweep over him horrified.

"The Counts are spared in such efforts, Skyla. In addition to my job demotion, they allow the Counts to proliferate their numbers. It's win-win for wickedness."

"Job demotion?" I mouth the words. It would almost be comical if he didn't paint such a scary picture. "This is huge," I whisper.

"I'm glad you realize the scope and magnitude of what lies before you."

"Why didn't you explain all this before?" I'm overwhelmed by the windfall of knowledge.

"You weren't in a proper place to hear it. Neither were you aware of your true heritage." He pulls me closer.

"What do I have to do with any of this?"

"Let me show you."

To my disappointment, I don't fight him when he sinks me into a kiss. It's like I have this calling to do something fearfully magnificent beyond the scope of the universe itself, and for the first time I feel the weight of its burden locked on my shoulders. The only way I could even hope to harvest a glance into the future is directly through Marshall's upper orifice.

It's a vision of me. I'm not anywhere or doing anything. I'm glowing. My entire person radiates a soft rainbow of light. It illuminates me from the inside like the soft flicker of a candle. My hair shimmers in waves of gold floss, my eyes speak a soulful language all their own. I don't believe I could ever look that beautiful.

A flash goes off, then a loud thump towards the doorway.

My eyes fly open to find Mia gripping her phone as she takes off running out the back.

I have a feeling all unholy hell is about to break loose. And it will be anything but beautiful.

44

I've Got a Feeling

In the morning, before breakfast, I consider the fact that according to Mia, not only am I pregnant—but I'm also cheating on Gage with my math teacher. She's loaded with dangerous half-truths, and right about now I wish it were in reverse. I'd much rather be pregnant with Gage's love child than let Marshall ply me with the future by way of his lips. I should have known the vision was going to be futile, they always are, except for when they're not, like the life shattering ones that came to fruition in a surprising way at my birthday party. Then it hits me.

Crap.

Not only am I Chloe's bitch—but I've been hijacked by Mia as well.

Downstairs, I find Mia and Mom huddled by the stove locked in a secretive conversation. Quite frankly I'm still too peeved at them for being Counts to really care what they're whispering about, but I'm guessing I can take a lucky stab at the subject.

Mia straightens when she sees me then makes a beeline upstairs.

Figures. Now all I have to do is wait for Tad to hold the next 'family meeting'. Tad and Drake walk in the room and take seats at the bar.

"So are you going to this—all school sleep, right after Christmas?" Tad looks perturbed by the idea.

That's right, I think Brielle mentioned something, but I think it was called something else.

"All school *ski*," Drake corrects, "and yes."

"Me too." I make myself a cup of coffee and pluck a banana from the fruit bowl.

"Sounds like a week long orgy if you ask me," Tad says. "I'm just calling it like I see it."

My eyes bug out at Mom. Did he just say the word orgy? It's breakfast for God's sake. I suppose Mom will use this as a springboard to discuss their efforts at creating a satanic spawn.

"Speaking of *away*," my mother sings, "our away time is next weekend!" She beams over at him. "I think we'll make a romantic rendezvous out of it, you know, really get the juices going."

"Oh, please no," I blurt out the words without thinking.

"Skyla," Mom sighs in exasperation.

"No, really, I'm all for it." The more they're away the better.

An errant thought floats through my brain. If Mom and Tad are up for hatching more larva anyway, maybe Holden could somehow get that body? Heck, I bet I could help cultivate him into quite the upright citizen, a potential presidential candidate, even. Plus, I wouldn't have to think about him leering at me every time I get out of the shower. Well, not for at least thirteen years.

I look over at Mom and Tad and wonder if I have the guts to try and pull a stunt like that. Doubtful, plus it reeks of stupid, not that I've ever let that stop me before. I blow out a breath. At least Tad hasn't uttered Holden's favorite word.

"Some*body*," Tad starts.

Shit.

He flexes the newspaper, "has got to clue this school in on what teenagers do behind their parent's backs."

I push my coffee aside and wait for it. He pulled the pin. It's just a matter of moments before...

The ground shakes, unnatural gyrations that rival a ride at the amusement park— buck and heave beneath us.

Usually it's just me privy to these supernatural events, so I hold off on a full-blown panic until I see Mom straddling the kitchen sink with her head pulled back.

"Earthquake!" She rips the words from her lungs in one lusty cry.

I can hear Mia and Melissa thundering down the stairs howling with fear.

The windows start in on a violent rattle, a tremor so powerful I expect the glass to explode any minute. As if on cue, the entire backslider, along with the windows in the dining room, ejaculate into the air forming a tornado of glass, with every last shard spiking right into...Tad?

The earth ceases all movement. The chandelier engages in a silent homage to the convulsions we've just endured, but we ignore it. We ignore the fact we've just bared witness to one of the most violent earthquakes we've ever lived through and stare down at Tad—at the thing of horror he's become.

ᴥ ᴥ ᴥ

The first response team, which consists of six firemen complete in bloated yellow suits, stare down at Tad as more of a curiosity rather than a victim. I swear I saw one snapping a picture with his cell, his hand was discretely hidden underneath a clipboard, but I saw the flash.

"Superficial wounds," one of them informs my mother. He's older with silver hair, bright blue eyes like Gage, and he has a comforting way about him, so my mother lets him hold her.

Tad rolls from side to side moaning while they load him onto the gurney, and the EMT tells him sweetly to shut up. It's more southern charm than it is nasty, but for all practical purposes I don't mind Tad being put in his place, not even in this bizarre state.

Mom gathers her purse and keys from the entry.

"I'm going to the hospital. Can you make sure the girls get a ride to school either with you and Gage, or Drake?"

I nod in obedience. I guess Mom isn't aware of the fact Gage hasn't really driven me anywhere in forever, and I guess this isn't the best time to inform her I'll be taking my driver's test tomorrow after school.

"It's so strange, all these things that keep happening," she mutters, riffling through her purse.

Her auburn hair is loose around her face. Her eyes are wired with bright railroad tracks that give way to tears.

"You know sometimes," she looks up in frustration, "I wonder if this wasn't meant to be."

The fury that surrounds Tad speeds out of the house and is replaced with a palpable calm. I feel terrible that she's doubting the foundations of her marriage, especially since it was me who inadvertently put a hex on it.

I think it's officially time to call off Holden's ghost, and I have a feeling it's going to be easier said than done.

A creak emits from the dining room, and the chandelier starts in on a slow swing, rocking from one side to the other. The drywall overhead cracks and splinters as the entire crystal-laden unit lands on the table with a crash.

On second thought I'm going to need a miracle, or the intervention of a very powerful Sector.

I know exactly how this is going down.

Marshall is going to eat my soul for breakfast.

45

Fierce

A dark curtain of a cloud stretches over Paragon smooth and rich as deep grey velvet.

Ms. Richards calls us into cheer lineup and claps until we're all facing front and settled into obedience.

"I received word today that the all state cheer competition will take place in Tacoma this year. We need to start a travel fund. I need you girls to put your thinking caps on and start up those car washes, cupcake drives, gift wrapping services outside of department stores, anything to help us get to the competition as a team." She gives a few wild claps. "Chloe!"

Chloe jumps to the front as Ms. Richards replaces her on the grass.

"The basket toss is the final stunt of the competition, and this is one event we've always been strong at. Skyla, you'll be the butterfly," she cuts me a devious look before babbling on about allegiance to our school and pride, but all I can think about is how much I hate heights.

"Um," I raise my hand. "I think technically Brielle is a touch lighter than me. Plus, she's got like way less hair, and—"

"Freaking shit, Messenger!" Chloe cuts me off. "If you cared anything at all about the team you'd hack your hair off like Michelle."

The bitch squad goes rigid. We all know damn well Michelle hacked off her tresses because she's gone bat-shit crazy, well, that, and the fact she's swimming in the deep end of the Fem pool.

"OK, everyone on your feet—lets go!" Chloe relishes playing the part of drill sergeant. It makes Michelle's wrath seem like long forgotten glory days.

She instructs the other girls to get in a tight circle.

"Not here!" She shouts and points hard over to the concrete. "There."

"That's not safe," Brielle clutches at her throat.

That's so sweet. Brielle must really care about me. Either that, or the thought of my head splitting like a watermelon takes her morning sickness to a whole other level.

Chloe gets right in her face. "Tell me, when was the last time you saw grass in the gym?" Her ponytail whips around her face like a wild python. "I thought so. On the cement, right now!"

We follow her over to the blacktop, and the girls get into a tight knit circle.

"Um, maybe we could get a few of the football players to help spot. What do you think?" I look right at Ms. Richards who barely notices us anymore ever since she's given free reign to the queen of treachery.

Ms. Richards twitches her nose then looks down at the far end of the field before calling the coach.

Ha! I won. I try not to gloat in Chloe's direction. I'm sure she's already plotting to douse me with kerosene and set me on fire. Of course, she'll probably save that maneuver for the competition in an effort to outdo the other team.

Logan and Gage run over with two other guys. Now this will be a pleasure.

I step onto the circle of their hands with Logan's just beneath my feet.

"On the count of three I want you to catapult her into the sky as high as you possibly can," Chloe screams. "Show the girls that you're better than them. I want to see Messenger's ass on the moon! One, two—

It occurs to me in that moment that perhaps it wasn't the stroke of genius I thought it was having four strong football players toss me in the air. As soon as Chloe said the word moon, my stomach leaped in fear—

"Three!"

I'm flying. I'm cutting through the wind like a rocket ship, a missile—a butterfly. West Paragon High retracts beneath me. It exposes itself in miniature as the earth begins to curve, my face buried in the thick of the clouds. I'm so frightened I don't flex my hands over my feet, or even think about any competition.

Then the earth comes up on me fast. I see the worried expressions of both Logan and Gage as a swarm of hands reach for me haphazardly with a gaping hole in the middle.

Oh shit.

I land soft in the arms of a wall of strength. My eyes open, and I'm greeted with an explosion of gorgeous dimples—eyes the color of the stratosphere.

"You caught me," I say breathless.

Gage presses a kiss onto my lips. "I'll always catch you."

✹ ✹ ✹

I wait until after cheer to present Marshall with the Holden debacle.

Gage is busy shuttling Catastrophe Chloe around, who I badly wish was Casket Chloe once again. Then he's driving all the way back to give me a ride home because he's really just that nice, and contrary to what Chloe believes, he really is my boyfriend. I so desperately miss Gage. I miss him driving me to school and walking me to class, the way he held me through lunch. Chloe needs to be boxed up—and fast. She's redefined the word miserable ever since her untimely return.

Mom sent a text during lunch and let me know they finished taking the final bits of glass out of Tad. She mentioned the nurses tried counting each shard, but gave up after two hundred.

"So he was literally encrusted in glass." I shake my head at Marshall. "He was like glass-man. He had this coat of glass, and if he got up and walked around it would have been totally freaky."

"Freaky," he mimics. "I'm rather impressed. Even I felt the quake this morning. You know it made the local news. Guess where they said the epicenter was?"

My mouth falls open.

He digs his cheek into the side of his face. "The grid read precisely under the Landon residence." He crosses his arms with the slightest irate expression.

"What?" I'm not sure, but it seems like he's trying to drive a point home, only, I'm clueless as to what the point might be.

"You, Skyla, have unleashed a category five disaster. Hurricane Holden has proven he's ready and willing to do whatever you wish to get himself back into a breathing body, because you, my dear, made a promise."

"Shhh," I press my finger to my lips.

"He's not here. I don't allow him near me." He gathers a stack of papers and sloshes them into his briefcase.

"So what am I gonna do?"

"I don't know what you're going to do." He snaps it shut and buckles the latches. "In fact, I don't believe you realize what it is you've done to begin with. You've given a wicked soul dominion over an area of your life."

wicked

"I'll take it back. I'll tell him to stop."

"Too late. He's accumulated all the power he needs. Let me give you a piece of advice, and please retain it. I'd hate to needlessly expel air for the benefit of having you nod absentmindedly."

I nod feverishly.

Marshall closes his eyes with great patience before continuing. "Whatever he does, however much it hurts, you must not pay him any mind. As far as you're concerned he simply doesn't exist."

"And that will make him stop torturing Tad?" I'm both hopeful and surprisingly disappointed.

"That's unlikely to happen," Marshall stands and motions for me to do the same. "Just be glad you'll be out of the house in a year's time and won't have to stick around to watch the show. You've bound them, Skyla, and now the only way to remove this bondage is to do what you set out to begin with. Find Holden a body."

"Will you help me?"

"No." He speeds to the door and flicks off the light.

I follow him out into the hall, down the stairs and out into a darkened world with a moth eaten sky.

"Gage won't be back for a few more minutes," I say. "You wanna hang out? We can go over the chapter test if you want?" I let my desperation linger.

"I've got a meeting." He winks. "Someone you know will be there."

"My mother?" My mouth falls open interrupting a smile. This is far better than a chapter test. "Can I come with you?"

"Are you interested in taking your last breath? We have a strict no mortals allowed policy."

"Oh, well, tell her that her daughter, the one being raised by Counts, says hello. Will my father be there?"

"I don't know." He begins to walk off into the murky shadows of the parking lot.

"Marshall?" I run over to him. "If the Fems have aligned with the Counts, who have the Sectors aligned with? Or have they?" It seems doubtful they would need to.

"Celestra." He ticks his head as though I should have figured this out. His face looks deeply tanned lost in the shadows, the white of his eyes call out like glossy beacons.

"There's not that many." And I hate to say it, but after the slaughter Logan imposed, I wouldn't be surprised if soon enough I was the last one standing.

"We don't need many." He leans forward and strokes my cheek. "We just need one."

"We just need one. We just need one," I whisper over and over again, alone in the dark at West Paragon High. I sing it to myself until my brain begs to split from the effort. It sounds like a chant, like a spell that has the ability to call something wicked into being by the sheer determination of the cadence alone.

Gage called and let me know he was on Main Street. That means about four more miles, and he'll rescue me from the armpit of my nightmares, which has seemingly morphed into West.

Cerberus gleams in the night like a relic from my rose-riddled nightmares. Six eyes stare into the dark, three tongues lash wild off the side of the boy's gym. The hound that guards hell, also guards West Paragon. I would have loved to have sat

wicked

in on that PTA meeting when the board approved this infernal wall mural of monolithic proportions. Obviously hallucinogenics were involved.

I peek over at the subject of my contention through slotted fingers. Three heads, each locked in fury, three forked tongues licking into the night. It reminds me of the Fem that replicated its horrifying effigy the night Chloe died—correction, the night I killed Chloe. Strange how the Fems intimately know your fears.

"Excuse me?" A kind male voice surprises me from behind.

I jump around and gasp.

A clown!

A shocking white face, thick and pale as paste, gapes back at me. His eyes are drawn in with heavy red shadow. His smile spreads over half his face with a grotesque lipstick grimace that has the distinct glossy trail of something far more sinister—like blood.

I can't breathe, or move, or think.

46

Run

I take off into the night, dropping my backpack, losing the sweater tied around my waist—my headband.

I run through the student parking lot clutching my phone with a death grip as though it were Gage himself, all the while breathing Chloe's name like a curse. I hate her more than I thought imaginable for holding both my bird and boyfriend hostage. I need Nevermore as much as I need Gage. It's not like Chloe's going to have Fems chasing her anytime soon with that protective hedge clamped around her neck.

The distant streetlights illuminate my erratic breathing into spastic paper white blooms. I hit the thicket just beyond the gravel parking lot and rush in at top speed.

An old cadence from childhood strums through my mind at a million miles an hour, *you're running through the forest and you're running really fast and you run into a tree.* I say it over and over until somehow the words comfort me. The idea of hitting a tree head on and having my skull fractured—my brain swell out through the crevices— actually soothes me compared to meeting up with the monster grunting behind me.

Something shifts in the forest. It breaks up the shadows with texture and movement. I can feel its heft unsettle the ground beneath me.

I pause behind a small fortress of ingrown pines, trying to ration my breathing as I lie still and listen. Then I see it, in the starlit clearing, a wolf-like creature the size of Drake's car

wicked

crawls to life. It maneuvers its way over to me, bearing its teeth, long as pencils.

I thought I knew my fears. I thought I understood their depths and how long I could last under their tyranny until I would succumb, but here in the cover of night, under the supervision of an anemic moon, I meet fear anew. This is a fantastic fear that covers me numb with shock. It asks nothing in return, as though I were an inconsequential target, just a passerby who stumbled upon an enormous wolf and a bloody clown.

A scream dissipates in my throat. A paralysis so strong grips me I have to remind myself to breathe.

The beast gives an unapologetic snarl in my direction.

I let out an unearthly cry and shatter the silence for miles.

A hard thump lands on my back and sends me crashing to the ground. I look over my shoulder and see a chalk white face, red oblong eyes—an exaggerated smile.

I've heard that one sure way to conquer fear is to face it head on. I'm no expert, but I'm guessing the person who said that was A. purely speculating, and B. an ass.

A thin trail of blood runs from its open mouth and trickles down my neck.

Shit!

I claw at the earth to get free from beneath it.

"Gage!" I call out like a wounded animal, terrified and helpless. The Fem cuts off my breathing, lays over me solid as a truck. Its stench burns into my nostrils and induces the urge to vomit. Strong rolls of nausea cycle through me until I start in on a series of unproductive dry heaves.

An audible grunt floats from up above.

"Gage?" I ask hopeful. It sounded distinctly female. Maybe it's Brielle—or Michelle in a tirade of insanity.

The dead Fem rolls off with its flour white face staring dismal into space. I jump to my feet and turn around.

A curtain of dark hair swings back like a shield before I see her.

"It's you!" I say, fascinated while staring at Giselle, Gage's long dead sister. She looks murky, taller than I remember, and a part of me is starting to wonder if I'm hallucinating again.

A low threatening growl trembles through the forest.

I take her by the hand and lead us towards the parking lot. Yellow glowing eyes zigzag through the branches. I can't tell how many there are. It could be one, but feels like fifty. The wolf-like creature touches down in front of us blocking our path. The fur on its back spikes up like porcupine quills as it reclines on its heels ready to pounce.

"I'm strong," I whisper trying to convince myself. Truth is, I haven't felt the need to test my strength or speed since I came out of the hospital, but if Marshall hearing my thoughts is any indication, I'm willing to bet my reflexes are more than a little off.

"Skyla?" Giselle pulls me back by the elbow.

The beast leaps in the air with distended claws, snapping its red angry mouth in our direction.

We're done. Really, I guess it's just me that's done since Giselle was done a long time ago.

It rises above us howling and scratching the air like a cat on fire. A shower of blood rains down from either side.

It is spectacular to watch, the elephantine beast exploding midair.

Gage!

He stands behind it with the spirit sword glowing by his side. He bolts over and spins me in a circle.

"You OK?"

"I am now. You always have that thing handy?"

"Never leave home without it." He takes a deep breath in the crook of my neck.

I lean in and meet him with a warm kiss. "Guess what?" I glance around the dark. I don't see Giselle anymore, and something about this frightens me.

"What?" he pants into my ear.

"I..." Maybe it was just another hallucination. God—I must really be insane.

"What is it?" Gage picks up on my trepidation—only he earmarks it as fear and yanks the sword back out of its sheath.

"Never mind." I push his arm down. "Get me out of here. I want to go home."

We tread our way out of the forest, Gage with his arm around my waist, and me with my sanity hanging on for dear life.

"Excuse me?" A weak voice strangles the silence.

I avoid saying her name in the event I've accidentally bonded myself to another spiritual appendage, some demonic imposter who's ready to take down the final pillar of my frail lucidity. But I see her. I see her pale face, glowing blue eyes, and the dimples replicated so well on her person that she looks like the exact female representation of Gage.

"It's her," I whisper. "It's your sister."

His hand goes limp, and he staggers into the forest a good five feet before pausing.

Giselle emerges into a thin sliver of moonlight, it washes over her like a supernatural waterfall of brilliance, and at the moment she looks every bit human.

He rushes to meet her, and they connect in an explosive embrace.

A loud hiss followed by a bright light detonates to our left.

The bloody carcass of the beast lights up the forest in a wash of quivering light.

I clamp my hand over my mouth in awe of its spontaneous combustion.

Gage pulls his sister over and grabs me by the waist. We run towards his truck with the engine still running and the driver's door wide open.

"I can't go with you," she says.

"Do you have a message from my mother? Is that why you came?"

Another ball of fire ignites behind her deep in the forest as the Fem bursts into flames.

I can hear Gage on the phone calling in the fire.

Her face contorts as though there were so much she wanted to tell me, and now there isn't time.

"Come with us," I say, getting into the truck.

"You look a lot like her." She squints into a pained smile. "I can't stay. She just wanted me to let you know there's a reason for all this. It's bigger than you, Skyla. She wants you to be strong."

Another vague pep talk.

I jump down from the truck as the forest erupts into a blaze as tall as a high-rise.

"Tell her I want to meet her," I try to swallow down my budding fury. "Tell her I'm in a shitload of trouble, and it would be really nice if my dead angelic mother could pull a few fucking strings for me." My sudden burst of anger surprises me.

"Testy." Her ears pull back in amusement.

"Testy?" I can barely get the word out. "The forest is on *fire*. I have the blood of a Fem all over me, and the one person I help bring back to life thanks me by stealing my boyfriend. *Yes*, I'm testy!"

Gage takes me by the shoulder and gently walks me backwards.

Giselle's face peaks in frustration. "I'll fill her in on how you feel." She blows a kiss to Gage and disappears.

"Fill her in?" I say disbelieving.

The shrill cry of a siren cuts through the air like a serrated blade.

We hop in the truck, and the doors clamp shut, and the engine starts on its own volition before Gage has a chance to insert the key.

"Shit," Gage mutters. "Get out, Skyla."

We thrash into the doors to no avail—the locks won't budge.

The truck spirals around in a wild circle before taking off as fast as the engine will allow—straight into the burning inferno.

47

Lost

White glowing walls, a stainless table lies in the corner with sinister looking tools sprawled out.

"Is this?" Gage pauses, taking it all in.

"The Transfer." I feel my way around the room until an opening appears that leads to a dark carpeted hall. "Emerson's here."

Gage wraps an arm around me as we drift down corridors clinging to walls. The hallway opens up to an incandescent light, and I lead him over to the tanks.

"There she is." I lay my hand flat on the cool glass.

Gage leans in and watches her slow dizzy spin.

"It is her," his skin glows a soft blue from the reflection.

"What is this place?" I walk over to the boy with short dark hair as he continues in his watery slumber. "Do you know this guy?"

Gage comes over and examines him.

"He looks sort of like," he pauses squinting into him.

"Like Drake, right?" Not quite like Tad, but almost. "Weird."

"That's more than weird." He stoops towards the metal band slapped to the bottom of the tank. It's turned in towards the wall making it impossible to read. "I can't see it." Gage plucks at the metal strip in an effort to remove it.

"Can you spin the tank?" I try to twist it.

"Doubt it." He pulls at the glass until it starts to turn.

"You got it!"

wicked

"I see it," he grunts.

A loud pop crackles overhead, and a trickle of blue liquid runs down the side of the glass.

Gage pulls me back a good three feet as the tank begins to shatter. Water gushes out with a hushed roar as the body drops to the ground in a heap.

"Time to go," Gage pulls me further into the facility, into another room lined with aisles after aisles of long glass tubes filled with bright blue water.

"Dear God," I whisper. Each tank is filled with a tangle of floating limbs, a halo of hair rising from each one.

An alarm sounds. A rumble of footsteps erupt in the corridor.

The scent of smoke fills my nostrils as the room turns strangely dim.

✺ ✺ ✺

A fiery slap commences over my cheek as my eyes struggle to open.

A man in a yellow hat telescopes in and out of focus until I realize it's a fireman.

I sit up shocked to find myself back in the soot-covered forest. My clothes are charred, and my hands covered in muck.

"Where's Gage?" I choke the words out.

"He's locked and loaded, ready to go."

To my surprise I've already been hoisted onto a gurney. We traverse through the woods, still burning in spots, as we make our way to the open mouth of the waiting ambulance.

I lean up as the bed collapses beneath me, and they glide me right alongside Gage.

His skin is covered with a thick layer of grime, and there's an oxygen mask securely fastened over his nose and mouth. His eyes are closed, and this scares the hell out of me.

I wait until they place an identical mask on my face, and the ambulance wails down the street before reaching over and clasping onto his hand, cold and limp.

I jostle and squeeze him trying to rouse him from his slumber—but nothing.

All of the kisses we have ever shared flash before my eyes. It is majestic, this love affair of ours, so powerful and regal.

It's the kind of love that fairytales are born of.

The kind that often ends in tragedy.

Smoke inhalation.

Both Gage and I sucked in a lungful of ashes, and now we're reaping the consequences.

I must not be that bad because they're sending me home, but they insist on keeping Gage for observation.

"You're awake!" I say, making my way over. As soon as the doctor said I was released, I made a beeline to his room.

Gage gets up on his elbows, his face still slightly smeared with grit.

I hop up next to him on the bed. "You should really consider becoming a fireman. You're way hot with all that soot on your face," I say.

His eyes pierce through like sirens as he coughs out a small laugh.

"I'm so glad you're gonna be OK." I lean in and offer a soft welcoming kiss, pull at his lips with mine as if we were anywhere but a hospital room.

"I don't know how we got out of there," Gage whispers into my neck. "Something tells me it was just in time." His eyes dart to the door before returning his gaze. I know he's talking about the Transfer. "I saw the name on the tank."

A loud rustle erupts from the doorway.

"She's in here, Lizbeth!" It's Tad. His hair is rumpled, and he's got a gown wrapped around him. His entire face is scabbed over with pinpricks.

Mom runs in and tackles me with a hug.

"Are the two of you, OK?" Her pea green eyes stare out in horror.

"Yes," I say. And judging by the way Tad's standing there with his arms folded in judgment, so is he.

"I just finished a nice conversation with an officer of the law," he huffs. "Turns out your romantic tryst in the woods burned down nearly a half acre on school premises."

"Our what?" I ask.

"They found candles," he directs it to my mother. "He said the two of you were tangled up in one another when they found you." He reverts back to Mom. "It looks like they were overcome with smoke from the inferno they set off."

"There were no candles. We didn't start a fire," I say to Mom. Some part of me still wants her to believe me.

Gage leans back, places his arm up over his head and closes his eyes as though the drama were too much for him right now.

"I want her on birth control," Tad barks before storming out of the room.

"I don't need birth control." I meant to say it to my mother, but instead I scowl over at Gage. It's not my fault his moral compass suggests we wait.

"Tad is being discharged." Mom pulls a pair of gloves from out of her pocket. "I'll be back in five minutes to take you home." She disappears into the hall.

"What was the name on the tank?" I ask Gage without missing a beat.

His groggy eyes look back at me like twin blue stars.

"Ethan Landon."

48

Somebody's Watching Me

Even though Gage was discharged the next morning, Emma insisted he stay home from school—probably doesn't want him anywhere near me. I bet she refers to me in horrible nicknames like Messenger-the-menace, or Scary-Skyla—Skanky-Skyla.

Marshall calls me over to his desk after class.

Chloe collects her things extra slow, assuring she's the last one to leave the room. She blows me a kiss on the way out the door. I don't think I've ever felt such an intense level of hatred for anyone before.

"She's quite enamored with you." Marshall doesn't look amused.

"The only reason she wanted to come back was to steal Gage."

"Sometimes, Ms. Messenger, things aren't what they seem." He scoops off the mess of paper on the surface of his desk and tosses it in his briefcase haphazard.

"You have plans for winter break?" I ask out of boredom. West gives three weeks off plus an entire week after as ski week. That's one, long, bliss-filled month.

"Shall I incite your mother to invite me over, Christmas Eve?"

"Will you play Santa?" I ask almost seductively. Maybe I can seduce Marshall into helping me kill Chloe.

His face relaxes, and he gives me those bedroom eyes. Marshall is far better at being seductive than I could ever hope to be.

"What are you after?" He looks me up and down with an appropriate amount of suspicion.

"Tell me about my mother." That's not really what I'm after, but it'll do for now. "She sends a dead girl to give me nebulous messages. Is my mother a coward?"

"I've already warned you not to slander celestial beings—your mother is at the very top of the list. Trust me, that is one woman you don't want to infuriate."

"Have you infuriated my mother?" The idea fascinates me.

"She's less than pleased with me attempting to procreate with her daughter."

That makes two of us. "She can find comfort in the fact it's not going to happen. Marshall? If I wanted to travel into the future I'm going to need a supervising spirit. Do you think she'd want to supervise me?"

"It's not as easy as picking a spirit out of the crowd. It involves great sacrifice on the spirit's part. But that's a conversation for another day."

He lifts my chin with his finger, draws me towards him as though it were a dare.

"Something is going to happen between us, Skyla," it comes out melodic like poetry embedded in that euphoric feeling he's emanating—hot, like a pleasure filled brand.

"What was that vision you gave me?" I wanted to say I could never look so radiant, but those were the only words I could afford without gasping for air.

"That's how I see you." His breath pours over me warm and soft. "Would you like another?"

"No—none of them were worthy."

"You might feel different about this one."

He dives down with an intense wild kiss. Marshall is starved for physical attention, parched for something far more than I'll ever be willing to give him.

I see it. It's me, walking down a long white aisle with flower petals at my feet. There's a man waiting for me at the end, he turns around.

It's Logan.

※ ※ ※

At lunch, Ellis and I watch with disdain as Chloe struts over flanked by the bitch squad.

"I hear your boyfriend's going to be OK," I say to Chloe with a half smile. I like the thought of beating Chloe at her own game.

"My boyfriend?" Her eyes cut across me with caution.

"Yeah," I sling an arm around Ellis. "I'm with Ellis now."

She gives a long exasperated blink and drags me towards the English building like she owns me, which she does, at least until I kill her again.

I don't know what kind of game you're playing, she says, *but I'm getting really tired of hearing stories of you and Gage fucking on the beach, fucking in the forest.*

"What?" I hiss. If there are stories of me and Gage doing anything that remotely resembles fucking I sure as hell want to hear about it—oh wait.

"How did you know about the beach? The forest?" I snatch my arm back. We certainly weren't *fucking,* but I like the fire it's ignited in her, so I really don't mind her thinking it. Judging by her seething anger, her heart is corroding at the thought of Gage touching me—wanting me that way.

"Call it an inkling." Her head twitches. "Let me lay down some ground rules. Hands off, keep your legs to yourself. I'm sure there's a nice steel bed with your name on it, and the Counts would love to have you fill it. Do you know what they do to Celestra like you? They milk you for blood. Rumor is, Pierce wants to have your baby. I hear the thought just kills your dear sweet friend Nat—so much so, she now has a vested interest in your capture, herself."

I swallow hard.

"Would you like me to take care of Nat for you Skyla? I'd do anything for a friend." Her dark eyes gleam at the thought. Chloe is a bubbling poison just waiting to spew out and cover the world in her toxin.

"No. Never mind Nat." The last thing I need is Chloe killing her and pinning me for Nat's death. Chloe's just that twisted, I can smell her insanity a mile away.

"Brielle is having a party tomorrow night." She washes over me with those warped lenses and takes up my hand. *Gage and I are going as a couple. I suggest you do the same, but it won't be with Ellis.* She digs into me with a satisfied smile. *I have another boyfriend in mind for you—our friend, the Sector. That's right, I saw the two of you feasting on one another's tongues. This eye you gave me? It really does see through walls. Besides, pissing off Michelle is one of my favorite pastimes.* The bell rings, and she takes off.

I have news for Chloe. I can't wait to see how helpful that necklace will be while I carve my initials into her chest with the spirit sword tomorrow night.

And I'll be sure to bring my new boyfriend, Marshall.

Once I'm through with her, he can take her straight to hell.

49

Baby You Can Drive My Car

Gage insists that I keep my appointment at the DMV.

Logan offers to drive me over in the Mustang. I run my fingers over the dry and cracking dashboard, fidget with the old school dials on the radio until I find a familiar song and let it bleed from the speakers. I can't wait to have this as my very own car.

"What am I going to do about insurance?"

"You have a job," Logan says, pulling into the DMV.

"Yeah, well, it's not turning out to be so lucrative."

"I'll front you the money. You can pay me back."

"Like a loan?"

"Like a loan."

"Deal." I should probably ask for terms or something, but I'm so excited to finally have my own car, I can't wait.

The fog lays thick over Paragon at this late hour in the afternoon. It seeps in through the opened door and cloaks Logan in mystery.

I don't really know what that vision of Marshall's meant. If I didn't already know I was marrying Gage I would have thought it was a wedding—our wedding—Logan and me.

He wore his familiar smile, but I couldn't really make anything else out. I walked a small eternity down a white aisle with what looked like flower petals at my feet.

My heart races at the thought. Maybe I'm accidentally going to marry Logan? Or maybe we'll be in a play? Or he's the best man at my wedding with Gage? Or worse, I marry them *both.* Good God, I'm going to be a polygamist! We'll have a reality show and twelve kids, and I'll have to support us all by modeling online in the nude—only no one will want to see me in the nude after twelve kids, not even Logan or Gage.

"You OK?" Logan shifts in his seat to get a better look at me.

"Yeah, I'm OK," I say, getting out of the car. Of course that was another lie. I've honed my skills on the art of lying.

I slam the door and head into the DMV. Let's see if I can hone my skills on the art of pretending to know how to drive.

🦋 🦋 🦋

OK, so I shouldn't be too surprised that I didn't pass my drivers test. It was like the forces of nature showed up and practically rammed me off the road—what with the wall of fog and vat of rain, the bionic windstorm that came out of nowhere. And I honestly don't remember that curve being there. All I have to say is thank you to the small tree that spared me from sailing down a steep embankment, which totally had instant death written all over it. Well, the administrator's death, not mine. I probably would have been vegging out, quite literally, in a hospital room for the next fifty years.

Logan drives me back to the Oliver's home, and we hang out with Gage who's convalescing on his bed, watching TV.

I crawl up next to him and wrap my arms around his waist. He's scrubbed clean and well rested, even though every now and again his chest rumbles with a tiny cough.

"So Chloe decided who my next boyfriend will be," I say plucking at a stray fiber on his shirt.

"Me?" Logan asks with more curiosity than hope.

"No, Dudley," I say.

An alarming silence hacks through the air.

"No way." There's a fresh rage in Logan. "I can't stand the thought of him touching you."

An image of Marshall sealing his lips over mine flashes through my mind.

"It's sort of a good thing," I say as the two of them snap their necks in my direction. "I mean he's faculty, right? It's not like she expects me to be seen with him in public or anything. It has to be a secret relationship. This is never going to be a big deal."

Their expressions soften as they consider this.

I let out a long drawn out breath.

Something tells me it's going to be a very, very, *big* freaking deal.

Back at home, fast food bags clutter up the Landon kitchen, and this shocks me because the last thing my fake family believes in is fast food.

"What's up?" I ask plucking out a burger and fries.

"Tad and I are leaving in the morning." Mom blushes like a schoolgirl. "The workup is done over a two day period, so we won't be back until sometime in the afternoon, Monday. Will you watch the house?" she asks, pulling out a stack of paper plates from the pantry.

"Yes."

Tad balks as he makes his way over, still purple and bruised. I'm starting to wonder if being inseminated is her preference. Tad looks like a villain straight out of a comic book. And since we're usually diabolically opposed, maybe I can be the super hero? Super Skyla? Sounds totally, meh. Maybe, medieval Messenger? Or how about the Angel of Annihilation? Speaking of names, I wonder how far Tad would jump out of his skin if I uttered the name, Ethan Landon. I guess I should ask someone far less volatile like Drake or Melissa.

Drake wanders in and it's not until he sits beside me at the bar that I notice Emily strutting in behind him.

"Everyone—this is my new girlfriend," he offers.

My jaw goes slack. Instinctively, I want to knock Drake off the barstool for being such an ass to Brielle and simultaneously thrust a napkin at Emily and ask her to draw me a picture, but resist the urge.

Mom and Tad wander over from the kitchen and stare at her like she's a curiosity.

"So you're a cheerleader just like Skyla!" The way my mother squeals, you would think we were the only two cheerleaders on the planet.

"Just like Brielle," I shoot a look over to Drake.

The air grows cold as Emily rolls her eyes to the ends of the earth.

"You'll have to excuse my stepdaughter," Tad starts.

I cut him off before he can fire off the zinger. "Yes, please excuse me," I say, leaving the kitchen.

I bump into Mia in the hall.

"I don't see your car parked out front." She sets her foot out in defiance.

"I failed the test. But it's not like I didn't try."

"Fine." She shrugs. "Just have your boyfriend drop me off on my date tomorrow night."

"No, Gage is not playing taxi." Unless you're Chloe. "Besides, you should invite him over here, and you guys can watch a movie or something." And I can totally keep an eye on this creep.

"Really?"

"Yes."

"You're the best sister ever." She bites down on her lip. "But you know who won't think so? Melissa. She'll be all alone and bored out of her skin. I think I'll invite a few friends to keep her company."

"Mia, no." I zero in on that mischievous look in her eye, and I am acutely aware of the fact she means more than a couple of friends.

"You can't tell me no." She plucks the phone from her pocket and waves it in my face. An image of me kissing Marshall burns on the screen. "Just give me one good reason, and I'll email this to everyone at West. I have the entire student directory downloaded and ready to go."

I've never hit Mia, but I have the sudden intense desire to insanely beat the shit out of her.

"Just a few friends," I hiss, making my way past her.

She's so damn wicked it makes me wonder if Holden already has a body.

50

Falling in Line

From across street, in the thick of night, the house looks docile—almost fragile. But I can hear and feel the faint sound of bass trembling beneath me while rows and rows of cars are parked haywire all up and down our street.

Clearly this is a recipe for a boisterous, balls out, call the cops because things are getting out of hand, wild disaster of a party. The air is rife with rampant teenage hormones of both the middle and high school variety. The cars aren't all here for the party at my house, it's the West slash East, it's almost winter break bash Brielle is throwing that has them coming by the dozens.

Not to be outdone by the party queen next door, Mia's get together actually has enough people to outfit a small nation. It wouldn't surprise me if the entire lot of us dropped into Paragon's infamous underworld from the sheer weight of hundreds of jostling bodies. My mind strays to the rooms in the Transfer that house Counts in liquid Drano. I wonder if Brielle knows about them?

"So you think there's still a chance?" Brielle hiccups into me.

I can't believe I'm comforting a Count—a knocked up Count no less, while Drake is in there pawing all over Emily.

"You can have anyone," I tell her. Brielle's mother is out at a conference, so she decided to have a few friends over. Funny how she and Mia classify a 'few friends' in the same manner, must be a Count thing.

wicked

"I don't want just *anyone*."

"Look, he's still into you. He just thinks you've lost it and are threatening him with a fake pregnancy."

"Really?"

"Yes. He hates puking, and when you kept hurling, he was afraid you were going to get him sick. It's not that he doesn't want you, he just doesn't want the stomach flu." I think.

"Really?" Tears gloss down her cheeks. "I totally know how to fix this. Thanks." She pushes in a wet kiss on the side of my face before taking off across the street.

A pair of headlights wink in my direction before parking high on the ridge.

Marshall gets out and struts on over. He's wearing jeans and a t-shirt pulled over a thermal. He looks hot and young, and oh freaking shit.

"No." I hold up a hand.

"I received a note stating you wanted to take our relationship public. Interesting venue." He glances over at Brielle's house.

"You know that note wasn't from me."

"Yes, but your name was attached to it, so I thought I'd swing by and appease the one who sent it. Come," he presses into my lower back as we make our way up the driveway.

A few guys in Ellis' stoner circle call out to him. He's like a rock star in this environment as we walk into a masculine choir of *Dudley*.

With Marshall glued to my side, we immediately garner the attention of, well, everyone as we enter the house. Logan is talking to Chloe in the corner as Gage comes back with drinks for the two of them. They all stare disbelieving. Gage glowers at us his with dark brows crouched over those electric blue eyes like a bat in flight.

I duck into the hall in an effort to ditch Marshall and run smack into Nat and Pierce.

Shit.

Her eyes have healed, and her skin looks even toned for the first time in days. Her hair's all wiry and locked in a kinky mess of curls that, in this dim light, actually gives her that Medusa effect.

I spin on my heels and land face first in Marshall's chest. I yank him along until we bypass Nat and her bloodsucking boyfriend and land in the cool night air right out back.

"You'd rather we be alone. I like where this is going," he growls pulling me in.

"No," I say, pushing back. "You have to help me."

"Why?" His eyes light up like copper kettles.

"You need me to fight a war. It's the least you can do, you owe me."

"Do tell." His features soften.

"First, a body for Holden. I don't like the thought of him leering at me all night long. Plus, I'm a tiny bit afraid of him. Second, deal with Natalie and Pierce. They're really starting to piss me off. Maybe humiliate them in the worst possible way." I close my eyes briefly. "And would you please get rid of Chloe? I'm sorry I ever thought she was a good idea. She won't let me near my boyfriend, and that's just…" I grapple for words, "wrong."

"Drama." His chest gives way to a sigh. "For your information, I don't *owe* you anything. In fact you've yet to thank me for hauling both you and your supposed boyfriend out of the Transfer."

"You did that?" I marvel.

"Yes, I did that." His cheek slides up one side.

wicked

"So it is called the Transfer. How did we get there in the first place?"

"I don't know," his lips twist when he says it while holding back a smile.

"You must have been there. Hey, are you watching me?" I blink into the realization.

"Am I watching you, or am I watching the Transfer?"

The moon casts a scant shadow down over the yard. It bleeds through the forest just beyond the property and dapples us in rich buttery light.

"So are you going to put an end to all these mysteries?" I ask dipping into him.

"Like?"

"Like what the Transfer is, why you need me to help fight the Fems, when I'll get to meet my mother?"

"Too deep. Let's get back to the task at hand. Holden gets a body, Natalie and Pierce suffer abject humiliation, and Chloe," he pauses, "nothing I can do about that one. You've made your bed, Skyla."

"You could humiliate Chloe." Everything feels hopeless. "What about the spirit sword?"

"You can't kill her, but you could try, the results might be amusing."

"I'll settle for whatever you can do."

"Very well." He takes in a breath. "I'll filter through your wish list, but you'll have to do something for me in exchange."

"And I want Nevermore."

He raises a brow as if to affirm this.

"Well then," I lick my lips. "I'll do just about anything."

51

Anything Goes

The windows shake in time to music turned up far too loud, booming out of crap speakers that replicate to perfection the sound of crumpling paper.

It's electrifying stepping into the crowd. I scan the room for signs of Chloe and Gage. A nagging feeling that things are about to go brilliantly wrong grazes along my nerves.

"Come on, Holden," I whisper. "Come out and play one last time. It's your chance to be the life of the party—make it memorable like only you can."

It's not that I need Holden's assistance in what I'm about to do. It's not that Marshall has asked me to do anything I've never done before—hauling Michelle into the crowd and having a cat fight over him—ditching the scene with him to prove a point—an open mouthed kiss as payment, but it's Gage whose heart I'm eager to protect. Hopefully Holden will create enough havoc that I won't have to.

I see Gage over by the window. His steel cut gaze bores through me with heart stopping intensity. His lips curve and ignite a smile that almost waylays me into forgetting my mission.

I scan the room for Michelle, her awkward haircut, that dim rose of hopelessness she wears around her neck.

Brielle catches my eye near the door, her hands wrapped securely around a dark figure, and she's laughing, dipping her head back as he nips at her ear. He turns just enough for his face to get caught in a narrow strip of light.

Drake?

They're back together! I'm completely caught off guard. Just seeing them in the same proximity brims me to the limit with hope for me and Gage. Love prospers. It doesn't dissipate under duress, it *grows*, affirms itself in ways we could never imagine. There's nothing Chloe can do to keep us apart.

"Hard right," Marshall whispers just before heading out the door. He wants his hands clean, and I can't say I blame him.

"*Body*—body, body, body, body, body," I whisper like an incantation on my way over to Michelle. I'm secretly hoping the Holden show will take over. I'm not really in the mood to kick some Miller ass at the moment, especially not while declaring my love for Marshall.

I step in next to Emily and Michelle.

"So what's going on?" I say rather unexpectedly, but neither Michelle, nor Emily seem to notice me. "Hey, where's Lexy?" She has this thing for Logan, and even though I don't want him, I'm not exactly optioning him out to other people.

"Excuse me, but we're trying to have a private conversation here." Emily's nostrils flare when she says it. She's obviously miffed about the whole Drake and Brielle reunion. Speaking of which, I should totally think of a couple's name for them, like Dreielle, or Brake.

"I was just looking for Lexy," I shout over the music. My gaze drifts outside the window where I find Marshall on his cell. "Oh, and Michelle?" I don't take my eyes off him. I hope he's incurring some incredible roaming charge for what he's about to make me do. I give a quick glance over at Chloe who's totally hijacking Gage at the moment. I hope she breaks out in hives every time she thinks of him.

"What?" Michelle barks in my face zipping the rose across her neck like a pendulum.

Emily leans in. "I realize you have no real friends, but could you leave us the hell alone, we don't want you here."

I stand there stunned by Emily's harsh words. Do I have any real friends? Can I trust anyone I've met while living on Paragon? How do I know I can trust Logan the Count or even Gage for that matter? Marshall wants to me to give him dominion by way of my uterus, and Chloe has already shown her true colors. What if the people that hate me are my truest friends of all?

I should grab Michelle by what little hair she has left, pull and run. But I don't want to get the things that I want by hurting people, not even Michelle.

Instead, I lean in and ask Emily something I'd really like an answer to. "So what's up with all those freaky pictures?"

The whites of her eyes flash, her hand reaches up and twists my shirt. Then she does the unimaginable and lifts it effortlessly over my head leaving me in nothing but my bra in front of all the kids from East and West.

Now, if I had worn my black lace push up, or my peach barely there see through, or even *no* freaking bra it would have been less embarrassing than the beige orthopedic number I threw on in a hurry this morning.

An echo of gasps whip across the room.

I pull down my shirt and push hard into Emily in one easy move. Looks like I get my throw down after all, just not the one stipulated by Marshall.

A hard knock comes at me from behind, and I fall on my face—it's Michelle, she did it. She initiated the fight. Oddly I'm filled with relief.

A familiar looking set of tennis shoes bolt in my direction. I roll onto my back and launch Michelle up near the ceiling before Gage could even hope to save the day. Little does he know that *I'm* saving the day, and doing multiple public services all at the same time.

Michelle lands hard on the floor just shy of my face and I pin down both her arms. "Oh, Holden," I whisper. "You have truly let me down," I grit the words through my teeth. I can feel Gage trying to pluck me off by the waist, but I'm so close to declaring my affection for Marshall I can't let him.

"Keep your hands off Dudley," I shout, sorely lacking the proper enthusiasm. Marshall steps into the house feigning a look of surprise. He's so obvious. I want to vomit all over Michelle first, then him.

Gage moves slightly, and I see the spirit sword flirting with me from beneath his shirt.

Without offering it any thought, I jump up and yank it free in one clean swipe. I run my finger over the back of the blade and feel it strum through me with a pleasing electrical current. The dull room lights up in a beautiful shade of astral blue as I dart over to a horrified Chloe.

It would be so easy to try and carve her just like Tad did the Thanksgiving turkey, so laboriously, painfully slow. But there are too many witnesses, and surprisingly even in all this fury, I can see the upside to not being locked in jail. Instead, I snatch at the necklace and give a quick swipe with the blade.

A clean line of blood erupts.

"Oh my, God!" Someone screams from behind.

Shit!

I think I just decapitated Chloe Bishop in front of God, and country, and a thousand fucking witnesses.

52

Shatter

A thin seam of blood quickly soaks Chloe's sweater. She stares down in horror as her face bleeds out all color.

It's safe to say I miscalculated the length of the knife. It's safe to say I...

A vacuum fills the room. Every orifice in my body is suctioned so succinctly that having my brain siphoned out of my ears feels like a very real possibility. In a sudden burst, the pressure gives. The windows all blow in simultaneously, and a rush of bloodied bodies explode in riotous screams. The floor moves, first in slow rolling motions then hard sudden jerks. Holden is really going all out, on this, his last night as a disembodied soul.

Pictures fly off the walls, people, purses, vases—bottles are jagging around the vicinity. The room whips up like a tornado, round and round until there's just one intense melting pot of color. Then, in a thunderous clap, everything crashes.

You could say free falling from Brielle's ceiling was something to behold—a weightless wonder, plunging into the startled world below. I land soft as a leaf into Logan's waiting arms.

Casting a quick glance around, I spot Ellis tending to an almost decapitated Chloe, so I head on over.

"Looks like that flying glass really did a number on you." I give her a hard look.

She swipes her hand over her injury and looks down at her glossy fingertips.

"That wasn't supposed to happen." She clutches at the pendant around her neck.

"Sure it could happen." Logan picks the sword up off the floor and gives it back to me. "She's a Celestra, pure as you."

"Really? I could kill Chloe?" I look over at her as she shrinks with fear.

Logan places his fingers on my bare arm. *You could if she wasn't wearing that necklace. You'd go to justice alliance. Also prison would be a real possibility because they don't defend killing within your own faction.*

So what you're saying is—I could kill you, no problem. I give a wry smile.

Sirens cut through the music, and the outside world ignites in a riot of patriotic colors.

"Let's go." Gage wraps an arm around me. "Chloe, I'm sure your mom will gladly pick you up from the hospital."

Ellis steps up. "I'll stay with her."

It takes everything in me not to scowl at Ellis for being nice to her.

"I hope you feel better." I lean over to Chloe and smack my hand flat against her forehead. *Press charges, and I'll cut a little deeper next time.* "You feel warm, you'd better get some rest."

She reaches up and digs her fingernails into my arm. *You're with Dudley now. Don't forget it. And Skyla? I hear the Counts would love to have you.*

A bitter breeze slices through the room.

I let my eyes linger over her as I rise to my feet. I want to remember her this way, feeble and bleeding.

I walk out the door with Gage and Logan on either side of me. Chloe's incision looked disappointingly superficial. With my luck she'll be sealed and healed by morning.

We come upon Brielle leaning over the rail yakking into the bushes while Drake stands beside her rubbing her back.

We head down the porch, and I turn to get a look at the house.

"Well done, Ms. Messenger." Marshall speeds me away from Logan and Gage over near the edge of the property.

"So, does Holden get his," I stop short of saying *body*, "you know..."

"Yes, he gets his, you know. I plan on collecting on that kiss momentarily, so give yourself a pep talk, psych yourself out, whatever it is you do to prepare for a touch of my resplendence."

At least his ego doesn't suffer.

"I can't give you that kiss." I glance back at both Logan and Gage openly glaring in our direction. "You forgot Nat and Pierce."

"Abject humiliation is hard to come by." He gives my hand a squeeze and looks up towards the roofline of Brielle's house.

"Oh wow." My mouth falls open.

Nat and Pierce are both straddling the rain gutter strangulation style.

"They're naked," Marshall is quick to point out in the event I hadn't noticed.

"Rutting on rooftops is sort of their thing." It's a reprisal of what they did at West a few weeks back—got Nat suspended for a couple days. Come to think of it, she's sort of suspended now.

The entire population of East and West watch as Nat and Pierce writhe in their discomfort. The fire department shines a spotlight in their direction, and everyone stares transfixed as though we were unexpectedly being treated to some X-rated movie.

"Good work, Marshall," I pat him on the back. "And Holden the not so friendly ghost?"

"Already resurrected."

"Really?" I bounce on the balls of my feet.

"Really," he mocks my enthusiasm. "I'll be by later tonight to collect your debt. The price of revenge is rather mouthwatering, wouldn't you say?" He looks past my shoulder into the crowd and gives a wicked grin. "Or shall we do it now?"

"Tonight," I breathe out in defeat.

53

The Chase

I see Chloe hedging around the corner of the house and not a sign of Ellis anywhere to be found.

What's she doing?

I step away from the commotion, circling around the crowd until I hit the abandoned side yard. The voices of the mob and rescue crews are quickly doused with the solitude of the forest on this narrow strip of land that leads to the open backfields of Paragon.

"Chloe?" I finger the spirit sword tucked in my jeans when I say her name.

I cut her once tonight and watched her bleed with pleasure. I'd love to repeat the effort.

Something shifts in the distance—a hand pushes out, then the shimmer of hair in the moonlight.

I pull the dagger out and take off after her.

Her footsteps quicken, she knows someone's back here. I can practically hear the self-doubt resonating in her erratic panting. She knows it's me—she must.

Chloe laughs as she runs.

"Catch me if you can," her voice echoes in the dark.

She wants this.

She's been waiting an entire year to lure me back into the forest—just Chloe and me, and the spirit sword—poetry in motion.

"Skyla?" It's Gage. His husky baritone echoes in the night. I hear my name again, overlapping—it's both of them.

I head deeper into the forest, away from the comfortable stream of moonlight to create a border of blackness between me and those willing to stop me from attempting to deliver one fatal blow.

So this is the big reprisal—the do-over ending that attempts to change everything. One of us needs to die tonight, and according to Gage, the odds are in Chloe's favor.

I can see her racing ahead of me, traversing branches, extending her legs over tree stumps like a track star. Chloe is exhausting all of her physical resources. I hope she's perfectly depleted when I knock her to the ground.

My side starts to cramp up. My shins are on fire. The night air cuts sharp icy jags into my lungs. I'm not up for this marathon sprint. Pierce and his thirst for my iron-rich blood has sapped my strength.

"Have to catch Chloe," I mutter.

We continue on, eclipsing the forest in its entirety, out to the embankment over Narrows' beach.

"Skyla!" The voice is distinctly Logan's—he's too close.

I muster every last stitch of energy to keep going—think of my father—how helpless he was when he burned. How Chloe used him to fuel the drive for her narcissistic urge for self-preservation. She barreled ahead at all costs, and now it propels me at super human speeds. Chloe looks like a thimble in the distance, but in less than a minute, I'm upon her, running in the fog-laden trail from the fumes of her undeserving breath.

The unthinkable happens.

Chloe stumbles. Her arms flail wild as she does a massive face plant into Paragon's fertile soil. I land on her back, pinning her down completely. I clutch at the knife with a stranglehold so tight, my fingers impress into the metal.

Chloe reaches back and knocks me in the side of the face with the force of a tractor. A searing trail of fire shoots through my jaw and up towards my temple.

She's going to crush me. She'll kill me if I let her.

It's a brawl of apocalyptic proportions as I try to control her wild limbs. The effort proves futile, so I swipe at her with the knife in earnest.

I slice through her sweater—her jeans, I get one clean cut into the left of her chin. Welcome to the club, I want to say as the thick seam of blood rises on her cheek. We wrestle and grunt, rolling over one another in turn.

Chloe overpowers me, rolls me on my back and sits hard on my stomach with a thud. It is an all out struggle for the sword, she won't quit, and I won't let go.

The handle of the knife inverts in my hand from perspiration, pointing the blade right down over my chest.

"Shit." I try and buck her off, but she grabs me by the wrist, holds the spirit sword over my heart and ignites it like a flame.

My elbows lock, my muscles tremble as I try to regain control.

"You're going to kill yourself, Skyla," she spurts it out with laughter. "Did you know this weapon has the power to kill? That even you could die by its blade?"

It's not true. I shake my head just barely. She's trying to scare me, throw me enough to land me in the hospital on a permanent basis.

"It's true." She bites down and studies me. "Shall we count to three?"

It takes all of my being to hold up that metal spear, but really I'm looking past it, past Chloe—up at the paper lantern sky, wondering if I could in fact be on my way to meet my father, my mother—leave this body right here on Paragon tonight.

Chloe lets out a magnificent roar, buckles my arms and sends the sword plunging towards me.

A shoe intercepts—Chloe is tackled from above.

Logan retrieves the knife from several yards away as Gage binds up Chloe with his body.

I get up on my knees and slap the dirt off my thighs.

"Enjoy it while you can," I chide. "That is the only bodily contact you'll get from him. And you know what? He hates touching you."

She looks up at him with heartbreak pouring out of those dark bitter eyes.

"You can hear him, can't you?" I ask. "He can't hide his true feelings when you touch him."

Logan steps over to her, unhooks the necklace from the back of her neck and holds it up for me to see.

I can't breathe. I'm so stunned I can't move. In truth, I had forgotten all about his grandmother's protective hedge.

It has its own magical charm. A large silver medallion hangs from it. The blue stone in the center shimmers with zeal as though it were celebrating the fact it was no longer around Chloe's neck.

Logan comes over, and I pull back my hair, bow into him. The pendant pats gently against my chest as he secures the latch, still warm from Chloe's body.

"Thank you," I say looking up at him.

It's done.

He taps his fingers over the pendant and I place my hand over his.

I'm safe.

54

Mia and Me

Logan takes Chloe to the convenience store down the street to clean up. I was outvoted when I suggested we butcher her into twelve different pieces, bury her flesh in the four corners of the island. I guess Logan and Gage are a bunch of bleeding hearts after all—that, and they're entirely not sold on the idea of spending the remainder of their time behind bars.

Gage walks me home through a blanket of darkness, dusted in luminescent fog. I love it like this with Gage—holding hands, safe.

I pause and fondle the pendant around my neck.

Gage presses out a smile that sends a hot bite of lust ripping through my insides.

"I love you," I say, dazed by his beauty.

He reaches over and removes the necklace with his class ring from around my neck.

"What are you doing?"

"I don't want it to catch, or anything. I want that pendant secure on you. I like the idea of no more exploding Fems." His dimples dart in and out. He places his ring in the palm of my hand and moves it close to my chest.

"Can I keep it?" I love his class ring. It's like having a piece of Gage wherever I go.

"It's yours."

"You're mine," I lick the smile off his face, and we fall into a timeless kiss. The world warps and melts around us, spins until it's dizzy with jealousy, until it's just Gage and me and the universe, breathing like one.

※ ※ ※

Gage and I step into the house still alive with the thumps and vibrations from the middle school event of the century.

Hundreds of baby faced seventh graders float around the house, each one armed with a red plastic cup. I snatch one out of the first hand I see and sniff.

"Are you freaking insane?" I shout over his squared off glasses. "This is *beer!*" He stares back sporting a full metal jacket in his mouth.

I send the cup sailing into the crowd as I storm through the downstairs in search of Mia.

Gage and I try to break up the party, and for once I feel like a responsible—moral adult, except for the part about having to kiss Marshall later. That will totally ding my morals and it makes me want to hang Marshall instead.

I see Melissa slumped over the counter, barely seated on a barstool, and for a second I think about checking her pulse. The weird thing is, I don't even panic. With my blood, and Marshall's know how, I feel strangely removed from the concept of death as I once knew it.

"Wake up!" I jostle her to attention.

She lets out a moan, and I can smell the alcohol on her breath.

Great.

"Where's Mia?" I slide a stack of paper towels over to her in the event she tries to invert her intestines.

She mumbles and points up.

Up? As in *upstairs*? Why would she be upstairs when there's a perfectly good party going on right down here?

Oh shit, oh shit, oh shit!

My hands push out in front of me as I speed my way through the crowd and up the stairs.

I trip over bodies rolling around in the dark hall until I stumble into Mia's bedroom. Empty. Thank God.

I breathe a sigh of relief as I shut the door. A vision of Mia tangled up in some boy sails through my brain, and I whip open the door to Mom and Tad's room.

A circle of kids sit on the bed, smoking, and judging by the very distinct Ellis-like odor, it's for sure not legal.

"Out!" I thunder scaring them all onto the floor.

I race over to my bedroom and open the door.

"Mia?" The light is on in my bathroom and the obvious sound of giggles emit from the other side of the door. God, what if she's getting it on with some guy in my bathroom? What kind of lowlife tries to get a girl on the freaking toilet?

I burst through the door fully pissed and ready to castrate.

"Skyla!" Brielle snatches a towel off the counter at a lame attempt to cover up her chest. Drake peers over at me from behind the wall. He's not wearing a shirt, which instinctively causes me to shut my eyes in the event he's got flesh colored pants to match.

"Sorry!" I close the door. "So glad you're back together!"

A hissing noise comes from the closet, and I jump, knocking over the lamp in fear.

"It's me," Mia hisses.

"Where are you?" I reach blindly towards my desk.

The closet light flicks on, and I go over. The first thing I glance at is the transom over the butterfly room, making sure it's securely in place.

"What are you doing?"

"I'm hiding." She pulls a long strand of hair over her face. "Gabriel Armistead wanted to do it, and I chickened out."

"Who the hell's Gabriel Armistead? Never mind, I don't want to know, and thank you for chickening out."

She shrugs. "I thought about you, and I didn't do it."

"Me?"

"Yeah." Her eyes glow in this gentle light. She's so beautiful. She's worth a thousand Gabriel Armisteads if not a million. "You know," she continues, "knocked up and stuff. I don't want to ruin my life like you did."

I want to correct her, but don't. "You made the right decision." Sadly I don't think it would *ruin* my life if I slept with Gage or had his baby. But I get what she's saying, and she's right. No reason to make life harder than it has to be. Not that I'm ever going to admit to Gage he's right in waiting for that perfect moment. Especially when it's tons of fun trying to convince him otherwise.

She walks towards the door. "Oh and Skyla?"

I glance over at her.

"I'm going to tell you had the party."

"I'll tell you had the party," I shoot back.

"They'll never believe you. No one ever does."

55

Lips Like These

Horrifying. Trashed. Decimated.

    I don't know how to even begin to clean this mess, so I don't. Instead, I convince Gage that I'm totally OK with him going home and wait for Marshall to appear over my bed like a glowworm.

    "Hello," he whispers, leaning against the closet.

    The next thing I know we're standing outside in the backyard.

    "How'd you do that?" I take in a sharp lungful of air from the surprise.

    "I can do anything," it comes out seductive with a trace of a drawl I hadn't detected before.

    He morphs into Logan.

    "No," I say, flatly. An image of Logan and I rutting in the backseat of his car infiltrates my brain, and I can't seem to stop it.

    He morphs into Gage.

    I let out a sigh. Kissing him like this would be easy as breathing air.

    His features sharpen back to his own.

    "This is the channel, Skyla. Sorry if it offends your viewing pleasure."

    There's something charmingly boyish about Marshall bathed in this stream of sterling moonlight. I stroke his hair back and pull him in close by the neck.

"I'm not offended. I'm just not the right one for you." My heart thumps like a jackrabbit. I've been this close to Marshall before, closer if you count his vision laced lips, but something about this is different, like I'm actually feeling something for him. But he's so far behind both Gage and Logan, I don't think there's a chance for us.

"You're touching me, Skyla. I can hear you."

My cheeks burn with heat. "I meant—"

"I know what you meant."

"Thank you for doing those things for me today," I stare down at the ground while I say it. I'm afraid if I look up at him I might get swallowed in by the moment. "I really am in love with my boyfriend."

"Boyfriends," he corrects.

"I just," I take in a deep breath ignoring his insinuation. "I don't want to cheat." I blink back tears.

Marshall bumps his forehead into mine before retracting. "Very well. I've left something for you in the closet. I was going to gift it to you regardless, sort of a belated birthday present. Nevertheless, in exchange for the kiss, to uphold your end of the agreement I'd like for you to wear it, Monday."

I nod eagerly. I'd wear less than a dress if he wanted me to. I'm so thrilled I don't have to cheat on Gage, he could throw in a pair of dusty angel wings for kicks, and I wouldn't protest.

His brows peak. "Next time." He lands a soft kiss on the tip of my nose. "Be forewarned, pop quiz first thing Monday morning." And with that he disappears.

That night I lose myself in a world of spasmodic dreams. Me chasing Gage— apologies drip from me like oil. I chase

Chloe with a blue flaming axe and hack off her limbs. I chase an entire school bus of boys out of Mia's bedroom, laughing because she doesn't want to be like me—but really she does.

In the final installment of my REM feature presentation, I see Logan's orange Mustang rocking in a dark lot overlooking Devil's Peak. It clots up my dreamscape like a guilt-riddled stain, beckons me over to it like a dare. I know full well what I'm about to see.

There we are—me in my ball gown and him without a stitch. It looks so primal, the two of us lost in our lust. I can hear the erratic breathing as our secret perfume lets out its scent through a crack in the window.

"Hello, Skyla," a voice rumbles from behind.

I jump back to see Logan standing there with a forlorn look.

"You just can't walk into someone's dream like that." It doesn't come out half as irritated as I want it to. "Didn't I banish you?"

"I don't think you banished me, and if you did, I don't remember—lousy memory." He gives an unconvincing smile.

Logan walks over and looks in through the fog-laden window. He folds his arms and watches unmoved with an undertone of great sadness at what's transpiring on the other side of the glass.

"I can't control my dreams," I say defensively. The possibility of dying from embarrassment in this subconscious world feels very real.

"No, they're usually uncontrollable," he admits. His jaws cinches as though he were in great pain. "You can't control your dreams, but they're really good at exposing deep-seated feelings." His fingers touch the glass, right over the hand on the other side. "Oh, and, by the way," he looks right at me and gives a sarcastic smile, "I have a birthmark on the back of my upper left thigh."

"Very funny." The air clots up with tension again. "Logan?"

"Yes?" He looks hopeful as though I might somehow decide to replicate what's going on in the car behind him.

"I just want you to know that I really do trust you."

"Thank you," he picks up both my hands and kisses them in turn—then disappears.

Mia and Melissa flat out refuse to clean up their disaster, and since I worked a long shift on Sunday, I don't touch the mess either.

So early Monday morning when I hear the front door open and the obscenities flow from Tad's scab encrusted lips, I haul ass downstairs to rat out my sisters before they do me.

"*Skyla*." My mother closes her eyes in a forced neurotic calm that I can only hope won't rocket into a well lathered fury.

"Wasn't me." I say proud of the fact I'm not lying.

Tad wades through a flotilla of plastic cups that rise from the floor like a foul red tide. The sofa in the family room is upside down. Gage offered to flip it back into position, but I decided it might be a good testament to the debauchery their little darlings were capable of.

Mia and Melissa file downstairs still wiping the sleep from their eyes. To my surprise Drake is already in the kitchen lapping bits of soggy cereal from a bowl.

"For two days we leave you!" Tad slaps his hand down on the counter, and a plume of drywall dust explodes in the air. Technically that's from Holden yanking the chandelier. It just keeps snowing like powdered sugar each time we move around upstairs, and there's not a darn thing we can do about it. "Who is responsible?" He snarls.

Mia and I exchange accusing fingers.

"OK," Tad balks through puffy cheeks. "We've narrowed it down to two, both yours Lizbeth." His hands fly up as though he were exonerated from the verbal gaff he's just committed.

A horrid groan comes from deep inside Mom.

"It was Mia and Melissa," I say, trying to balance the Messenger to Landon ratio.

"Drake—Melissa?" Tad looks soberly over at the two of them.

"It was Skyla," Melissa shrugs in my direction.

I sigh. "Of course she's going to side with Mia, they're emotionally conjoined."

"No, it was really Skyla." Melissa's face turns a bright shade of pink. "And she made us stay up in our rooms all night."

"What? You were sitting right here about to puke your guts out when I found you. I even gave you an ice pack before I left for work yesterday to help with the hangover."

"You let my baby drink?" Tad takes a bold step in my direction.

"No, she did it herself. Right, Drake?"

"I'm Switzerland," he says shaking his head.

Figures.

"Skyla, we had an agreement." Mom tosses her purse on the counter.

"A signed legal document with real ramifications," Tad states regaining his composure.

"What's he talking about?" I ask Mom. I need her to decode his stupid speak for me.

"The contract, Skyla." Her eyes close in frustration. "The one you signed when we first arrived?"

The way they're talking about it makes it sound like some sacred document signed in blood, but it's not. It's that ridiculous statement of oppression they rigged, making me swear I'd never smoke pot or open my legs.

"Oh that." It was totally stupid and probably qualifies as child abuse. The consequences probably have something to do with turning me over to the Counts. Although at the moment I'm feeling rather turned in by my sister who is a Count, and imprisoned by the ones appointed as my legal guardians.

"Yes, that." Mom shoulders up to Tad.

"Pack it up, kiddo, I'll have you shipped, lock, stock, and barrel by the first of the year. There's a boarding school on the East Coast that will gladly take you mid-semester." He strides over to the junk drawer and pulls something out before slapping it on the counter. It's a brochure with the picture of some haunted looking castle on the front. It reads *Ephemeral Academy, where legacies are created.*

"I'll run away." The words fly out of my mouth before I can process them.

"You can't run away," Mia interjects. "What about the baby?"

The entire room depletes of oxygen as everyone sucks in a lungful of air.

"You have crossed the line, Mia," I say with a controlled anger. I snatch the curtain rod off the table and lung towards her just as Drake intercedes.

"Whoa," he gives a sly smile. "I knew it. It was *you* Brielle was covering for."

"No," I shake my head. "It's not me." The tight building knot in my throat restricts my protests.

"She's got a bunch of baby growth pills in her room." Drake folds his arms.

"Prenatals," I correct.

"Oh, Skyla," Mom's face bleaches out. She holds her hands out in an effort to balance herself from the shock.

"Well there you go, Lizbeth. Your own daughter is trying to eclipse your glory. I bet she did it just to steal your thunder."

"Mom—are you having a baby?" I ask, quick to glom onto anything that has nothing to do with the lies propagated against me.

She shakes her head.

"And she doesn't know who the daddy is," Melissa points hard in my direction.

"Skyla?" Mom clutches at her neck.

"It's either Logan," Mia presses down a finger, "Gage, or that creepy teacher we take horseback riding lessons from—I caught them making out in the barn."

Fuck.

My mother slaps her forehead.

"Now *that* is just a flat out lie." I needle Mia with all of my wrath. Marshall is the catalyst for the utter disgust I'm feeling towards my sister right now. Then an ingenious thought comes to me. "She's just saying that because I caught her smoking pot, and she knows I'm going to rat her out." Two can play at the lying game. I give a little smile.

I'll plant pot all over her room before they ship me off and set the damn thing on fire if I have to. Thanks to Ellis and his never-ending supply, I can rival any marijuana bust in modern day history—make it look like Mom and Tad are nothing but a bunch of reefer farmers.

"Mia, I want you to take back what you said about Mr. Dudley." Mom's tone lets her know she's not shitting around.

"He's a very good friend of the family and I won't have you slander him that way."

Slander? I squint into my mother. Marshall has said more than once, you don't slander celestial beings.

"It *is* true," Mia whines, "They were all over each other in the backyard Saturday night, too."

"That was Gage," I'm swift with the lie.

"Ah-*ha*!" Tad slaps his hands together before pointing over at me. "Bam! She's guilty, and I bet good money he's the daddy."

Just perfect.

"I tried telling you months ago we had a problem on our hands," Tad assumes a posture of superiority. "She was sleeping around the entire time," he narrows into my mother accusingly, "and you chose to believe her lies. I hope that illegitimate child she's carrying stamps your passport to reality because I sure couldn't."

I glare over at Mia.

"Get ready for school," Mom whispers. "We'll figure this all out later."

I head upstairs wondering if I let Holden out of his spiritual bondage a little too soon. Or perhaps I should have asked Marshall to hit the mute button on Mia.

"Thanks for taking the blame for the party," Mia traipses up the stairs beside me. "I still have the picture, so don't mess with me." Her lip curls to the side. "Look," she blocks the door to my room, "I feel like shit, OK? I'll split the fifty bucks with you."

"It's more like a hundred," Melissa says, heading down the hall.

"Not interested." I push past her.

The only thing I'm interested in is staying right here on Paragon.

56

Me and My White Dress

Monday is West Paragon's official last day of school before winter break. Yes, Monday. The rest of the week is replete with pupil free days, and everyone knows you don't go to school on pupil free days unless you have a crush on your teacher, or live in a house full of hostile Counts.

Gage is nice enough to pick me up, and I relay the series of events on the way to school including the immaculate conception of our nonexistent child, which both Mom and Tad firmly believe exists.

We take the long way and have to park in the student overflow near the charred forest.

"We burned this down with our love," his dimples ignite on either side as he helps me down from his truck. "You look gorgeous." He leans back and takes me in. I give a little spin in the stark white dress Marshall gave me. It's arid and loose, but sexy with alternating rows of intricate lace inlays.

"*You* look gorgeous." I run my fingers through his damp hair.

"We never did go snorkeling." He brushes his lips against the side of my face, and it sends a shiver up my spine.

"I owe you for your birthday. I think we should *do it* at Rockaway Point, you know, finish what we started." I bite down a smile.

"Maybe we will."

"Really?" I hop up and kiss him full on the lips. "I love you!" It's like I won the lose your virginity lottery and to the love of my life, Gage.

"Maybe, being the operative word," his brilliant blue eyes hide a smile.

"As soon as I can clear up this mess about our fake love child, I think I'm going to talk to my mom about the Countenance, you know, about her being a card carrying member."

"You sure?"

"I'm sure." I drag my eyes along the muddy tire tracks digging through the gravel.

"Nev came back." He releases a wild grin. "My dad has him. His wing is broken, but he's healing."

"Oh no."

"We think it happened when Tad trapped him. He'll be good as new in a few weeks."

"Great. I'll probably be in the belly of Fem by then," I pull a face. "Oh wait!" I swing the pendant from around my neck.

"You almost don't need it." Gage fingers the coin shaped piece of metal. "Because I'm not taking my eyes off of you." He gives a slow lingering kiss, probing me carefully as though he were just discovering the landscape of my mouth.

The bell rings, and we pull away.

"What made you wear the dress today?" Gage wraps his arm around me as we head to first.

I lean my head onto his chest and take in his clean scent, feel the bionic force of his affection.

"My love for you," I say.

It's more than true.

By the time second period rolls around, I'm tired of people gaping at me like I'm some kind of freak show. I'm not sure if it has to do with the fact I accidentally slit open Chloe's throat, or this costume Marshall is having me wear, which is really starting to itch. Nevertheless it's a small price to pay for keeping my lips to myself, Holden and et al.

"So what's up with you and Chloe?" I ask Ellis as I take a seat behind him.

Marshall is filtering through his briefcase with his back turned to the class, so he hasn't seen me sporting the celestial special.

"I hear she's in the market for a new chauffeur," Gage says as he reclaims the seat behind me.

"Me and the ice queen? Don't think so." His eyes look decidedly glossy, and a tangled network of crimson wires spread over them thick as spider webs.

"You replenished your stash," I say as my head magnetizes in Chloe's direction.

Her hair is stark as night—black-in-a-box—freshly dyed.

"You went on a light drive, didn't you?" I can't believe Ellis would go anywhere with her after the way she treated him.

"Maybe—maybe not," he says.

I glance back at Chloe. She pulls a lock of hair through her fingers over and over as though she were patiently waiting for me to put the puzzle together.

"What did Chloe do while you were getting your stuff?" The words filter out my mouth, numb like pulling cotton.

"Who knows? What did you do when we went?" He turns back around as the bell goes off—drills into my bones with the prospects.

I trashed Carly's car. I kissed Gage, met up with Holden's ghost—killed Chloe. The possibilities are innumerable.

You look ravishing. Marshall beams unapologetically at me.

"Everybody—pop quiz." He claps his hands together and motions for the desk clutter to disappear.

Be here at four-thirty. I have plans for the two of us.

I knew it. It's some freaky wedding dress. Just putting on the gown was probably a seal of our unity, and now he's going to try and consummate the union right here in his room at four-thirty.

I'm so stupid. I should have settled for the kiss.

Don't look so enthused. He gives a bleak smile. *It has to do with your mother.*

My mouth falls open at the thought. I flicker a private smile at him as he hands out papers.

"I'm going to meet my mother!" I whisper in excitement over to Gage.

"What?" He leans in. "Not without me. Swear to me you won't go without me, Skyla."

I spin back around in my seat.

I'm going to meet my mother. The idea alone feels like a sun-drenched dream. God, I miss her, and I never even knew her. How wild is that?

I can't stop surging with happiness. First, the prospect of sex with Gage, and now meeting my real flesh and blood mother? Well, probably not flesh and blood, but nevertheless this more than makes up for my crappy morning with the Counts.

I'm going to ask Marshall about Emily and her deathly diagrams, see if he'll confirm it's the same war he showed me in a vision several weeks ago—that, and about the lion, the ox, and the eagle. It must mean something if there are statues of them in churches, if Emily Morgan felt the need to etch it onto Drake's back.

Chloe raises her hand. Her back straightens, and she audibly taps her foot against the floor in an effort to gain Marshall's attention.

I look back at Gage and frown.

Chloe is such a kiss ass. I wouldn't be surprised if she volunteered to lick his shoes after school.

"Yes, Ms. Bishop." Marshall returns to the front of the class and ticks his chin up a notch.

"I was just wondering," Chloe cuts her gaze across the room at me, slitting the air with her hateful vengeance. She returns her attention to Marshall, "What exactly is a Sector?"

57

Killing Time

Marshall pulls his hands out in front of him with great effort as though he were stretching out a rubber band.
 The room grows still. A hollow noise fills the void—not a soul moves or breathes. Chloe is locked in an obnoxious fixated gaze, her hand still frozen in the air.
 I turn around to find Gage with his eyes opened in horror in Chloe's direction, motionless as a statue.
 Shit.
 Marshall's face brims with color and not in any good way. He grits his teeth and penetrates me with a menacing stare.
 "Gather your things, Ms. Messenger. You'll be coming with me."

✺ ✺ ✺

 I don't remember the walk to Marshall's car, only vaguely do I recall him taking my backpack and tossing it into the dumpster before locking me in on the passenger's side. He confiscated my cell just before we took off.
 I sit and watch the road stretch before us at dizzying speeds. Cars stall on the highway in silent, stale configurations. The people inside them unaware of the fact they're suspended in motion, unable to progress with their lives until Marshall releases them from this comatose state.

wicked

We weave in and out of the inert traffic at speeds that defy the automotive technology that the four-wheel beast we sit in is capable of—*gravity*—we're defying gravity.

"When will it start up again? You know, time?" I listen to the strange naked sound of my breathing. Important things were happening somewhere, babies being born, planes, cars, trains, a pop quiz in math class—and now they'll have to wait until Marshall hands me over to the Counts—until they're sucking the life out of me by way of Pierce's fangs.

"Ms. Richards will take over my class. Your seat will remain empty. I've given the illusion we've stepped out together. A Fem will take your place momentarily and walk out the door with the Fem that looks like me. Does this amuse you?"

"Yes." I hardly have the energy to digest this all, let alone dispute it.

They say fear is mitigated by your perception of reality, that what you fear is no bigger than life and death rolled into one. That seems pretty damn big if you ask me, and I'm sure as hell afraid of being locked up in Ezrina's lair for good.

"Will you visit me?"

"Perhaps."

Gage might be able to as long as he doesn't get caught, as long as there isn't a binding spirit to prevent him from doing so. But I already know Marshall will.

A lone tear makes its way down my cheek and gets caught in the scar Chloe gave me in honor of Logan. It trails down with the finality of a gutter ball.

We pull off onto a dirt road just north of the Falls of Virtue. I recognize the brush, remember the night Logan saw me here dripping wet and naked. The same night I killed Holden.

I wipe my face clean and straighten in my seat.

Marshall accelerates up the side of the mountain until we hit a clearing full of lush green grass—blades as tall as a man.

"Get out," he says, making his way around to the trunk.

I follow orders and extricate myself from the vehicle. Circling around back, I peer into his opened trunk. A bow—thick with glossy varnish, comprised of layered espresso colored wood. Marshall whips out a quiver full of arrows and straps it to his back. He reaches over his shoulder in one swift motion and plucks one loose. He sets it on the string before pointing skyward.

Marshall grunts as he draws back the bow, and launches the arrow straight into the clouds.

Moments later a large black crow spirals down to earth, landing just shy of his fender.

"I'm a good shot," he shakes his head with pride before reloading. He sends the next one straight into the heart of a pine fifty feet away. "I could slice a fly in half if I wanted."

Somehow I believe this to be true.

"Chloe never did ask if *I* was a Sector, now did she?" He gives a calculating smile. "What's a Sector, Skyla?" He shoots off another arrow, partially disinterested in my answer.

"It's the highest order of angels." Actually I don't know how many orders there are. All I want is to get away from him right now.

"Incorrect." He draws another arrow from over his shoulder. "A sector is the distance between two radiuses. Does a pie slice within a circle, ring a bell?" He shoots at something moving on the ground in the distance.

"Oh," I pant with a huge sense of relief. "That's right."

"But that's not what she meant. Is it?" He doesn't bother to look at me, just keeps shooting in the forest over and over.

wicked

"The Counts have a bounty on the both of us, Skyla. I made a deal. It was my price for coming down to earth. It always costs to stray from the ethereal plane."

"Is that what happened to my mother? Can I meet her? If you let me go, I'll be your wife," I hold out my wrists in front of him. "I'll do anything not to be handed over to the Counts," I plead.

"Skyla," he lets his bow slip under his arm. "I'm bound by my word."

"That's it? Some stupid promise? People break promises all the time."

He tugs me in by the dress.

"Humans break promises. All of creation seems to understand the heft of breaking away from a covenant with God other than yourselves. Why he chooses to entertain himself with the lot of you is staggering. You should feel honored and stupefied at the privilege bestowed upon you." His features soften. He cups his hands over my shoulders and pulls me in until his face nuzzles into mine. "I'm going to offer you one last chance at freedom." He gives the same peaceable smile he did the night I met him in my dream.

I could try to be happy with Marshall. I could try to be happy in his world, as long as I was safe. My fingers reach up and carefully caress the side of his face.

"I know something." It speeds out of me in desperation.

"What's that?"

"Brielle's not having your baby. It's Drake's. You don't have to tell the faculty."

His face contorts. "I was warming to the idea."

"I'll give you a child." God, what am I saying?

"Now you bring it up," he says it curt as though the offer offends him.

"Then show me something," the words crackle out of the baseball size knot in my throat.

I lean in and kiss Marshall. A pure unadulterated kiss that tries to convince him I'd be the best bride, that our children could have dominion if only he'd keep me, let me love him in exchange for refuge from the Counts.

It's the vision I wait for, the clue into the window of my world. I want to see that I'm marrying Gage to affirm his fantasy, Logan, hell I'd take Ellis right about now—just show me something, anything. But there's no vision for me.

The wind picks up, it floats the skirt of my gown in the air like a kite, and I wonder what we must look like kissing on this grassy hillside, a girl in a white flowing dress, a man so tall and handsome.

Marshall pulls back and examines me with an ice-cold expression.

"I'm going to teach you a lesson, Skyla," he pauses, "if you run I may not catch you. Now go." He spins me around and gives a swift push. "Run."

The rain starts in as I begin to move.

"Run!" His voice thunders past me, swift as a bullet.

The arrows come. They come in pairs, in groups of ten, manically fast, precariously close. An entire shroud of darting black flames slice through the wind as they whistle by. They call out victory over me—taunt me, as I drift through the pouring rain.

They whisper the word, *run*, over and over.

And I run like hell.

58

Count on Me

It is a season of hopelessness, of being lost, of wishing I could turn to dust and melt with the rain. Dreams and nightmares swell into my world, blur my vision with the broken boundaries of reality.

The storm passes. I wake up cold, sopping wet with my arms wrapped around my knees, tucked in a thicket of trees. I had covered myself in branches like a hunter stalking his prey. Only, I was the hunted—the hunter's eyes were fixed on me.

A never-ending quiver—Marshall is a damn good shot. He killed that bird midflight with minimal visibility, but me he couldn't touch with the tip of a thousand arrows.

He let me get away. Perhaps that was the plan all along—perhaps he truly loves me. Or maybe he's out there, stalking me still.

I close my eyes and try my best to light drive back to the time of my father, the beginning of time, anywhere but Paragon. I open my lids carefully. Still here—in my wet dress, the thick scent of nature filling my skull.

"Binding spirit," I whisper. Marshall wants me here. I won't be leaving, ever.

I shake the dirt off the back of my legs and stretch out my limbs. The hard rain of the afternoon has given way to a lavender sky, a beautiful dusk, with the remnants of light dipping over the ridge. A bright moon crests behind the hill. I'll need it to illuminate my path if I ever hope to get home.

I could live in the hills, stalk the Falls of Virtue and wait for Logan or Gage to find me. Nevermore will heal soon and let Gage know where I am.

I set out on the muddy path, filled with arrogant hope.

"Hope never dies," I whisper. Ironic because it comes out rather hopeless, diluted.

I walk near the spines of the trees, lose myself in the murky shadows afraid of the slightest movement, every creak of nature that buzzes through the air, rattles my jangled nerves.

Then I hear them—a stark laugh, the distinct sound of a woman. Voices—elevated, humming—many.

I follow along the outskirts of the woods until the sounds pick up intensity, until I can almost see them, feel them, touch them.

Maybe it's a search party? But why such uproarious laughter—the sifting of footsteps in one small location? If they were really looking for me they'd call out my name.

I creep in as close as possible, cut through a clearing and crawl through passages of open brush to be near them, hopeful to catch a glimpse of someone I might know—see if I can borrow someone's cell phone to call Gage.

Legs move in the distance, quickening, stopping, more laughter. I adjust myself in the bushes until I'm leaning against the warped trunk of a centennial evergreen.

It's an entire group of people wandering around an enormous round stone the size of dinner table.

I can't make out their faces. Everyone stands still while an arrow flies across the field in their midst. A round of applause breaks out.

It figures. Marshall's probably training Fems to hunt me down by the dozens.

At once everything stops. People gather towards the stone and simultaneously stoop low and pick something up off the ground.

They're getting, dressed?

Long dark cloaks are pulled over their clothes.

"Oh my God." I seize with panic.

It's some kind of satanic ritual.

I strain to make out their faces as they gather near the stone. Some of them look about my age, familiar.

One of the cloaked figures snaps his neck in my direction, stares into the bushes as though he knows I'm here. He breaks free from the crowd and slips away undetected.

In the back of my mind, I can hear Marshall's charge to run, but my feet won't move. I swallow down a scream.

The cloaked figure hides in the shadowed periphery as he moves in my direction.

He comes upon me with yellow glowing eyes. His dark hood drips to the ground. His face is merged with the shadows. He pulls the hood back and gives a wicked grin.

"Logan!" I lunge into him, bury my face in his neck, and take in his familiar scent.

Relief a mile wide swells through me, and I pull back, soaking in his regal beauty.

"Are you OK?" he pants. "We thought he took you." His chest rises and falls in spasms.

I give a quick nod as he pulls me into an electrifying kiss. I can feel the sizzle of movement coursing through his veins. I try to push him away, but he overpowers me until I can't move my arms.

Logan pulls back and examines me. I want to scold him and remind him I'm with Gage, but more than that I just want him to get me home.

It's a meeting, Skyla. He darts a glance over his shoulder.

I see them now clearly, the faces of men and women—oh God—Nat and Pierce! I bet Pierce has an entire bag of kittens ready to sacrifice.

It is a sacrifice, Logan says, rubbing his thumb against my cheek, *a blood bonding.*

"Creepy." I strain to make out the faces of those milling around in flowing black robes.

I shift my gaze to Logan. The purple velvet lining the inside of his cloak gives off a sickly hue upon his skin.

He looks from me, to the gathering, then back again with the glint of an idea.

I interlace our fingers and try to pull him in my direction, but he's quick to release my grip and clasp me by the wrist instead.

The crowd turns towards us.

"It's OK. I've got you." He pulls me out into the clearing.

"No," I pant.

Logan pulls me forward in large gaping strides, brings me tripping right into their midst.

"What the hell are you doing?" I struggle to break free from his grip.

His eyes light up like golden embers, his face cold as stone.

The crowd examines us with blank dead stares. I lock in on a pair of familiar faces, take in a breath and forget to let go.

Chloe—and *Brielle.* She knows. She's always known.

I can't breathe.

My entire body trembles with hatred. I have to get away. I have to run. My fingers pat around as I ease my way backwards. I accidentally tap the stone and it shoots off the intense sting of an electrical current.

Shit!

I snatch back my hand and look up at Logan the boy I thought I knew.

"Help," I whisper.

His features sharpen, hard as marble. He says nothing in return.

Feels like a bad dream.

They pull their hoods on one by one—except Chloe. She makes her way over with a smug look of satisfaction.

"We've been waiting for you," she says with a sterile look that goes beyond hate and jealousy—something entirely foreign to me. Her fingers thread through my hair as she unhooks the clasp on my necklace and places the protective hedge back around her neck, swift as a magician.

Chloe resumes her position next to Brielle and the circle closes in as they take one another's hands.

"Demetri," Logan says, tipping his hand above his shoulder as a dark figure from behind, lays a dagger on his palm.

My entire person freezes. It's him—the man who initiated the death of my father—my family. I try to make out his features, but the cloak has him locked in shadows.

Logan grips the handle of the knife, never breaking our gaze, and gives it a light swing in my direction.

Seeing him like this, in all of his Countenance nobility paralyzes me. Thoughts of what he plans to do with that blade gleaming pridefully in his hand suffocates me.

"This will only hurt for a moment." Logan's voice is layered with savage ambition.

It was all an act right from the beginning.

I have never known him.

"We'll need you to lie down for us," Demetri says, stepping out from the shadows.

Logan's lips curve into the slightest impression of a smile.

"Welcome to the sacrifice, Skyla."

Thank you for reading, Wicked (Celestra Series Book 4). If you enjoyed this book, please consider leaving a review at your point of purchase.

Look for the next book in the Celestra Series, VEX (Celestra Series Book 5).

About The Author

Addison Moore is a *New York Times, USA Today,* and *Wall Street Journal* bestselling author who writes contemporary and paranormal romance. Her work has been featured in *Cosmopolitan* Magazine. Previously she worked as a therapist on a locked psychiatric unit for nearly a decade. She resides on the West Coast with her husband, four wonderful children, and two dogs where she eats too much chocolate and stays up way too late. When she's not writing, she's reading.

Feel free to visit her at:

http://addisonmoorewrites.blogspot.com
Facebook: Addison Moore Author
Twitter: @AddisonMoore
Instagram: @authorAddisonMoore

Printed in Great Britain
by Amazon